About the Author

Millwood Thomas is an Australian writer who spent her childhood making up stories. Nowadays she tends to write them down. When she isn't tapping away at her computer, she can be found reading, researching or listening to extremely nerdy podcasts.

ACROSS THE HALL

Millwood Thomas

ACROSS THE HALL

Vanguard Press

A CIP catalogue record for this title is
available from the British Library.

ISBN 9781784656 95-9

*Vanguard Press is an imprint of
Pegasus Elliot MacKenzie Publishers Ltd.*
www.pegasuspublishers.com

First Published in 2020

**Vanguard Press
Sheraton House Castle Park
Cambridge England**

Printed and bound in Great Britain

Dedication

For:
Rebbeca, Hayley, James.

And
especially for Adam.

INTRODUCTION

Journal Entry: No. 287

Why Lilly? I don't know?

Maybe because she looks like a little lost sparrow cast out of her nest and forced to fend for herself.

Maybe because the love that pours through her eyes can light up the night brighter than the moon and all its stars.

Maybe because time stops as she walks from the bus to her front door.

Maybe because the red apples that she eats are colourless, next to her lips.

Or maybe it's because she's my Lilly.

Written by Adam, year 10

Journal Entry: No. 288

I am Adam, my name means 'to be red'. Red as the earth is red. Red as the colour of my people's skin. A common name, that sprang from the earth. Adam, commonplace, so plain I camouflage with the backdrop of my life. I, who secretly thinks about dying, more than living. Who believes that poetry, no matter how bad it is, in fact, is a worthy

expression of the human condition? Also, I wish my mother
would hug me more, but am too insecure to say it out loud.

The above was from a small piece of yellowing folded paper I found in the back of my sock drawer the day I left home. I must have become embarrassed about writing it. I could imagine myself shredding it from my journal and hiding it. That was me as a teen. Honest only long enough to write, then quickly destroy my work. Not that my words are worthy enough to be considered work.

Now I'm standing, throwing the last of the drawer's contents half-assed into an open gym bag on the floor. I pick up the scribbled note written in almost invisible pencil, after years of lying hidden. I could have easily mistaken it for an old scrap of nothing, instead of it being everything. It's attached to my first clear memory of her… Lilly.

Standing in my childhood bedroom, this little room, until recently was all I knew as my personal space and home. I dig through old books for no reason in particular. I find a worn paperback of Emily Dickinson's poetry. It was a hidden staple of my teens. I turn to the back cover, my secret attempt at honouring Lilly after seeing her with John at the school dance.

Journal Entry: No. 351

In a room full of people,
    There was she,

No one else,
Not even me,
Only her,
But that pair of hands,
They were there,
Those hands,
Highlighted, blue-white, hands,
Illuminated by light,
Hands cut from the bodies with the darkness of the room,
Clenched around her waist,
Cutting her in two,
Music popping my eardrums,
He's running in valleys and mountains,
She's quiet,
Compliant under those hands,
I am not here,
I'm invisible,
His hands are unsupervised,
Once, she wasn't tamed,
His hands locked into place,
Pinned like rocks on the string of a balloon,
No more spinning or twirling,
Confined,
Voiceless,
There's hands dig into my brain,
That plant themselves ready to grow,
I will see those hands for a thousand years,
In the dawn,

In the dusk,
Awake,
Asleep,
My hands empty,
Hidden in my pockets,
You have the lightest of touches,
That's all he needs,
Pure white hands,
Their ownership of what is mine,
But now there's a fire,
It's rising,
It's burning,
It sees no sense,
And knotted fireball in my stomach,
Beads of sweat on my forehead,
Signal their warning,
Like a red flag,
Like a green flag,
My feet begin to move,
Fire is rising,
It spreads along with my arms,
I'm a bushfire,
Uncontrolled,
Those hands squeeze tight,
I'll rip them away,
My palms filled with heat,
I clench them tightly,
They steal,
Lava moulded into fists,

I step into the darkness,
Light skims my surface,
I am a volcano,
I have all the force of hate,
My spine clicks into an animal's curve,
I am only purpose.

This is what I wrote, this is how I felt, but what did I do? I did as I always do. I did nothing…

The moment I saw it, I cast my mind back. Resting on my childhood-bed, my consciousness neither here or there. The paper in my hand felt light as a feather, only heavy as a rock on my soul.

My single clouded thoughts of her are jumbled, without shape or order, timeless. I do, however, see her in my mind. This time, she's a tiny bird jumping from branch to branch, trying to fix her nest with a broken wing. Heartbreaking yet beautiful. Sorrowful yet accepting. I open the paper forcing my eyes to focus on the bad handwriting.

I read in my head, then, out loud so the words will resonate through the speakers that are my ears. It's almost tangible, they conjure up true-life images, almost like flicking through a scrapbook.

I read louder, slowly I savour each word, pausing to emphasise the spaces in between each line. The gaps have stories, some hidden, some untold. Quietly they have laid waiting for me to dig them up.

CHAPTER 1
FRUIT OF THOUGHTLESSNESS

I'm creeping, making myself small. Pushing back into the tiny space between the staircase and the wall. Hoping the blackness will gobble me up. Have I made a mistake? My stomach says I have.

There she is… across the hall, Lil. I had followed her home. We were about twelve or thirteen. The fact is; I know her to say '*hello*' only the way you'd say hello to a neighbour you see sometimes, or someone behind the counter at the corner shop. She's a classmate, that's all. I remind myself of that fact all the time. Whenever I find myself trying to smell the scent of her shampoo in the lunch line. Whenever our legs brush against each other, while we sit on the study benches in the library. Though deep in my bones, I feel she is my missing rib, sculpted from clay just for me. I know this to be fact; as sure as I breathe air.

After school, I had stayed at least ten paces behind her, through the busy market street on which she lived. I'd hidden behind a garbage bin at one point, terrified she would see me. I watched her squeeze through the main doors of her building, trying to spy the code she tapped into the keypad. She didn't touch it, instead she jiggled the door handle and it pushed open — stiffly. The lock must be broken, I surmise while my left -hand covers my nose with my sleeve, in an attempt to block out the cigarette butts and rotting food congealing in the heat. I watch every movement she made intently until even her shadow was inside.

I continued on to my bus stop. I stood there with half a dozen other people, all waiting to get aboard. They will be taken to what the locals call *The Fringe*, which is the city limits, or the first line of housing rather than apartment buildings.

The evening was coming in fast. The cold wind licked at my collar until I pulled it up to meet my hairline, covering my exposed ears.

The bus arrived. The doors swing open with the familiar whoosh sound I expect. Some habits and routines become so ingrained you can feel them happening before they actually do. I watched the others climb on, one after another, letting myself filter through them until I reached the back of the line. My feet seem glued to the red-painted concrete. My brain paused as I felt the arms of people brush past me. Slowly it took form; an idea came to me, and as most bad decisions do, it came suddenly without any real warning. It sneaks up on you, leaving you without the inclination to say no.

The old crinkled bus driver knew me, with a plaid shirt and raspy- sounding voice hovering over the steering wheel waiting for me to climb on. I travel with him every day after school like clockwork. He asks me, '*Are you coming or staying*?' not really a question, he says it calmly expecting a '*yes*'.

I look down at my palm for a second. My fare sits in my hand like shiny pebbles. I look back at him shaking my head and waved him on saying:

'*Not right now*,' so quietly it's like I'm afraid of my own voice. I put the money in my pocket and zip it in tight, tapping twice on the outside of my pants to make sure it's there. It's more than money, these fifty cents are a lifeline to home.

I stand for a moment, not quite believing my own actions. I've never disobeyed my parents before. I had to wait for my head to catch up for a second. Could I go through with it? Could I walk up to her front door without pausing or running away, without choking on my words? Could I stand in front of her with my eyes wide open looking into her face? Could I move right now out of this bus bay; stomach flipping? Could I keep going all the way down to the other end of the street? One thought of Lilly was enough to swallow hard and decide *yes*.

I looked down towards the ground noticing a stain on my K-mart pants. My floppy, loose-fitting home brand clothes matching my half-done, home trimmed haircut. I was mostly happy being classed as dorky, it wasn't like I could be anything else anyway. I'm too skinny for most sports. I seemed to fluke ability in basketball. I'm not in the same league as the school team or the gang that hung around on the playground after school. However, I could keep up with the others like me. The nondescript kids who fill in the gaps. The kids who no one can remember; a lost name on an old school photo.

Looking up the street to her apartment, I didn't have a plan as such; I just knew I wanted to see where she lived. There had always been rumours about her family. They buzzed around school like a swarm of bees only dying down long enough for another to start. I didn't care; I never cared about shit like that. Suddenly, with nothing to stop me, I turned and walked to her building. My chest inflated, my chin out like I'd seen the upper school kids do with their long striding walks and, to me at least, their invincibility.

The door was still unlocked when I reached Lilly's building. There were blue and red wires hanging out of the keypad. The box inside itself sat a little lopsided. I felt like a thief, even though I had no intention of any wrongdoing. The wind inside me, that puffed me up, disappeared as reality set in. A pain hatched in my stomach, dull, but gaining strength. My whole stomach set to flipping nervously, suddenly dropping with an objection to what I was about to do.

Stop hesitating, it looks suspicious, I told myself. My legs wouldn't respond to my command. A man behind me pushed past, making me jump. It jolted me enough to unfreeze my feet. I squeeze through the gap, not even touching the doors. Entering the building in silence, quiet like a mouse, I crept carefully making sure my sneakers didn't squeak on the floorboards. A couple of other inhabitants of the building were hanging around the mailboxes, and I looked down carefully not making eye contact, hoping that it would stop any questions. Just as I got to the first step, I heard a man shout in a gruff tone, proceeding to turn into a splutter and cough.

'You got a dollar?' When I didn't turn, it came again in my direction, 'Hey, you got a dollar?' I didn't know if he was talking to me, but I don't stop to find out, instead, I picked up my pace and sprinted up the stairs. I tiptoe. Holding my breath up the old wooden staircase, I tried desperately to avoid any step that looked like it might crack under even the lightest footstep. I knew she lived on the top floor. As I climb each stair carefully, I couldn't help but notice how dirty the stairs are and how unsafe the rail is coming away from the wall precariously. Large sections of the wood were missing, forcing me to place my hands on the crusty surface. I try to avoid the patches of paint peeling from the walls and ceiling, hanging down in some places, like large strips of old Christmas decorations. The further I go into what feels like a rat's nest, the darker it gets, with not one of the light bulbs working as they swing from exposed wires and I'm careful not to let them touch my skin.

When I get to her floor, I hover, ears pricked, suddenly sensing danger. Without a sound, I back down a few steps, standing on the staircase below her floor enabling a quick peek. I peer up through the rails without being seen. Her front door is in sight, it looks like the bottom panel has been kicked in, but still I want desperately to knock on it; however, something feels off. I know, I shouldn't be here, and I have no excuse.

I find a little hiding spot, a small nook where a fire hose should be. Only the fire warning sticker with the sharp protruding nail and a loose swinging bracket hang there. I wait... I wasn't sure what for. The door opened, a handful of kids poured out all at the same time, pushing and shoving into the hallway with a worn-out soccer ball. Filling the hallway, they start running up and down, playing in the small space as if it's a backyard. One boy opens a door at the opposite end of the hall. It had the word 'bathroom' written on the battered wood with a black marker pen. There was enough light to see that it was gutted and was an empty space with chipped plaster and broken fittings on the floor. It now became the soccer goal. Mark, the only kid I knew out of the bunch (I knew him only because I had overheard Lilly moan about looking after him when she was forced to bring him to school last year), was now the goalie. He was pretty good, only about six or seven, thin as the rest of them, with messy straw-like hair but still stood out; he was a natural with the ball. He could predict where the ball was going to be before it got there. The other boys, some a little older, all tried to get one past him in vain. The shouts converged with mayhem echoing off the walls; making it sound like there are a hundred kids playing. For a moment, I forgot I was invisible, forgot I was hiding and got lost in the game.

Before long Lil appeared, like a hammer to the heart. She evoked thoughts of myths, like a water nymph tossed from the sea. Much quieter than the other kids and the only girl, I had never seen her out of school uniform and seemed out of place. The cotton dress she wore was slightly too small, stretched tight across her chest, cutting in under her arms highlighting her small breasts. A sight that should have driven the thirteen-year-old me crazy, but my focus turned to the painful-looking rub marks under her arms, which made me wince. The other kids were still making a lot of noise screaming and shouting, Lilly didn't seem to fit, standing quietly watching absent-mindedly. The wind howled through the landing hallway where the kids played. From this angle, from this hidden vantage point, half a staircase above me, Lilly looked as if she had been cut and pasted from a storybook.

A tall, spindly man appeared on the bottom stair, he strides past me, taking two stairs at a time. I remain hidden. He smelt of cigarette smoke, and his hair was greased back into a ratty ponytail. There was a silver chain hanging from his belt to his pocket, and his leather jacket was cut at one of the elbows, leaving a small hole. On reaching the apartment door, he knocked with some urgency. Although I can't read the situation, it felt off — shady. The guy was welcomed in by Lilly's mother with a grin, almost pushing his way inside, which surprised me. It didn't however seem to surprise Lil who didn't bat an eyelid. From my hiding spot he hadn't noticed me, why would he?

The front door was reopened; another child was pushed into the hallway kicking and screaming, a small toddler, which from what I could tell had been awoken from a nap. Lilly quickly grabbed him trying desperately to calm him under the glare of her mother. She was such an imposing woman, to me it seemed plausible that she could breathe fire or break Lilly in two with no effort. The man hovering inside paid no attention to the distressed child. It was shocking for me to see children treated badly coming from a family who treasures them. I saw the fiery red hair of Lil's mother bend down to Lilly's eye line. I could feel the tension in her every movement.

'Keep… Them… Quiet…' A fierce low growl rumbled through her chest filling the air. It sent shivers through me to the bone. I held my breath, pushing hard up against the wall thinking she might smell me out, like an attack dog after a rabbit. It was petrifying and it took all my effort to hold my muscles tight enough to stop the shaking.

Lilly tried to hush the children frantically, but they weren't listening. She ran around in circles herding them with one arm, while the toddler, still screaming, hung from the other. There she was, a tiny sparrow trying to organise crows. It seemed like an impossible task. Feeling helpless I sat back wondering how this could arrive at a positive end.

It was draughty out here, the wind howled through the broken window in the demolished bathroom; making a low whistling sound. Lil pulled the sides of her skirt around the now whimpering child, which she held close to her body, rocking from side to side. Soon, he fell into a sleep-like trance. Lilly too stared out into the black abyss of the stairwell without blinking.

After a while, the scruffy man came out. He was smiling to himself; there was something sinister about his expression. I felt a shiver run through me, like someone had walked over my grave.

'Your service is good as always,' he said, giving the bloated-faced woman a peck. Lilly's mother had money in her hand. The crumpled bills were promptly pushed under her loose bra strap, which she readjusted onto her shoulder. She scowled at Lil in defence of unsaid things. He didn't say anything, he who scratched the back of his head so vigorously I waited for the skin to burst open. There was a look that past between him and Lilly; like she had a mouthful of lemons, and he wanted to suck on them. She took a step back. He sniggered. Although I wasn't a hundred per cent sure, I vaguely got the picture. My stomach turned, a hundred rumours flew through my head.

He saw me squashed into that little hiding-hole between the stairway and the wall; giving me a wink and tugging on his fly as he took the steps downwards, two by two.

A loud roar bellowed across the landing as the kids were directed inside for dinner. The kids' noise shut off like the turning of a tap: instant. A cold shiver ran through me, like ice cubes stuck in my shirt. The kids scrambled past their mother. Except for Lilly; her mother's hand reached down grabbing her by the scruff of the neck, scolded her violently and indenting her chest with a sharp finger, then shook her by the shoulders as if to wake her up. I watched through my semi-closed fingers.

'Why didn't you keep the kids quiet?' the red-haired dragon demanded. I pushed my hands over my ears to block out some of the thundering echoes, only daring to look up at an angle. Lilly's mother's temper boiled over. Her face was as red as her hair; sweat appeared under her arms in large rings. An inch from Lil's face she bellowed, letting all kinds of madness fly out. The noise reverberating from the walls, Lilly just stood there taking it, her eyes like two giant blue marbles. Fists screwed into her skirt like tight balls, holding onto her sanity. Her punishment for what? I didn't quite know. My hands shook; I tied them in a knot in my lap. The tremble seemed to transfer itself to my stomach, then my back. I stiffened, pushing myself against the wall; worried the sound of my bones rattling would give me away.

I heard the order, '*Stay in the hall.*' She was told to think about what she'd done. The words poured down upon her; selfish, useless, clumsy! All thrown around like they weren't destructive on her fragile, emerging soul. Helpless I sat, watching each word rain down on her blow by blow. I didn't understand what was happening, or why she had singled out Lil when she was trying to help. Nothing was making sense. Her mother stormed inside yelling at seemingly whoever was in front of her, slamming the door behind her.

Emptiness fell over the hallway. My eyes struggled to see her at first with the doors at each end of the hallway now closed. Slowly, my eyes adjusted seeing only her outline, after straining a little, piece by piece her frame filled in. Lilly fell against the wall. Sliding down it as though all hope had been sucked out of her. She was an empty husk sitting on the floor. It was then I noticed she wasn't wearing shoes, and her feet looked blue with cold. I saw silent sadness run down her face. I desperately tried to search my brain for a way to uplift her. I needed to be the crutch that held her up. She is no more than a tiny figure sitting across the hallway; tear-stained and delicately beautiful, still, like part of the building.

I am as quiet as the bricks and plaster, hiding across the stairway. Her face rests on her knees, arms protectively around her legs. I looked up onto her level, ducking down I reach into my bag for a piece of paper. She still had no idea I was there. I wrote her name in large letters and then reached into my pocket where I had three wrapped sweets. I lay the paper down between the rails without her noticing, placing the candy upon it and pushing the tiny gift out onto the landing, inches from her toes.

I snuck back to my hiding spot and waited for Lilly to spy the note. Needing to see her face. I needed to make what small alleviation to her pain I could. When she raised her head, the paper sat at her feet. Searching desperately from side to side to see who could have possibly placed it there; she looked a little nervous. I watched as she edged to the empty bathroom, poking her head around slowly checking for monsters. When the room was empty, she must have assumed it was one of her brothers, and an easy calm seemed to come over her. She uncoiled, letting her legs drop, taking the hard-boiled sweets, one in her mouth, and two in a pocket. She pulled at her tight dress in an effort to find comfort. Shifting slightly, she settled in for, what I could tell, she assumed would be a long time. She sat wet faced with an enormous smile, eyes closed, focusing on the flavour. I had a surge of sunshine race through me at that moment. I knew from that point on it was my job to make her smile.

I waited a few more minutes until the coast was clear, and I snuck away out of the main doors catching the later bus home. Perfectly aware, I'd be in trouble getting home so late. Knowing that my actions would be worrying my mother half to death but despite this, it was worth it to me, knowing that I'd given her a smile.

CHAPTER TWO
THE JOY OF BEING ME

To Be Added to Journal: Entry No. 3791

Thinking of my father, riding on the train home; on the stub end of a pay cheque, I wrote:

If I could be half the man he is,
Gentle is the wind,
Still is the morning,
Clear is my vision,
Strong is my belief,
Calm is my mind,
Steady is my hand,
I am the father,
Never the son!

Is my life my own? Nope, but whose is? A man is not an island, I've heard that so many times. It's not healthy to live a solitary life. I truly wish I could live in a lighthouse alone. However, according to my therapist I need to socialise with a greater cross-section of people, get a hobby, and try to meet someone. I see an island, that's what I see. I'm not depressed, not anymore. My sadness no longer pushes me down; I don't openly wallow or mope. It's more of a pale blue misery rather than an all-encompassing blackness. That's what it is to live in my head.

I've cut down on the pills but my drink levels are up. I'm doing a little better, I think, but it's hard to tell. Isn't it better to be more drink, fewer drugs? Not counting the prescription stuff of course. It's not easy to be objective about these things.

My mother noticed when I went to see her on Saturday. I took the chocolates she likes to hopefully cast a sense of optimism. I even combed my hair and cleaned up a little. She believes it's the new promotion that I fabricated to stop her from fretting. There's no new job. How could there be, with a face like mine? I'm still in the warehouse packing trucks. It's honest work, does that make me a good man? Probably not. My mood is so low, for the most part; it's almost impossible not to see the dark clouds that surround me. Or maybe I hide it?

In truth, what has lifted me isn't anything at all much worth talking about. Below the third-floor apartment that I rent, a new bar has opened, that's all. Now on the way home from my job on the warehouse floor, I can stop and get plastered before rolling home only to start over and do it again. I have worked in that damn warehouse since I was sixteen. My father begged me to go to college, he thinks I'm smart because I like to read and scribble nonsense down from time to time. I'm not. I like to hang out at the bar and blend into the background.

I like the bar more than any place I've ever been (not that I've been so many places), that's sad I know, but true. It's quiet, but not so quiet you stand out or get seen. There's always a fight on the big screen or sports of some kind. Someone to make a comment or two but not in your face, and the beer is good, well cheap. I'd see all the boys that come through the door work on the dock too. A couple of them work in the warehouse, like me. Sitting at the opposite end of the low-lit room, they raise their glasses in my direction when they begin to feel the drink flow. The barman knows most of us by our first names, he makes it his business to; I like that, and I also like how he leaves me alone. I just sit and watch, enjoying the place and it's become like a second home.

This world of pills and alcohol had become my universe. Not a home I choose exactly but where I dwell nonetheless. Its doors and windows are locked, with the curtains drawn.

So here I am standing in the doorway, looking over to the spot I slouch every evening. It's empty, and I'm filled with contentment a little too big for such a small thing. Felix, the barrow-rounded barman, pulls me a beer and a whisky automatically before I sit, and I thank him with only a nod. Pete and Joe are warming their seats too.

They raise their eyes as I sit and lean over my whisky. That's my boys; they pull a smile for me, even after another long day doing the same old shit. We have been friends since high school and we can read one another with a mere glance. We used to do this stupid handshake, Joe still tries to re-instate it now and again, we leave him hanging, laughing.

'Game's shit tonight,' Joe grunts, and takes a swig.

'Only cos you put too much on it again, how much pay you got left?' Pete prods. Joe's owl-like eyes don't leave the screen. Pete and I both laugh, and then Joe joins in with a self-defensive smirk.

'Ahhh, I could win yet.' He's laughing like it doesn't matter at all.

I block out the world as the beer hits my empty head. The pinging thoughts that fly around are at last subdued, for at least a while. My gaze locks on the game but I'm not watching at all, deeply lost in the buzz instead. I hear Joe and Pete talking some crap about girls they don't have, could never have, then my ears prick up as I hear the name Lilly. I turn.

'You've talked to Lilly... Lilly Kern from Market Street... you've seen her...?' I ask with obvious interest. My body stiffens, every cell on high alert. The familiar tingle of arousal streams down my spine. They fall all over each other with sweat and slur, drunkenly howling.

'Yeah, we've seen her. What's it to you?' Pete scoffs.

'Lilly the peg... are you sure?' Passing over the banter, trying to get them to focus. I lean in to make sure I hear them right, getting a waft of sweat for my trouble.

'Yeah, that's the one,' they laugh at my enthusiasm. I shrug it off wanting to know more but knowing better than to ask. They let me stew on it. They're calling my bluff, waiting for me to ask, no, waiting for me to beg. Bastards! My feelings are written all over my face.

After five or so minutes — an agonising amount of time! — I bite the bullet and give in.

'So, where did you see her?' I ask in what I believe to be a nonchalant way. They look at each other with smirks on their faces, Joe lets out a snort and beer shoots over the counter; not that anyone but me seems to care.

'Who?' They're going to make me say it.

'Lil.' I shift on my stool understanding it's a game now.

'Gee, I don't know, let me see?' Pete crows, overacting and scratching his head.

Joe, seeing the fun, joins in as I knew he would.

'Well now.' Pete pauses for effect. 'I think... yep, that's where it was...' He winks at Joe, all subtlety evaporating.

'That's right, I left her at home in my bed, all naked and wet, begging me for more.' Pete proudly stands, miming his stroke on a chair. I shake my head scowling into my now empty glass. They roar and shriek as though it's the funniest thing ever said, slapping each other on the back. I stare blankly at the pair of them, not even a hint of a smile.

'Oh no don't be like that!' Joe blurts out seeing my face; he's on the softer side despite his rough edges.

'It's OK buddy.' His giant hand slaps my back. 'I'm just having a joke, the truth is, she works in the titty bar on Fourth... just serving!' He puts his hands up as not to offend. But then Pete pipes in, looking at Joe as he speaks, then back at me, calling us in close with his hands.

'Rumour has it — she's one of the voices on the sex line they have over there.' I see Joe shift his eyes as if to shut Pete up. Pete is far too wasted to care and continues as if in the middle of some important speech. 'The one you call up after nine p.m. The posters are up all over.' Pete gave me a wink like he was doing me a favour. He reaches into his pocket and pulls out a flyer, big red numbers printed on it and a girl with knickers up her ass. I look down at it placed in front of me. It's not her; inside I feel a sigh of relief, this I'm careful not to show. Pete pulls the paper from my hands, points at all the smaller printed numbers at the bottom disclosing real names of the women he knows. 'I have a talent for putting voices to faces,' he announces proudly. He sits back in his chair like he's solved a riddle, as he taps the flyer.

'This new girl is Lilly the peg. I'd put money on it. Pete's got years of research up his sleeve,' says Joe, not wanting to be left out, smugly.

'You'd put money on anything Joe, you know if you had any…' I state, trying to get one in as we get back down to the business of drinking.

CHAPTER 3
DARK PAST

- ✓   *Note to self:*
Add to Journal! no. 3812

The only paper I can find, a ticket with bold print font:
Dock platform 9.
Invoice ticket no. 7385:
Pack 'n' stack inventory
Small and large crates
Pen lines are shaky, scribble in the top corner where
I try to make the ink run more freely from the biro. It's
hard to write on shiny paper:
Why am I, so addicted?
I ask myself a thousand times.
Why does she stand out above all others?
What is this uniqueness that fascinates me so?
Others could walk pass her not seeing what I see.
I am aware of that,
To me, she is the answer to every riddle,
The melody in every song,
So delicate and pure,

It's almost a sin to touch her,
To invade this sacred space.
Pierce my soul with longing,
My hunger, my craving, my addiction.

Later that night, I search in my pocket for the flyer now covered in beer — I smuggled it away from the boys earlier. Now in the safety of my place, I study it carefully under a lamp. I look at all the numbers, about twenty in total.

I haven't seen Lilly in years since we were about seventeen. Her mum died, and she went to live somewhere with her brothers, an aunt or something? No one actually knows. One day she was here and then she wasn't like she was a mark on paper that someone had erased. I asked around and went to her old apartment in an attempt to hunt her down. It was empty, apart from some old junk, more run down than when she lived here. I stood in the room that I assumed was hers, small like a cardboard box, with lemon wallpaper. Then I forced myself to face the fact that she was gone. More than that, I forced myself to accept she was never mine in the first place. My sadness was palpable, real, like watching sand fall through my open hands. Sand that wasn't mine yet should have been. Then without warning, something moved in the hall, a cat, rat or a kid? It shook me, I suddenly felt wrong being there, as if I was intruding on sacred ground. Muddying my precious memories, flustered I left quickly. At the time, I couldn't think of anyone that might know where she was or leads to find her. I made my peace with it or at least I tried. That was until a couple of weeks ago, I heard mention of her at work.

Some guys were hanging around the vending machine, it wasn't my conversation, I only heard a snippet; a spark of hope. She was working somewhere around here. I had been on high alert ever since, hoping I would see her in a cafe or at the markets. But when I didn't, I thought I may have misheard the boys at work. Wanting to hear news so badly, my brain was tricking me into hearing anything that would keep me going.

Sitting at the same bus stop I had as a kid, the memories of sneaking into her building and following her home all came flooding back. The detailed plans I concocted came back to me as if I were still thirteen. I remember wanting to see inside her apartment so badly. I thought if I could see her room, the things she liked that maybe I would know her better, well, enough to strike up a conversation and become friends at least. What I saw, time and again, were kids in need of a bath. Filth covered the stairs and Lilly standing in the hall with one or two crying children trying to rock them to sleep in one of those big old-fashioned prams. I remember her unfocused stare; it was void of all emotion, almost like one more tear would be the drop that sank her. Tired, she leaned against the wall to keep her upright. I managed to run out before she could see me, each time feeling relieved I hadn't been seen. These are the images scorched onto my visual memory.

At night, sometimes for weeks after the event, I would wake up at three or four in the morning after seeing her. I cried lying there in my bed. That expression, her pure exhaustion played over and over in my head. The helpless feeling that accompanied it tying me in knots. Recalling her fear or worse, complacency to her poverty, which suggested it was normal to her. I still don't understand why it affected me so much, or why I couldn't let that shit go. Poverty wasn't unusual to me. Even now in adulthood, I feel it hovering. Taking its place at the forefront of my mind anytime something lightly hints at a memory.

I went to a therapist for a while. Despite the framed diplomas on the wall and her pleasant disposition, she still couldn't dig that twisted shit out of me. My mother had demanded the sessions when I became too moody for her to handle. She never knew about Lil, I never told her where I went after school, I never told anyone, even though they all tried to find out. After all, it's not like I felt close to my family apart from my dad. Saying it out loud, talking about affection in high school made me feel fake and inauthentic. I find it hard still, it's not that I don't have the language to express myself, when it comes down to it… it lodges in my throat.

Lilly and I were in the same year at school, the same homeroom too, not that she'd remember me. I started watching her from afar because I was riveted. I couldn't bear not knowing what she was doing, and I worried about her constantly. I was like a satellite spinning around her atmosphere without ever touching down on earth. Sure, I

36

may have got a wave from across the street, or a '*hello*' on the bus, a smile if we both got to class at the same time, nothing more. It was a crush that's all, my crush not hers. High school stuff, yet it's never left me.

I blame my face, the way I dress it's like an accidental camouflage. I have the superhuman ability to disappear into any crowd, but I noticed her, she stood out. She did not see me. She was like a tiny spider too fragile to be in the violent assault of high school. With not too many friends, she sat alone mostly. I had a few buddies but then I've always thought that it's easier for a boy, what with sports or chess or whatever. The girls at our school always seemed vicious, like tigers with claws. Scratching away at the vulnerable private parts of delicate developing spirits. Until they finally broke through to the soft underbelly.

I would watch her walk home to her building, knowing she would go all the way to the top floor. Her mother was a strict Irish Catholic when it suited. Wearing a gold cross, which fell hidden between her large breasts most of the time. She was on a small pension, left with seven kids to feed. She had the entire roof space, dirty and shabby as it was, in the centre building in the markets. I found out years later she only rented a small room, but she claimed the rest as no one else wanted to live there.

Lilly's father was gone, that's all I knew. By the sound of the banshee screams from her mother, I don't blame him. On the bus in the morning, I would see her emerge. With her screwed-up face, fire-red hair and her flower apron so tight it was practically grafted to her skin. She was a fierce sight. I wondered how something like that could possibly have yielded such a delicate creature as Lilly. Each morning I would save a seat for Lil in hope that she would sit next to me, not that anything came of it. She would stroll down until she saw a safe spare seat next to an older person or office worker. She would then lean her head against the window and close her eyes looking drained. She worked for her mother not only with her siblings but also on the roof of her building.

For extra money, Lilly's mother would take in other people's washing. She hung it above the market street below on long wire lines. I saw her mother meeting people on the building steps, mostly taking drawstring laundry bags full of bed sheets from the nursing home. That face, she couldn't hide the contempt for her lot, to the point of almost loathing those who gave her work. I understood her life had not amounted to what she believed she was due. Undeserved blame placed at the feet of her children, considerably more at Lilly's.

Quite often you could see Lil up there on the roof with pegs pinned over her shirt, pushing out the lines with rope pulleys. Thinking about it, I was a little obsessed back then, but no more than the girls with their boy bands. It's not like I had her face on a T-shirt, or scribbled her initials on my school bag. I derived so much pleasure from watching her. She seemed quite happy while she was busy, maybe because the task was keeping her mind from other things. She liked to run under the drying sheets. The wind would catch them, sending them flying up parallel to the wire. They pinned against her body, turning her into a clean white cut-out. She stood there with her eyes closed, sun shining down, letting the cool white linen gently pass over her. She was calm like a pale statue. In these unguarded moments, my eyes were free to roam. Until the orange sun turned her into a silhouetted puppet show, I mentally recorded every inch. The words would come to mind then, I couldn't keep my hands still. I wrote on whatever was in front of me. She was truly angelic, radiant... perfect. Not like at school, where she was shy. I only heard her speak a dozen times of her own accord during school.

John Rossi was a demon of a boy in my year at school. A huge Italian kid twice the size of the rest of us, he was built like a bulldozer. I hated him on sight. His family owned everything around here including the police or so they say. He had a group of leeches, which followed him around, copied everything he did. He thought he was invincible and why wouldn't he? A large number of teachers owed his father for this or that. One teacher, who wasn't from our town, gave him a detention for not handing in his homework. Her contract was not renewed the next year, coincidence? Maybe I'm reading too much into it. It's funny though, that these occurrences disproportionately happen around Johnny. That parasite is now my boss, owning the company I work for. I wish, I could say that at twenty-six I can stand up to him but I spend a great deal of time avoiding him. Pretending he doesn't exist seems to work for us both, if indeed he knows who I am.

This one day, one winter term on an icy cold morning when we were about fourteen or fifteen, all us kids were waiting to be let into our class. If memory serves, it was something to do with lost keys or a broken lock. The snow piled up against the walls. Even though the path had been cleared and salted, I found myself hopping from one foot to the other to keep my feet warm. Lilly was standing, quiet as a mouse. She'd pulled her woolly hat down low, arms wrapped around her, but she was still shivering. Johnny locks his eyes on her, my stomach dropped. I knew what was coming. The dilemma in my head began. I'd caught him looking before; she was an easy target. He barked an order at her, expecting her to jump.

'Stand next to me!' She didn't look up. 'Hey, you hear me, come here, and keep me warm.' He made a gesture to his crotch. She didn't move, looking straight ahead. Being shy, her only defence was to act deaf, pretend it wasn't happening. I knew I had a window to do something. If I wasn't such a pussy I would have gone over there and put my arm around her, claimed her as mine but I am, so I didn't. I held my breath instead. This is how it starts with Lil; with others. 'Are you fucking deaf? Move your ass here!' Johnny's face turns red with the effort of yelling. His buddies now watching with interest, he couldn't back down.

Her tiny face still looked straight ahead, clearly frightened. My heart pounded, I just wanted it to be over.

He walked over grabbed her coat with his large shovel-like hands. Yanking her hard in his direction, making her stumble into him, she only let out a meagre gasp, her body rigid. The coat ripped open with a loud tearing sound followed by the popped buttons hitting the snow. Even John was shocked by his strength, and for a second there was a pause. Then John points, and with a bellowing laugh, rallies his friends to join him.

'Fuck look!' Lilly is pulling her coat around her, fighting back tears, struggling, trying to break free but still pinned by John's fists.

'What?' His friends gather around; she is cornered. I can only see glimpses; their bodies block her from view.

'What, I can't see anything?' One kid pushes his way in. The coat peeled back open as he pinned her in place, her feet only just touching the ground forcing her to tiptoe. All I can see is the tips of her toes.

'Like a washing line! Pegs pinned all over her shirt!' squawks a lanky boy I don't really know. He wraps his arm around John's shoulder. *Ass licker*, I think as I stand out of view.

'Fucking pegs, all over her. Fucking pegs!' The gang of boys all pushed and shoved around her, trying to get a better look. I almost moved, I was almost brave when I heard a small squeal. Then a glare from Johnny's buddy had me looking the other way. A stab of guilt.

'Did you say something, Jew boy?' I shook my head.

'A washerwoman,' another said, nodding at John who spurs them on. He secures her against the wall, coat open.

'Why you got pegs all over you?' A shorter kid with braces unintentionally spat in her face with a roar of laughter.

'I was helping my mum wash this morning, I forgot they…' She uttered in barely a squeak, trembling from the cold or fear?

'Like a fucking gipsy, hey Johnny?' another added, tugging at her shirt making a peg or two loose and fall. Laughter followed by grabbing and poking.

'Don't be like that boys. I've got a soft spot for my little Lilly. She can't help being poor, right?' John's insincerity made me cringe. With each second that passed another scar was added to my heart.

'Fucking dirty like her mother with ten kids!' A greasy boy pulled at her skirt, lifting it up showing what was underneath. As horrific as that moment was, my brain took a snapshot of her legs, thin, long and shapely and the lace on the edge of her knickers. I couldn't believe what was hidden under all those layers. Johnny must have liked what he saw because he sent that boy flying backwards, taking ownership.

'He's sorry Lil, aren't you?' he slurred, not turning his head to look at the boy now sitting in the snow. Pushing himself into her, he licked her face. A long, wet lick from chin to eye. Then with a smirk he held her face in place because he could. In my head I was screaming, stomach flipping in sick waves. I was so rigid with fear for what could possibly happen next, I could hardly breathe. My fists clenched so tight I left marks in my palms that lasted a week.

'My little Lilly the peg,' he laughed.

His friends slapped his back, hooting and carrying on. All I saw was the repulsion on her face, too afraid to lift her hands and wipe it off. She stood there with the saliva line like a snail had crawled across her face. She fixed her eyes solid, staring into the snow as if she were trying to wish herself away.

The name stuck. Lilly the Peg was born. I felt ashamed as if a deep chasm had opened up inside me. I stood with my hands in my pockets wishing I could kill him with my bare hands. Instead, I leaned against the frozen drainpipe trying to look like I didn't care. All due to the odd rules of survival in high school, I did nothing but hated myself more each second.

The keys were found, the doors were unlocked, and nothing was said. I picked up the buttons out of the snow and put them in my pocket. I watched her all lesson as I turned the buttons over in my hand. Only thinking about John's greedy hands. Each second of Lilly's ordeal ground against my own self-condemnation. Her miniature frame was perched on a stool too large for her. Her hands constantly smoothed down her worn skirt, an act I'd witnessed each time she was recovering from her mother, John or the girls that stopped her from using the bathroom. Johnny and his boys sat at the back of the room squawking away. I thought about going to the teacher and then I thought better of it. I wanted to hold her hand, to let her know it was OK and she wasn't alone, but I would have been lying. It wasn't OK, and it wasn't OK for a long time after that.

After school, I followed her home. I was looking for an opportunity to return the buttons — it never came. She ran home fast that afternoon, coat flying open with nothing to hold it shut. Running so briskly her feet didn't seem to be connecting with the ground. I saw her barge through the front door not looking back. I knew she was crying. A few minutes later I looked up to the rooftops. Lil is sitting there on the ledge, looking over at the street below, barely holding on. My stomach dropped and I let out a gasp. I thought I was watching the end. I thought she had finally had enough.

For one awful hour, I sat underneath praying she wasn't thinking of jumping. 'Please don't jump, please don't,' I said under my breath over and over. She swung her legs freely over the side and surveyed the market below. I thought if I could hold her together with my mind, she'd find the strength to scramble down.

Finally, I saw her mum grabbing the back of her coat, nearly ripping it from her body, screaming at her… always screaming. I couldn't hear the words, only the volume. She was in trouble, probably for not doing the washing. I stayed, long after I should have been home, watching she didn't come back to the ledge.

I still have those little wooden buttons in a box next to my bed. I get them out when the night's silence is too loud and I can't sleep. I roll them round the palm of my hands remembering how small and alone she was, I still feel ashamed, like a coward. My mind always wonders... occasions like this, where I wish I had acted braver, more empathetically, kinder or with a more generous spirit. They stay with me, never far from my waking mind. Almost like a smudge on my insides, I never really feel clean. I can't escape them. Their shadow still looms over me, I suspect until I can rectify it in some way.

Back to staring into space... I think of that moment a lot, with half a dozen other moments just like them. All gathered and stuck in a collage labelled wimp, somewhere in the back of my mind. Every single one involving Lil, each leaving me wishing I'd been something that I'm not. It's impossible for me to jump back in time and be that kid watching her, traumatised and frozen. There's not a day that goes past when I don't think of it.

CHAPTER 4
THE GETTING OF HONEY

Journal entry no. 3825

More scribble written on a scrap of paper:
The sweeter memories are like honey they soothe me.
Rock me to sleep like affectionate, mothering arms.
However, these memories are like barbed wire.
They cut and grate away, clip and prod.
They are impossible to remove without hurting.

I should collect all these scraps of paper, stick them in a notebook rather than leave them around my place. I find them in pockets, down the side of my armchair and around my place. I always intended to gather them up and stick them into my journal.

Isn't that the point though, to write all the shit in my mind down on paper, to screw it up and throw it away? Why would I keep it? To hang on to the twisted shit in my head, why would I ever read it again — to prove to myself how fucked up I am? I know that much is true already. No reminders needed.

The market was alive with shouts, calls and peppered with strongly worded orders from brawny-looking men covered with tattoos on their arms and across their throats. They pushed, pulled and stacked crates, filling the air with the urgency of preparing for a day of work. The smell of fresh flowers lingers, mixed with the sweetness of bags full of coffee. There was something honest about it, the authenticity of hard work. This is the picture in my head when I talk about home. This place with all its sweat, chaos and grime, warms my heart. I was a seed. I sprouted here. I survived despite myself. It's a victory surviving this place, a mix of tough with a hushed softness. To put my feet on the same bricks my mother did when she was young reassures me. To buy fruit from the same stalls my father did is an anchor I am glad to have. Fresh fish off the local dockland boats, farm-fresh produce being unloaded from trucks straight from the dirt. The banter amongst traders is flung across stalls. The families working this street have been here for generations. Passing over the reins from father to son, or mother to daughter. Birth, life and death pepper this place with the reality of cycles continually moving forward. When I was at school, I assumed I would work on this street one day. That was before I even knew of the warehouse and the drudge of packing freight.

I stand still for a second closing my eyes. Sounds, smells and tastes converge. This place soaks through your skin. The odour that can't be scrubbed off with soap and water, it becomes part of your tissue, the makeup of your skin and bones. I begin to feel the beat in my foot, instinctively, almost unconsciously. It strikes me as poetic. Then right on time, a tapping in my brain, like a knock at the door, *write it down* it urges... then demands, *write it down*. I pat my pockets hunting for anything I can use, back pockets, jacket, shirt, wallet... nothing. I feel the flow of the words begin...

Mental note, add to journal:

Humming with life,
The rhythm, the flow, the scramble,
Standing up, we can't lay down,
The clanging, the banging,
Counting the beats to shape a country's rise,
Like the ringing of a bell it starts,
Out of our corners,
Swinging, singing, optimism's voice,
Surging forward with all its might,
It corrupts, it overwhelms with its force,
Ticking time bomb,
It hunts with all its might,
Ships spilling with sweatshop plastic,
Blow by blow they hit the concrete,
The doors ripped open,
Inside, it yields wealth, a title, a life,
Unbalanced, uneasy,
Where does it stop?

Again, I hunt in my pockets for anything to write it down with. Not finding anything, I committed myself to singing it in my head all day as not to forget it.

Awoken from the spell of my gentle daydream, I hear movement, heavy boots and the squeak of wheels that need oiling. I stand in the way of some guy with cartons on a trolley. I am thrust back into life like a smack upside the head. *Adam work*, I tell myself as to turn the key and get myself started. I hasten my pace.

Although my family home stands outside of the main streets of town now, this is the street I grew up on. My school marks one end, and the grim aesthetic nothingness of a twelve-storey 60s building marks the other end. That was where I lived until my father scraped together enough money to get us out. Lilly's apartment block was the smallest, only five storeys somewhere in the middle of the street. It wasn't really fit for people to live in, however, the down-trudged did. The poor, the addicted, ex-cons and Lil's mother all found shelter there, along with market rats (people and animals alike). The local council turned a blind eye to building codes, having nowhere else to house the occupants.

This meant Lilly's mother and the other tenants couldn't escape the roar of life in the morning. Followed by the traffic and noise all day, even late into the night, when the bars and clubs bring it to life. The building my family lived in before getting the house faced into the next street on one side. So at least it was talked about as the good building, something completely nonsensical to me. It was true, we did escape a little of the noise, and the police cars didn't tend to come down to our end but, only by a couple of buildings.

This street was named First Street, but better known as 'Market Street' for obvious reasons. Leading off this street was Second Street, then it divided into Third and Fourth, making a Y shape and a lot of traffic jams. Third Street was not the greatest place in the world but Fourth Street had a reputation. If you were seen heading down that way, it was assumed you were doing something shady. One of the biggest insults in school was: you were born on Fourth. It had three bars, a pawnbroker, hookers, a tattoo hut, a couple of gambling shops and a place called The Cage that was rumoured to belong to the Rossi family. There were no streetlights all the way to the docks. It was Pete that pointed that out to me and told me not to be stupid enough to repeat it. To think of Lil walking along these streets in the daylight was bad enough but the idea of her working here made my skin crawl. I still couldn't believe it. Strange because for all Pete's showing off and his big mouth, he was normally right. In fact, I can't remember a time when he was wrong.

I checked over my shoulder to see if anyone I knew was around, God forbid it should get back to my mother that I was here. Then I hurried along the path onto Fourth, trying to look inconspicuous. The Black Angel bar, otherwise known as the titty bar on Fourth, sat a little way back off the walkway. A piece of cheap red carpet invited you in through painted gold doors. The blacked-out windows were covered with poster-sized photos of the delightful girls you could find inside. Every girl looked young, but one especially, I'd put money on her being under sixteen. I had to make a continued effort not to think about their circumstances and concentrate on it being part of life, here.

I came here for my twenty-first with Joe, Pete and some buddies from work. It blew my mind. It was the first time I'd seen a girl naked that wasn't in a movie or dirty magazine. I didn't have the money back then to come regularly. I'm glad, or I could have become addicted to the body glitter, knickers and slow erotic movements. The bulky guy at the door is friendly, inviting me in and putting a free drink token in my hand. It's dark and smoky, which I'm grateful for, the last thing I want to see is another guy jerking off. It's hard to see through the waves of smoke being pumped onto the bottom of the stage, especially with the blinking rainbow lights. I circle around the edge of the stage, which only has two greased-up girls at this time in the afternoon.

I make my way to the bar keeping my eyes peeled for any glimpse of Lilly. I pull up a sticky leather stool when I get to the bar, and call out for the barman by knocking my knuckles on the dark wooden counter. I turned my head, checking every girl in the place. A few hover around men they think they can get a lap dance out of. A couple of topless women serve drinks on trays and I can't help thinking this scene looks like the inside of my teenage mind.

My eyes get stuck on the stage for a moment. A girl slowly slides down a pole to the joy of five men intently watching. She throws back her head sending her long bottle blonde hair flying back in a wave. I can feel the gasp of delight from the men from here. Then, I turned back around. I see a small figure on the opposite side of the bar in a white, tight stretched T-shirt walking towards me.

'One whisky, one beer,' I say reaching for my wallet.

'Sure,' says a wilting voice, I immediately recognised it and my head whiplashes around. I stare for a second in disbelief, then unable to stop my mouth I blurt out.

'Lilly is that you?' She pushed her face forward straining to see me in the dim light.

'Do I know you?' She poured out the whisky. Smacking the stopper back in with the base of her palm, she pushes it back on the shelf.

'Um yeah, we went to school together. I'm Adam, Adam Silverman.' I pick up my drink trying not to let her see how unsteady my hand is. I shift nervously in my chair and I can feel sweat forming on the back of my neck. She's more beautiful than I remember. Age seems to have enhanced her allure, which is a fact every fibre of my being has picked up on.

'Oh, sorry I don't remember you.' Shrugging her shoulders, she places my beer down and takes the money I laid down for her.

'That's OK, I'm pretty forgettable,' I joke, my stomach flipping like an overloaded washing machine. Drifting, my eyes catch sight of a flyer with phone numbers but not the same as the one I have. She catches me. 'I wasn't looking at taking one.' My feeble lie met with an eye roll. She pushes one in my direction.

'And you've never phoned one either, right? This one has all our latest girls on it.' I take it and put it in my pocket. She shakes her head and walks to serve another guy at the other end of the bar. A waft of her perfume grabs me, impelling me to draw breath, holding part of her in my mouth.

I down my beer fast, chilling the back of my throat. I can feel my blood alcohol rising, it starts to steady my hand, a familiar warming feeling. A growing confidence, which is most likely psychosomatic, spreads throughout my being. I feel more myself than I have all day. I have to order another before she's off shift. With an unfaltering hand, I tap the bar again. She walks over.

'Another?' she says, taking my glass to refill.

The music changes behind me signalling the alternation of girls on the stage. I automatically turn my head: bad move, now I'm just another lowlife here for cheap thrills. I rotate my head back to Lilly. 'Beer thanks.' I throw a twenty-dollar bill down, in an effort to seem relaxed. She takes it and opens the till to get my change. I watch her for a minute or two, my eyes trying to pierce the dark to mentally photograph every inch. Pete clearly has it wrong. She only works behind the bar, not on the phones. She's such a nice girl, I can tell. It's still there in her eyes... like in school. 'So how long have you been working here?' My small talk has a lot to be desired.

'A while, a year I guess.' She stacks the glasses that she pulled from a drying rack. Then rearranges bottles of liquor that need finishing, putting them to the front of the case for easy reach. I watch, not quite believing that Lilly is right here in front of me. Not only has she been back for a year and I'm only finding out now, but also that even in the dark, even though we have only spoken a few words, she still has that indefinable quality I hunger for. The faded edges of my insides start to fill with hope.

'You getting ready for tonight?' I smile in hope to seem friendly.

'What?' She struggles to hear me over the music.

'I just said, are you getting ready for tonight? You're stacking?' I pointed to the shelves behind her. She gave me a half smile and nodded to be polite.

'I suppose Friday is busy around here. Big crowds.' She nodded again. She seemed completely disinterested.

'So, it was a nice day today, right?' She looked at me as though I was either crazy or drunk. I shifted. 'The weather I mean… it's nice, sunny. I walked here because the weather is so nice… it's good to have nice weather.' I could hear myself repeating my own words. Why couldn't I be halfway normal for just a few minutes? She looked at me for a second, then said:

'I wouldn't know. I get here in the dark and leave in the dark.' She hung up the cloth she'd been using on a brass peg. Then stepped through a little doorway and disappeared out of sight through the back door, where I could just make out the edge of the kitchen.

'It was nice talking to you…' I called after her. I don't think she heard me, or at least, she didn't acknowledge she had.

I didn't hang around after Lil left. I didn't come here for the girls, although more of them fill the stage, none of them catches my eye. There would be something wrong with me if I didn't find them sexy; swinging around poles with pouting faces. This is not really what I'm into, only in times of complete drought do I find myself here. I find it hard to forget the girls are show only and I imagine what they talk about out the back in the changing rooms. It doesn't even come close to the sweetness of Lilly. I pretty much down my drink and go. There is still a little light left in the day as I clamber up the doorway steps. Crossing over the little patch of red carpet, I observe it's starting to fray in one corner and surmise it's a perfect metaphor for summing up the strip club experience. On the way in, everything is bright and exciting, on the way out, you're drunk, broke and a little frayed. At this time, as I find my way out, I notice a change in atmosphere. Couple that with the speed of my drinking, it hits me, and I sway, grabbing out for a street sign to steady myself.

'You OK, buddy?' the doorman calls out with a laugh. I nod and gather myself. Using all my will and concentration to stand fully upright.

'Fine thanks,' I mutter, gruffly waving him off. Then, I hurry to get back to Market Street in almost a straight line. I pass groups of guys in threes and more heading into the bar. A shiver passes through me at the thought of Lilly dealing with rowdy men, fired up with their pay cheques to blow. It's a sobering thought.

The market is closing with just as much noise as when it opened. The slamming of truck doors as the stock is packed away. Brooms and hoses are worked over the street returning it to order for tomorrow. A sign for fresh honey grabs my attention. The stall is a staple of this street, therefore, a staple of me. I walk over with the intention of grabbing some for my mother. As I get closer, I see the stall has a large and bountiful range, more than normal. I hate change. A woman pops up from behind a table.

'Can I get something for you?' She sounds a little preoccupied. I notice she's trying to stack boxes into the back of her van. She seems to be having trouble making them fit. I automatically help her lift them in.

'Oh sweetheart, I would have been there all night. Choose something.' She points to the jars in yellows, reds and oranges.

'No, you don't have to do that.' I wave off her offer.

'Yes, I do, they're the rules around here — now what do you want? I don't have all night.' Seeing I won't win, I agree.

'OK thanks, what's good? It's for my mum.' She picks up a dark golden-coloured jar and puts it in my hand.

'Now you give this to your mother and it will cure her of everything; back pain, neck pain, a broken heart — you know everything except maybe a pain in the ass husband. There's no cure for that!' she laughs.

I grin back. 'OK thanks again.'

On the way home, I hold the jar up to the streetlight to look at the deep intense colour, strands of light illuminate the swirls like marble, pouring forward beckoning me to taste. '*Cures a broken heart huh*?' I say to myself before dipping my fingers in the runny liquid and letting it drip on my tongue. Kind of gross yet delicious. She'll never know, I think as I repeat the manoeuvre.

I felt the flyer in my pocket. I've never called a sex line before — could I? If someone else answers the call, is it OK just to hang up? What's the protocol? Worse, what if they recognise me? The shame it would bring to my mother is unthinkable, in a small town like this it would be inescapable. It would be followed by rumours that float around growing in strength. So much risk, all of this just to prove Pete wrong. He's an idiot — he doesn't know what he's talking about. There's no way. Lil is not the voice on the sex line.

CHAPTER 5
OBLIGATION

Every Saturday, I go with some cheap present for my mum, all the way out of town to the Fringe. It's more the thought than the gift itself. I'll place it on the table; she'll act like it's made of gold. I know, if I don't, she'll be disappointed. It's the only real ritual my mother and me have.

The Fringe is the suburban neighbourhood on the edge of the city, where I spent the last half of my childhood. Visiting is like a step back in time, like I'm putting on my childhood clothes, walking around in my old skin. The houses are small and packed tightly together, like toys with quaint courtyards rather than the gardens of the outer neighbourhoods. It's a quiet place now, filled with mostly retirees and families, women with double prams, and kids on bikes hanging out on the corners. It has such a different feel from where I live; the atmosphere changes me instantly at a molecular level. Within seconds I am a different person; calmer. The trees have grown tall on both sides of the street and there's no hustle and bustle. At first, it seems almost dead with the absence of loud, boisterous movement. But as your mind's eye adjusts to its new context, you see people taking care of their small front yards decorated with pot plants, prized flowers and small shrubs. I always see at least half a dozen people I know. It's strange that most of the kids I grew up with on this street now have kids of their own. There's a strong sense of belonging and my parents have always been happy here. There are more of our people here, as my mother puts it. Although I knew this as a kid, I never understood why cultures flock together.

This week I've brought the honey that I got at the market, which, thanks to the rustic screw-on lid, doesn't look opened. I feel it in my pocket, with a little remorse for putting my fingers in it earlier. In my mind, I can see my mother spooning it into her tea with anticipation and I can't help laughing out loud to myself.

When I arrive at the house, I know what she'll say. There will be something about being too thin and needing new clothes. Something about her needing to feed me or I'll fade away because all I eat is muck, apparently. All leading up to her grand finale: pure guilt over not having a girlfriend at my age and her lack of grandchildren. It's OK she just worries! She's a woman that even when everything is going smooth seems to live on the edge of her nerves. At fifty-seven, she's still slight of figure with hair dyed black. She's warm but stern, if not a little meddlesome. Tradition is of the utmost importance to her. We eat together at three every Saturday. My sister comes in straight from work. My mother doesn't like that she works on Saturday. However, she doesn't say anything any longer, just glad that she comes at all.

I have a brother too; he comes when he feels like it. The only one of us that is married, he has a slightly bossy wife, two kids, and one on the way. My mother doesn't like his wife, they argue. She starts every conversation about her with: 'That woman...!' she never uses her name. Then comes the list of complaints starting with: 'She doesn't care for your brother at all because...!' which I don't think is true. She just doesn't care for him the way that my mother took care of him. Which involved her practically spoon feeding and dressing him, or propping him up on pillows to be worshipped. He was always the favourite, not that that bothers me. I've always been closer with my dad.

As I sit at the table, I wait for it.

'So, Adam, when are you gonna bring a girl home?' my mother questions. My father rolls his eyes at me, so she doesn't see. I stare at the almost mocking, pure white tablecloth. I shuffle my fork from one side of the napkin to the other.

'Why would he bring one of his girls home?' The emphasis was on one. My mother was silenced for once. 'He's a young man. He's only twenty-six. He is busy playing the field.' My father searches for words in an even tone. 'They're not the kind of girls that you bring home, nothing wrong with playing the field a bit before settling down,' he says to me with a wink. He asks me to pass on the bread with a hand signal as he speaks. I nod my head at the obvious lie.

My sister keeps her head down. She wants to stay out of the line of fire and continues to eat, offering nothing… bypassing the chance to tease me, which strikes me as odd. She is loyal and obligated to our parents' will. That's why she's here; to do her duty mostly, but as soon as the dishes are done, she'll be gone. I will be required to stay. I'll help my father fix whatever needs fixing and hopefully get a few moments alone with him. My father and I are friends. He is a Prince among men and I would think so even if he wasn't my father. He has an easy way of being, he's funny and his life hasn't managed to turn him dark as it easily could have with what he's seen.

After eating, he and I sit out in the garden on chairs that smell of tea tree oil in the doorway of his shed. He has a small heater that, most of the time, he is too frightened to turn on as my mother will complain about the gas bill. He's a man with few needs, but even he needs heat, I think to myself. He passes me a cigarette from the hidden packet and winks in the direction of the house; another of our secrets. Mother runs a tight ship and cigarettes are contraband around here. She's not too fond of drinking either.

'Is there any girl that you have your eye on, I don't mean to pry?' my father smirks. 'I'm only asking because you remember my friend Isaac?' There's a short pause while I wait for the punchline, 'He has three daughters, all still single.' He nudges me with a grin. Isaac is my father's best friend.

'Yes, and we both know why they're all single!' I joke back with a laugh under my breath. He nods his head still laughing.

'Poor Isaac, he is a good man but… oh, those girls. What will he do?' He chuckles placing his hand on his forehead.

'I could take one out on a date,' I point out. 'Knowing my luck, I'll get one pregnant and have to marry her. Then I'll be stuck with three ugly daughters of my own,' I say under my breath.

'No, no,' says Dad, shaking his head and chuckling,

'But if you think it'll shut Mother up for a while!' I'm only to happy to take a bullet for him.

'I think she would be happy if you bring home anyone at this point. She has her heart set on grandchildren from you since the last fight with your brother's wife… you know.' I nodded. 'So, it's all I hear all week long. Why doesn't Adam have a girlfriend?' I pat his back in empathy. My mother can be a handful and stubborn when she digs her heels in. I hear her voice in my head as he says the words.

'It's hard for me to meet girls. There aren't too many where I am.' I shrug off the awkwardness.

'Surely there are some OK-ish girls who work in the warehouse offices?' he offers, passing me over a whisky, the bottle also hidden under a blanket in the shed.

'Not where I work, at the north end, only men… so nope. Unless you count Ivor Selberg.' I snicker. He laughs and nods, nearly choking on his drink.

'Ivor Selberg? I remember him. Weedy fella. I think you could even bring him home and she would be happy!' Patting me on the shoulder, he pulls my head close to his and ruffles my hair like I'm still five. 'No... no... you know, I'm joking. Better not bring home, Ivor Selberg. I don't think your mother would cope with that at all. Unless you agreed to adopt, that is.'

We sit in quiet silence, comfortable and relaxed. Scanning the backyard, I realise nothing has changed. This place feels like my father, from the plant choice to the little paths going nowhere. I get brave with the whisky in me, with a deep breath in I start.

'So... Dad...' I lose my nerve for a second, choking on the honesty of what I wait to share with him. To say out loud and make real I go on. 'There might be this one girl.' My father laughs and slaps me on the back.

'So, there is a girl after all. Oh, that makes me so happy.' His excitement comes from deep inside, genuine happiness. His hands begin to wave, encouraging me for details. He is suddenly alert and sitting bolt upright.

'Don't get excited and don't mention it to Mum.' I try to calm him down, but it's a lost cause. I can't help smiling with his excitement.

'No, no, of course... So, have you spoken to her yet?' he says quietly, his face close to mine as if someone else could be listening to our conversation.

'Not exactly,' I explain, trying to hide the smile I know decorates my face like a clown's painted grin. 'We went to school together, you know. So, I have spoken to her but I get the impression she believes I was just passing time with idle conversation.' A sigh escapes from within me.

'So, think of something to say, you're good with words when you want to be,' my father encourages, waiting for more details.

'There's something else… She works in the bar on Fourth Street,' I say plainly, knowing he will swallow his real reaction. My father's face turns down then immediately he hides his disapproval.

'Fourth you say…? Interesting.'

'Behind the bar, Dad.' I try to sound confident. 'She's a lovely girl. There aren't so many jobs at the moment.'

'Yes, I'm sure if you like her, she's a nice girl,' he offers, trying to sound positive. I continue, endeavouring to bring back his excitement.

'I was hoping that she would recognise me from school or remember my face… but she didn't. So, I sat there talking about the weather.' Saying it out loud made it feel even lamer. The bloodbath that is my small talk made me cringe.

'So, do you plan to talk to this girl again?' Offering me another drink, he hears the hesitation.

'Yes, but I'm not sure how to do it yet. There are others that want her so I have to think of something a little better than weather to talk about.' I leaned back letting the last mouthful of whisky pour smoothly down my throat.

'But what chance do others have standing next to you?' He is forever the optimist. He smiled clinking his glass into mine. I look at my father sarcastically and he lets out a laugh, 'There's nothing wrong with you.' He points his finger at me letting me know that he means it.

'If only everyone thought like that,' I reply to the ground, rolling my eyes.

'Well, when you take this girl out make sure you drop by to say hello to your mother. You'll keep her off my back for a while.' We laugh nodding in agreement.

CHAPTER SIX
CALLING

Add to journal (I like this)
Entry no. 8827

She is the lantern, a promise of hope,
The touch of light, when clarities needed,
Barer of a delicate flame to be guarded,
With my whole self, I commit to task.

I only have two small windows in my apartment. They look onto another block of drab buildings, offering only a view of bricks above the alley where the garbage is locked up. This homeless guy lives there on and off. There's a crack in the top corner of the glass where the wind screams through, scaring the shit out of me at night. I sigh upon entering this place the boys call my '*Rat's Nest*'. The walls seem to close in on me entering, small and dingy as it is. Old orange curtains hang at the windows, given to me by my mother last spring clean. I hated them when they hung in my mother's house, now I hate them even more. They remind me of a seedy middle-aged man's divorce pad. I wrote this thing about it, I'm not sure where it is now. I have a drawer full of bits I've written; I don't know why I keep them. I should throw them out. Then there are linoleum squares that peel up in places, the kitchen that has two doors missing from the wall cabinets, and the ceiling has more cracks than plaster. There is one ceiling fan in my bedroom. It makes a buzzing sound that could drive a person insane. So in the summer, I am faced with a choice; either be driven mad by a buzzing sound, or sweat in stifling heat.

However, most of the time I don't care. I live like a pig anyway, but tonight it seems shittier than normal. I don't wanna be here. I feel restless, it's dread, actually. It comes from the horror of time spinning crazily by while I live the same day over and over. It's suffocation and frustration bubbling up only to be quietly suppressed while feeling ungrateful for having a job and life that sustains me. I get this way sometimes. A strong feeling of free-falling or hanging in limbo with all its complexities. As though I could walk out my front door and just keep walking. I don't know where, just walk until I get somewhere that's not here.

It's hard to live with myself in this mood. In fact, it's hard to live with myself most of the time. There are times when I wish I had multiple personality disorder. At least I would get some relief from my monotonous, circular paralysis. I force my body up and I try to keep busy, calm myself. In an attempt to clean up a bit and shake this feeling, I move stuff around. I wipe stuff with a damp cloth, a little half-assed. I do the dishes and hang up my clothes. It doesn't make that much difference; it's still a shitty apartment. I don't have visitors, so it doesn't usually bother me. But after being at my mother's house, all clean and cosy, then sharing a drink in Dad's backyard, it feels so claustrophobic. Like there's no air and everything is too tight. I don't know why I bothered.

On my fridge, which I bought for only fifty dollars, second hand from a guy at work after his girlfriend had left him, I'd stuck a large advertisement from a travel magazine over a dent. I told myself it was there to cover up the large scratches, not wanting to admit I needed to see it, that it gave me hope. The picture itself shows a silver-sanded beach, complete with leaning palm tree, a half-naked girl strolling alone with an umbrella cocktail in her hand, calling out for my company. The sky is an endless, pale blue with kite-like birds dotting the horizon. I can almost feel the warm breeze on my face. I'm not sure a place like that really exists, probably it was edited with a computer. In my whole life, I've never actually been to the beach. Not a beach without pebbles and driftwood from boat hulls or filth from the docks anyway. In fact, I've not really left the city, just to my parents' place, and they don't exactly live in an exotic location. I tacked the glossy picture up over six months ago, determined that this would be the year that I put my feet in the water. It's not gonna happen.

With some order in the place, I sit down pouring myself a whisky, although I've probably had enough for one night. Sometimes I have these moments of clarity where I see myself so I grab a drink to push it back where it belongs — hidden. Grabbing the flyer from my pocket, I look over it. The phone is on the table in front of me. It's impossible to think of Lilly on the other end of one of these chat lines. What if I could hear her voice? She wouldn't have to talk about anything dirty, I'd just like to talk to her, maybe get her to say my name. I'd like that, hear her say, Adam. I feel myself smiling.

I pick up the phone and look at my hand, questioning if I have the balls to do it. Dialling the first number, I wait for a second or two.

'Two dollars a minute...' announces an automated voice. I take a deep breath, a woman's voice answers. Not Lilly!

'Hey honey, what can I do for you?'

'Nothing, thank you, I think I've got the wrong number.' I hang up quickly like I'm fleeing the scene of a bank robbery.

I let a deep breath out of my chest. My hands are shaking slightly. I dial the next number. The same protocol, a slightly hoarse voice answers this time, an attempt at being sexy.

'Hey, I'm Alice, you feeling lonely? You wanna talk to me for a while?'

'Um... no that's OK, I'm all good, thank you.' Oddly disappointed I hang up.

I repeat the routine through about six or seven more numbers. Punching the numbers in one after another, I realise that Pete is absolutely wrong about Lilly. She is far too innocent for this even if she does work in a strip joint. Maybe innocent is the wrong word. I just know there's a huge gap between bartender and sex worker. Is that too harsh…? Is phone sex really that bad or just…? Next number… I have to stop my mind now it's beginning to roll in waves, thoughts are starting to crash in the front of my mind. What if, what if, what if? Focus on what you're doing!

'Hey…' a tiny voice answers the phone. It reminds me of a little sparrow. 'Hello is someone there? Hi, I'm Jen,' I'm stunned to silence for a second. A million thoughts flash across my brain. Speak. I think to myself… Speak now.

My voice comes out a little shaky,

'Hey… hello Jen, how are you?' I hold the phone tight to my ear.

'I'm good, thank you, do you wanna talk to me for a while?' I've never heard her speak so many words at once. Her sweet little voice enflames my imagination. I am instantly hard. I clear my throat.

'Um… yeah sure,' I sit up in my seat, my stomach flips. It's her for sure. I would recognise that voice anywhere. I don't know what I'm saying yes to. I want her to keep talking.

'Your name's Jen, right?' I'm fighting every urge to say, Lil.

'Yeah that's right, so are you all alone in the house tonight?' The way she spoke had a playful edge. I'd never heard it before and it was driving me insane. She was

70

talking to me like she knew me like we were really flirting. Almost like things had gone well at the bar.

'Yeah, I'm all alone.' Clearly, she'll be doing most of the talking as my head felt like a traffic jam, too overwhelmed to think.

'So… do you wanna know what I'm wearing?' I could feel my heart starting to pound hard, like a hammer in my chest. As though it was trying to break its way through my ribcage, smash its way out of my chest and dart down the phone.

'Sure, you can tell me what you're wearing.' I sit up straighter nearly snapping my spine, I wish I was better at this stuff; I just wanted her to keep talking. She could be reading out the dictionary and I still would be satisfied.

'Well, you see… I just got home from work. So, I took a shower… I only have a towel on,' she said shedding some of her innocence. I felt my temperature start to climb. My phone hand started to sweat so I swapped sides as my pants became tight and uncomfortable.

'Yeah…' I say, leaning back in the lounge. 'You only have a towel on?' I swallow hard. Just hearing her voice is making my hands sweat. I know, I should take a greater part in this conversation but I don't know what is polite to say. There is a moment of silence again and then hearing my shallow panting, she adds:

'Would you like me to tell you what I look like?' The words are slow and deliberate, rolling slowly off her tongue.

71

'Yes… yes do that,' I say excitedly, starting to breathe heavier, aware of myself but unable to stop.

'My hair is long and blonde with highlights. I have blue eyes. Big full lips,' her voice gets deeper, throaty, with a hint of desire as she pauses and I wait for a shallow moan to end, hoping another will start. I let out a grown, I don't mean to. I wish I could shove it back in. I've never been this turned on before and it's hard to stay sitting.

'Would you like me to talk about my body?' A shiver of excitement goes right through me. I fight to keep my eyes open as my head naturally tilts back.

I stammer, 'Yes.'

'I'm small, my legs are quite long, shapely.' Instantly I'm cast back to the day her skirt was reefed up. Just like that, she was in front of me. I could see her… every detail… my imagination working in Technicolor.

'Keep going,' I mutter.

'Like I said I'm tiny, small waist, small hips, my tits are a handful but they are cute and perky with small pink nipples.' I couldn't breathe hearing her breathy voice describe herself, saying the word tits to me. The word repeats a few times in my head like an echo.

She was there. Standing in front of me in a soft white towel. I could picture her pulling it open. Letting it drop to the floor, showing me herself. Letting my eyes wander all over her, taking me on a tour with her fingers. I undid the button of my pants with one hand, thinking of that creamy white skin inching closer, struggling with my jeans. Wanting to tear them from my skin as quickly as possible.

'What else? Tell me everything.' My words are coming out more confidently as my demanding became stronger.

'Soft skin... flat stomach...' she giggled, 'I'm running my hand down my thighs, wish you were here to follow my fingers with kisses.' The fever took over me, burning white hot. I could see myself tracing the lines of her stomach, hips, then inner thighs with my lips lightly touching her.

'God yes... Please keep going.' I took hold of myself... throbbing... I couldn't help it, the picture so clear in my head.

'My fingers are moving to my thigh.' She gave a little moan. She must have known I was close. Like an expert she made me wait a few seconds, making me beg.

'Now what are you doing?' It was getting too much.

'Mmmmm,' she responded with only a moan, forcing me to ask.

'Tell me, please,' I choked out, my hand tighter, moving faster. I spat on the palm of my hand before my cock caught fire.

'I'm slowly opening my legs,' she sighed like speaking was too much, pleasure dripping from her tongue.

'Are you wet...?' I said gasping. It was out of my mouth without thinking. I'd never said anything even close to that to a woman before but I didn't care. I wanted her so badly I couldn't stop myself.

'Oh yeah! You're making me so wet. I want you inside me,' she moaned with a heavy breathy voice. It was too much for me. A sudden realisation of whom I was talking too, of the words I'd always wanted to hear coming out of that sweet mouth. A surge of need, unstoppable need. In a rush of heat and excitement, I erupted. It was over with a groan. I dropped the phone. My sticky hand getting tangled in my pants. Trying to catch my breath I fished around the floor to retrieve it.

'Honey are you done?' came from the other end of the phone. 'Do you want me to keep going... you done?' she said, returning to her almost normal voice.

'I'm done... er... done thank you,' I answered not knowing how to conclude the interaction. I waited. Listening for a clue as to what came next.

'Call again, honey,' she hung up... silence... It was over. I gasped sucking in air with the surreal realisation what had just taken place. I sat there surveying the mess, I relaxed back, a laugh of relief and shock rumbled its way from my chest. I just had phone sex with Lilly.

Feeling myself almost comatose and growing heavy with post-ejaculative satisfaction, I picked myself up, taking the bottle of whisky and my half-full glass to the kitchen. I swilled the glass letting my normal liquid sleeping pill wash away down the plughole. I didn't need anything to drift off tonight. The picture of naked Lilly had tattooed itself to the inside of my skull and I could see it with my eyes open or closed. I lingered for a second on the thought of her lying next to me in bed as if it had been real.

So Lil is a woman, not as innocent as I believed. There is a freedom in that knowledge. I don't have to feel quite as guilty as I have done in the past, dreaming about the things I want to do to her.

CHAPTER 7
MORE THAN THE WEATHER

Do I like this? Unsure?
Journal entry 3828

I am a microscopic dot, reduced to less than a speck
of dust.
Insignificant.
All hope is lost.
I am so compacted,
Dehydrated of all that is good.
My spirit has been drawn from me,
I can no longer find my way

I race home from work, bypassing the bar. As tempted as I am to get a drink in me, I resisted despite being consumed with the anxiety of the '*perhaps*' changes on the horizon. The minute I get inside my apartment I take off my clothes and jumped in the shower. I am out of shampoo and used soap in my hair, it might not make my hair shiny, but at least it will be clean. I look down at myself. In the last couple of years, I have gained muscle, broadened across my shoulders, my arms are powerful, legs feel strong like a boxer, even my core is hard and ready. For once I am thankful to work with my hands. It's kept away the layer of heredity roly-poly fat that my office-working brother has gained. The hot water and steam clear my head. I am at last at zero. The floor is slippery stepping out; skidding sidewards I collided with the doorframe, bruising my arm. I don't stop to rub or even look at it; the dialogue in my head is too loud. There are too many *what ifs* and too many *maybes*.

I hold a five-minute discussion with myself on how much aftershave I should put on to smell manly, yet seem casual. After more deliberation, I decided to splash on a palm full, second guessing myself the moment it touched my skin. I stood in front of my wardrobe. I had nothing to wear. There was nothing that would make me stand out. For some reason, I thought a well-put-together outfit would just appear on a hanger. Like in those men's magazines where the men do one-handed pull-ups while smiling for the camera. I pulled on jeans and an ironed shirt, which were at least clean thanks to my mother nagging for my washing. I looked in the mirror.

Same face, same hair, same clothes. Let's hope my conversation is more engaging or at least a little brighter today, I catch myself talking aloud again. She had been on my mind constantly, obsessively so. I replayed each and every word she had spoken. That voice, the image of her playing on a loop that I couldn't and wouldn't turn off. I can't help but toy with the idea that maybe when she sees me she would realise it was me on the phone last night, that she will feel the connection between us. Lighting will strike, she will leap over the bar straight into my arms, we would walk out into the night ready for our new life. I'd suddenly be witty and cool, and not so broken. She would adore me the way I adore her… we'd go to my place, she'd stand in front of me, I wouldn't need to tell her a thing. Slowly she would peel off the layers… she would stand naked, allowing me to look at her, I'm left breathless. I catch myself. I'd had that same thought, in a variety of scenarios, throughout high school. It had never ended up even close. Why would it be different now?

Taking one last look in the mirror, I see myself, sigh at the reflection. My hands are shaking slightly. It's a rare thing to notice my own jitters, most of the time I don't stop long enough to notice. I make a point of not looking in the mirror. The sadness in my reflection scares me. If I stare too long, I can see the dark hole running right through my chest cavity and out to the other side into the abyss. Holding my hands up close to my face I inspect the rough skin on my palms from the dust and years of ripping used cardboard. My knuckles are out of line from punch-ups I can't remember and being completely reckless at work. Glancing in the mirror sideways so I only get an impression of myself. I force my spine straight, it hurts thanks to my continuous habit of slouching but the stretch feels good… like a cool shower after a long day. I look closer at my face. The lines on my forehead are a road map of apprehension, of trial and error, of night terrors and pills. I am undeserving. I am unworthy and I wish I hadn't looked.

My stomach rolls in waves, lapping the back of my throat as a warning of what is coming. The anxiety is returning. I can name it now, if only in my head. What am I doing? Closing my eyes, I count to ten trying to find my centre. I slowly open them, hoping another image will meet me in the mirror. I shake my head at what I have to work with. I give myself *a snide thumbs-up* with a crooked half smile. You look like a prick, I say in my head. I know it's true. A well-timed cat creeps along the windowsill taking my attention. I watch for a few seconds, breathing in and out. It sits licking its hind leg with great care. A pep talk is all I need. I can't bother Dad again. I rally myself, '*Come on Ads, you can do it this time*'. Even the voice in my head had a sarcastic tone rather than being encouraging.

I jog rather than walk across town, aware that my armpits are staining my shirt. Breaking out into a cold sweat I am aware of everything… another warning sign. The night has a chill to it with a smell of musky Chinese takeaway in the air. Regardless, I take my jacket off to prevent creases and to dry out the wet sweat on my back. My shoes feel too tight for running. My jeans rub against the inside of my legs. I could feel my spirit starting to deplete. The warning signs of a panic attack are all lining up. I hate saying it, even in my head. It reeks of teenage-girl melodrama. I stop for a second, perching on a hip-high brick wall. The feeling, like a rolling thunderclap, begins up from deep in my stomach, pushing past my heart setting it to burning. It gathers into a ball of scorching heat, making my face pulse. It's going to happen here, out in the open. I haven't got time to find a bathroom. I tap my finger to my thumb, then the next finger, then the next, over and over, trying to stop it. It's too late to block it, to late to turn back home. The only thing I can do is try to slow it down. I realise I am sweating hard now, aware to a passer-by that I look ridiculous. I pant like a dog without water, looking down at my hands, forcing focus on the tapping.

'*Think about each touch*,' I hear my therapist's dry voice telling me to stop. *Forget the world; tap one finger to the next. Adam breathe out, don't hold it in. One finger presses tightly to the next. Faster, tapping... only think about tapping... nothing else. Over and over,* I feel the compression as I squeeze my fingertips tight. I am blind, must keep my eyes shut until I gain my equilibrium. I suck in air, I increase the pressure, the pain cancels out the burning in my face. Focus on the pain, make a fist, and squeeze as hard as I can. The heat lessening, only to be replaced with a queasy feeling. I dry heave, standing, leaning over the wall; well past caring if people walk past, yet ever conscious. A small gust of wind catches a curl of hair that's flopped in my face; I push it back and stand upright. Using the wall to prop myself up, I fill myself with oxygen; too much, I'm light-headed. It begins to pass, not a full-blown attack just a tremor; the full-blown quake is on its way. Not tonight hopefully but soon, I must delay it.

I know the cycle well. I can't think about it or I'll bring on another attack.

***

I must have sat for thirty minutes before I started to daydream about Lil's face. Some of my previous excitement returns, accompanied by a handful of butterflies. I can't focus on the fact that people have probably seen me freaking out, the embarrassment's enough to cripple me. The music pumping from the other end of the street made me quicken my step, setting my mind back to the task at hand.

I don't have to line up, but I'm lucky to get in before the doors close. Seven thirty p.m. and the place is packed already. Men crowd around the stage, which runs right down the centre of the building almost cutting the room in two. High-backed chairs and tables are placed for prime viewing pleasure. Around the edges of the room, the floor is slightly raised in order to see over the crowd and men hang over the wooden partition. A few booths at one end curve for more private viewings and lap dances.

Six over-made girls in the middle of their sets are gyrating on the stage. The long fake nails of a girl under twenty-two hold every poll. Some of the men are already drunk, smothering themselves in a topless waitress or two. All patrons know to behave, there's a code of conduct to follow. You never stiff a girl. You can smack her ass as she passes, but never grab. No fingers, but face diving is fine (top or bottom). The manager doesn't tolerate rowdiness, especially during Friday night routines, the biggest money-maker of the week. I walk straight over to the bar filled with men from the docks. I squeeze in between two men that look like they're getting ready to leave. Soon enough, as a place opens up around the stage, the two men wander down there as I predicted they would. I wanna keep my head down. I don't want Lilly to think I'm here for strippers; I'm just a guy looking for a drink. A guy I haven't seen before comes over to serve me.

'What can I get you?' I order a beer and whisky, which I intend to drink slowly — it won't have any real effect. I need a cool head to talk to Lilly. I didn't realise this place got so packed, I usually get here later. The bar staff weave around one another serving drink after drink. Behind them, an array of colourful alcohol bottles is lit up with spotlights.

Two men are exchanging words over one of the girls — it looks a little hostile. I see the manager give the bouncer a wink. *They're out of here the second the bouncer can kick them out without causing too much of a scene*, I think to myself turning back to my drink that is disappearing quickly. Even after last night, I couldn't believe that Lil belonged in a place like this; flashing artificial lighting, men in business suits slumming it, lugs from the shipyards and me. I'm here. This place has some poetic justice to it. The potential inspiration for a million novels begging to be written. Each person here could be an exaggerated character from a third-rate movie.

It's a show, a performance, yet the guys in here preen and show off like peacocks to get the girls' full attention. As though it was reality. As if they convinced themselves that the twenty-two-year-old butterfly in front of them could ever look at the drunken, greasy fifty-two-year-old in front of her with anything but disgust or pity. Don't know if they forget they paid at the door. If they push to the back of their minds the fact that until they shoved a fifty in her knickers... she wasn't looking his way. They believe that even with their beer belly brokenness and their thirty extra years on this planet that somehow when you grunt for her to sit on your knee... she wants you. I fill with loathing; I hate all of them — animals. I hate all this shit, life, the way it works yet I'm here as lousy as the rest of them. A shiver ran through me at the thought that one day I could walk into this place and see Lilly on some drunk-ass guy. I promised myself, falling asleep late last night, that I would do all I can to get her out of here and I caught myself in that second, my body stiffening. I'm getting too far ahead of myself. Lil, isn't my Lilly yet. I still need to win her.

It was then I caught sight of her at the other end of the bar. She was pulling beer feverishly, one after another. As I study her, I realised that there are other men that clearly feel the same way as I do about Lilly. A growl of ownership gurgles from deep inside of me, jealousy, pure and simple. I could kill each and every bastard looking her way. She is a beautiful woman, none of the skinny, muted girl left in her. I was a fool to think that it would be easy, that this romance was anything more than a dream I have in my head. But standing so close even with the impossibility of her becoming mine, I know, I have to try.

I had spent most of my day trying to figure out something reasonable to talk about when I activate my plan, not so much a plan as a hope. I haven't managed to think of anything yet. I'm capable of winging it for once, surely. Something will come to me in the moment. The noise starts to build in my head again. The nag of uncontrollable things, things out of reach, things that shouldn't be. I push them down like swallowing a bad pill. My stomach swishes, another drink to get me in control again.

Amazed to find a small table and chair in the back corner of the room, I sit to wait out the next few hours. There's a time frame involved in this plan of mine. Although one or two girls come over to me I am able to sit virtually undetected. It needs to be this way until around eleven o'clock, that is when I will get up and set the wheels in motion.

***

Having spent the evening watching Lilly from across the bar I am eager to finally have my moment. It never became boring, not for a second. I could never get sick of studying the way she moves, her gestures, the way she flicks her hair back when it gets in her eyes. While I sat, I re-formulated the plan; going over and over it in my head…

I'll wait for her break at eleven fifteen p.m. All employees take their breaks in the courtyard's side alley. It's hard to get in with locked gates from the street but there is another door that the employees use in the wet area behind the bar. The plan was to pretend to be slightly tipsy. Make a wrong turn into the staff toilets, cross the hall into the store area and end up outside in the courtyard. Not the most brilliant plan but I hoped it would work. I could be out there with her, hopefully alone. I could talk to her a bit without all the noise. I'm sure something witty would come to me.

At eleven fifteen on the dot I watched as she handed over her post to a tall guy with tattoos and started to make her way to the exit. Taking a double whisky with me, I stand. The plan to keep a clear head had gone a little awry, but it had stopped my nerves being a hindrance. I start to make my way to the toilets, then took a left turn through the storeroom, and opened the door to the alley.

The door shut behind me, the sound of it clicking shut made my decision final. I paused, waiting for my eyes to adjust. I see her sitting on some upturned beer crates, staring up at the stars peacefully, with a bottle of water in her hand. The enormity of the moment hit me. This is my chance. Could be the only I'll ever get. I must be bold. Women like a man who knows what he's doing. I draw in air, filling my lungs with the cold night chill. I can do this, I tell myself in the same sarcastic voice that continually lives in the front of my mind. I step down into the courtyard alley, I feel my whole being open up, my raw heart waiting for any response to my approach.

'Oh, hi, I think I took a wrong turn,' I say, faking the confidence I hoped to start feeling.

'Yeah, this is staff only, sorry.' She laughed lightly in reply adding, 'Oh, you're that guy from the other night!' and second glancing in my direction.

'You remember me?' I was shocked, stepping closer careful not to sway as the fresh air hit my head, standing so she could see me clearer under the outside lights carefully, not to scare her.

'Hi,' she said again as I got closer.

'I'm Adam,' I said, putting out my hand, she shook it loosely. It was like ice from holding the water bottle.

'Lilly,' she said automatically.

'Yeah, I know, Lilly Kern, right?'

'Oh, that's right, we went to school together. I can't believe you remember me, it's been years,' she said looking up, shielding her eyes from the bright overhead lights.

'Of course, I remember.' I took another steady step forward.

'Do you want me to open the door for you? You need a key. It locks automatically.' She started to get up.

'No, don't get up, I'll go in when you do, take your break.' I realised I was standing over her slightly and took a step back.

'Are you sure? Really, it's not a problem.'

I shook my head.

'No, I'm fine,' I said, signalling her to stay seated.

'OK then, at least sit down, I can't relax if you're standing.'

She moved over slightly so I could sit down next to her on the crate. I sipped my whisky in an effort to hide my excitement at her invitation. I sat making sure I left a gap between us. I felt her shiver, causing me to shiver too. I tried to hide it by rubbing my arm as if I were cold. There was a little silence. I was about to break it but she spoke first.

'So, Adam, tell me about you.' Here was my chance to impress, I had waited all night, in fact, and I've been waiting my whole life for this. True to form my mind was blank. Don't choke now. My eyes flickering across the expanse of the alley, hunting for even a hint of a conversation starter.

'Well, I work on the docks.'

'Oh, you're a tradesman… Docker or…?'

'Not exactly, I work in freight… in the warehouse.' My small existence hit me like a punch in the chest, swallowing it down with a mouthful from my glass. There was a pause as I search my mind for something interesting to say, noticing she was watching the sky. Looking at the lines and patterns that the stars made dotted out before us, between the roofs, ariels and aeroplane warning lights. 'I used to like reading about the stars when I was young,' I stammered out. She looked toward me in acknowledgement. 'You know about the myths, the gods and goddesses. It was kind of fascinating, they were all very human for gods,' I said, trying to shrug off the feeling of being stupid.

'I would like to read about that sometime,' she replied, speaking softly but genuinely.

'I like books... I read a bit.' This is the best I could come up with, my nerves still pushing me around. She smiled in answer.

'I thought you were smart, I could tell. I wish I could read more. I read *Dracula* once. There's a time constraint thing, you see. I don't have any spare time. I'm always here — tell me something else about you, Adam?' She glanced as she said my name and I knew I would replay that moment every night for at least the next week. Her hands screwed up in her lap like she did when she was a kid, almost like she was nervous. What does she have to be nervous about? Do I scare her?

'Another fun fact... I play the piano as well — is that something?' I said adding, 'I need to practice a bit. I haven't done it for a while.' I took a mouthful of whisky as I could feel the effects starting to wear off, and I needed its alcoholic comfort more than ever.

'Do you play in church or anything?'

'No, it's just for me. My mum taught me. And as far as church goes, I'm actually Jewish so no church.'

'Oh,' she said apologetically. I saw her fists tighten again and take a large swig of water.

'I help my dad with wood carving sometimes... I'm good with my hands and he has a garden.' *Yep, you're bringing out the big guns Adam*, I think to myself. Nothing says sexy like helping old people with their hobbies.

'Garden?' Her eyes suddenly springing to life, 'I love flowers. I wish I could have a garden. I have a couple of sad pot plants on my windowsill, but that's about it. When I was little, I used to help my mum grow vegetables on our roof, until the manager of the building told us we couldn't because of the amount of water that we used. We still did but we had to be careful.' I shifted around to face her rather than continue to sit side by side. The small lights on the outside of the building cast shadows across her face, and it was as though she had turned into a living black-and-white photograph. Every inch of her was perfect, moving in slow motion. She smiled at me. I realised I was staring and looked away.

'You know, now that I'm looking at you closer Adam, I think maybe I do remember you. Didn't you have long hair?' Her hands loosely held the bottle and played with the lid as I pretended not to watch.

'Yeah, that was me — I hated haircuts.' She laughed. A warm honey-covered sound that made my heart flutter.

Her face was so close it became agony not to touch it. I'm staring again. I look away, but I could still smell her with each tiny movement she made. It was like a summer's day dancing across my senses. Catching sight of my watch from the corner of my eye, I realised her break was nearly over and our time was quickly coming to an end. I had to do something memorable so I had reason to come back.

89

With sudden inspiration and nothing to lose, I became more laid back with the situation. I remembered a trick one of the boys had shown me in the bar one night. Although I'd never tried it before I believed I could pull it off. It is going so well, how could I fail? I tell myself getting up. I look down at her face, her eyes following me questionably. I take note of her expression and try to put her at ease.

'OK, this will be fun. I'm going to show you something,' I reassure her. Her face is a little blank, but I can't stop now. 'So, I bet you must be wondering, what a nice boy like me is doing here alone?' I lent in slightly nudging her arm playfully, feeling a little braver.

'Well, no I wasn't wondering that, but go on…' she said giggling, seemingly relaxing too, still a little confused.

'Oh, I see, you just think I'm a pretty face, all looks and no substance?' I couldn't believe it, I was being mildly funny, and she was laughing with me.

'Yeah, yeah. That's exactly what I was thinking,' she said joining in.

'Well, let me prove to you I'm more than that. On top of my boyish good looks and my addictive charm, I can also do this.' I jumped up balancing my half-full glass on the back of my hand. Then, with a flicking motion, I launched the glass as high as I could into the air. I spun right around catching the glass on my opposite flattened hand without spilling a single drop, shocking myself as much as Lil. She claps and laughs, spitting out the mouthful of water she'd just taken failing to suppress her laughter.

'That was an amazingly impressive trick,' she said wiping her mouth with the back of her hand.

'Thanks. You reckon I can go around twice this time?' Keen to continue the act.

'Ah no, I don't think you're in any condition to try that.' I am indeed a little merry from a couple but I'm not that bad, I think to myself.

'Challenge accepted!' I set up the glass again completely overpowered by the moment.

Unfortunately, I am so eager to prove myself to her, — I wobble. The slanted glass went up fine but leant over, turning on its side on the descent. I watched in slow motion as it fell, helpless to stop the inevitable from happening. I watched as most of the glass's contents spilt over me, splashing straight down my shirt. Unable to do anything about it I freeze in horror, my mouth open waiting for contact. The first thing I hear as the liquid hits me is Lil bursting with instantaneous laughter. The second thing I hear is the glass shattering into a million pieces, despite my best efforts to catch it with my limited drunken balance.

'You idiot… do you know what you look like?' Lilly was howling with laughter and struggling to stay upright as tears started to run down her cheeks. A little embarrassed, I stood up shaking off what whisky I could.

'Impressed right…?' Taking a bow and surveying the mess I was covered in. She nodded still finding it deeply amusing, covering her mouth in an attempt to stop and failing miserably.

I decided any attention is good attention. So, I curtsy. This is not the best decision I can make. Before I knew what was happening my feet tangled, I stumble around then trip, landing on my ass, which only makes Lilly bust out laughing once more.

'I'm sorry, I can't help it,' she says apologising for her behaviour. She stands, reaching out her hands, pulling me up still laughing.

'Thanks.' I let out under my breath, not knowing what else to say.

'That was quite a show,' she snickered looking up at me. We were inches apart. My heart throbbed in my chest still holding her hands. Was this my chance, could I risk it? Lil looked straight back up at me unflinching. Her hands tight on mine, *kiss her*, my heart screamed. I drew my head down slowly holding my breath as my heart verged on explosion. Just as I did, a small gasp from Lilly as she turned her head... someone was there... watching.

CHAPTER 8
HUNTED

To depressing for journal?
Entry no. 3854-maybe?

The living death
I'm alone in a hole,
No traction,
I can't climb up its sides,
No friction,
Bang my head against the sides,
Still breathing,
Kill some brain cells,
Beyond trying,
Razor sharp pain,
Holding tight,
Hunting for a reason,
I'm screaming,
Walls closing in,
Am fighting,
Darkness,
Don't numb it,
Still living.

I heard shuffling of heavy feet to the side of us. Straining to hear, frozen, I didn't register what it was at first. I got the impression it was a large man. He stood back just inside the doorway so only his shadow was exposed. He cleared his throat, his feet shuffling forward. My blood went cold. I felt Lil stiffen, her spine snapping straight. The outside door flung open with a bang as it hit the wall. The noise made both Lilly and me jump. I grabbed her hands tighter and encircle her body with my shoulder in a natural protection over her.

'Hey Lilly, sorry about that, you know I'm a bit heavy-handed. You're back up out the front, bars waiting and John's out there checking things over so you might want to... I didn't mean to interrupt.'

'Thanks, Dan.' Lil flushed with embarrassment and stood back instantly, breaking our connection. The overfed security guard backed away as quickly as he had arrived.

'Only a heads up,' he called over his shoulder disappearing.

'Well, that's my break over. Come on... I'll let you back in.' She held the door open for me, signalling where to go to get back to the main floor, but I noticed she couldn't quite look me in the eye.

'This was nice, Adam,' she spoke quietly, almost in a whisper so the guard couldn't hear. She hesitated like she was about to say something else but didn't get the opportunity. She smoothed down her shirt and tucked her hair behind her ears, eager to return to her post. I knew it was my chance, now or never.

'So, it was nice talking to you too,' I said sidling up to her, keeping my voice low.

'I was wondering…' But before I could finish my thoughts the towering statue of John came around the corner. I had worked for him for a long time but had escaped ever having any personal contact, with the exception of a handful of factory meetings; although it was never one on one like this.

'Hey Lilly, get your ass back out there,' his gravelly voice demands, walking towards us from down the hall. I'd seen him around of course but from a distance. His true control wasn't so intense, up close I'm reminded of his sheer power. I still hated him… man do I hate him.

Ever subservient, Lil nods her head obediently rushing out to the front bar, grabbing a tea towel on the way through. Checking over her shoulder to see I'm not following, looking panicked. Lilly squeezes through the narrow passageway past Johnny. He subtly smells her hair. My stomach turns with revulsion. I look at my shoes, which are covered in dirt and whisky. It all seems too absurd to be real, this repeat of circumstance. I try to fill my mind with anything but wanting to hit him. I know it will show on my face and my scowl will be met with a fist. Starting to walk back to the bar, there is a huge pull on my arm like an anchor had been dropped. It pins me in place, evoking more fear in me than I can ever remember feeling, my mind clangs shut automatically switching off my voice.

'Ay, what are you doing out here?' I realised John was talking to me, imposing and authoritative, still truly terrifying; king in his castle, the rest of us here purely for his amusement.

'I took a wrong turn and got locked out, the girl just let me back in.' I joked with as much self-assurance as I could muster. Not wanting any trouble, I tried to continue on only to be stopped once more by strong fingers pushed firmly into my chest. My body hit the wall behind us with a thud.

'Don't I know you?'

'Me? I don't think so… well, I work in the warehouse, that's probably why I look familiar.' I look at the fingers with their white strained knuckles pushed into me.

'I see, you work for me, do you?' The owner of the hand relaxed and leaned back arrogantly.

'I think most people do,' I laughed, trying to keep things light-hearted, almost gagging on my cowardliness. Johnny wasn't in a joking mood, he must have seen the way I was looking at Lil and, clearly, he still had the hots for her.

'I know you from somewhere else. I never forget a face.'

'I think we were at school together, Johnny.'

He nodded. 'Yeah that's probably it. Well, don't let me catch you here again.'

'Sure.' My compliance made my stomach roll. He glared down at me a little too close to be comfortable, pushing his face into my personal space. Then giving my rib cage a final dig, he turned to yell for the security guard to, 'put a fucking sign up in the hallway before more assholes stroll down this way.'

I walked down the dark hall back out onto the main floor. I find a spot at the bar. The bartender walks over to me, 'Beer?' I nodded.

Lilly's not far, if I hang about here for a while, I should get a second chance at asking her out. Johnny, however, had other ideas. I could see him in my peripheral vision, standing over Lil like a dog guarding his bone. She saw me waiting and continues pulling a beer. Johnny's eyes tracked her every move. Without looking at John, who is practically perched on her shoulder, she brings the beer to me. She pushes the drink to me without emotion, straight-faced and rigid.

'You need to go,' she lipped silently then walks back to her tap and starts serving. He eyed her off from the other side of the room. I could feel his eyes moving from her to me and back. The excitement of the bar could not compress the tension between us. Johnny's temper was increasing steadily, although he did his best to taper it. His temper blazed through his glare. Lilly was thirteen again, staring straight forward serving drinks, not moving her focus from anything but her task; fearing eye contact. I kept my head down, *'leave it alone it will pass,'* my father's voice spoke in my head.

I made conversation with the bench warmer next to me. Yet inside that familiar anger boiled like hot oil, it spat and bubbled with that same rage from childhood, as if it had never left. This time it rose up not content to stay lying in its pit. I breathed deeply through my nose in an attempt to control it. Have some restraint over it. The wittering fool next to me, half-drunk on booze and lust became an insignificant blur, a muted tone in the background. My veins flowed with poison, with only one cure — ending John. As I chastise myself, I knew the only person to feel my scorn would be me.

Johnny has gone. Disappeared? Where? Why? My mind races through stories which maybe just rumours from the docks. *Johnny was gone, then as if by magic, popped up again with a knife.* You never saw it coming. My eyes search the room as the hairs on the back of my neck stand up, half expecting him to be behind me.

'There's a booth just opened up over there,' the returning barman said, pointing to the place in a darkened corner. My stomach churns, this is not a request, I get that. I looked at Lil, she's uneasy, controlling her moves, retreating into herself until she's mechanical.

'I don't want to cause her any trouble.' Admitting defeat, I walk away wiping sweat from my top lip. I reach the booth and sit. A girl immediately comes over, I assume sent by John, she parks herself on my lap even though I waved her away. Glitter-covered arms snake around my neck, up close the gaunt dancer is almost plastic. Thick make-up tries to hide the girl's twig-like vulnerabilities. But her eyes with their blank euphoric stare gave it all away. Another crack baby, I think in my head. I want to pull up my collar to prevent her skin touching mine. Where has my empathy and humility gone, when I'd rather wipe my neck with the ashtray then have her arm on it?

Johnny watches me sip my beer, unashamed of his glare; it's intense and laser-like, beaming straight at my head. He returned with some of his mates who were loitering out the back. I watch them lay their plans, handshakes and clinking of glasses. I try to read their lips — an impossibility with the flashing lights and artificial smoke.

Lilly pulls her beer from the gold tap so precisely, she hardly spills a drop. The shadows around her exaggerate the speed of her hands, slowing the task down to a graceful dance. Evidently, with John using his body as a buffer between me and Lil, I can't even see her outline fully from here. It's no accident a girl is sitting on my knee. The only question is, why? Was I being amused? Is John planning something?

Still feeling his eyes bearing down on me, my imagination is running wild. I looked over at the stage as I was expected too. I drank about half the beer, leaving the rest on the table. Fear is keeping me sober. The threat hangs in the air with the smoke, like cheap perfume. I need to bolt — now!

***

Some time passes — slowly. I wait for the right moment, checking the location of the bouncers before edging out as undetected as possible. I get out the front, pulling my hood up over my head to hide my face. Zipping up against the cold of night, I start walking at double my normal pace. Is paranoia setting in? There's still the element of crazy to all this. I'm on a regular street. I'm a regular guy. Yet I know with the drop of my stomach it's not paranoia. I sense someone jogging up the steps and across the red carpet a few paces behind me, a second person, side by side. The individual is far too light on their feet to be drunken patron. I turned slightly to see two of John's mates a couple of car lengths behind me. I nearly choke on my tongue. Maybe I'm not ridiculous, maybe I am. People have to go to places, including Johnny's men. I quickened my speed, stepping off the pavement and walk right down the centre of the street. There's no traffic this time of night, and I need to avoid the entrance to any alleys. I imagine myself being shoulder-barged down some dark lane, never to be seen again. My imagination sets to work. Every over exaggerated story I've ever heard on the docks beats a hole in my brain until I almost feel the wind whistling through it. Mind racing from one thought to another as panic grips me.

Earlier in the bar... was that handshaking about me? My pounding chest beating in my ears, I must think quickly. I feel the pulse in my neck and a trickle of sweat down my back. There doesn't seem to be another soul around. No witnesses. Perfect conditions for a beating, reality hits me like a punch in the chest. The sound of their polished shoes hitting the pavement behind me, takes hold of every hair on my body standing them to attention. A clear, defined sound like the clapping of hands in an empty room. My mind hits the panic button, as even without turning my head to look behind me, I'm sure, there's definitely a third man who's joined their nightly walk. Quickening my speed, I search for a haven. I need a direction, somewhere to hide or run to. There is no one to help, not one person, no shops, not even bums in the alleys. My spirit starts to decline slightly with despondency. It can't end now, not now that I've spoken to her. Not now she knows who I am.

There it is — a maybe, a lifeline. The yellow glow of party lights, thumping music, rowdy people and an open set of doors. I see it. Can I reach it in time? A brightly lit bar ideally placed on the corner, full of patrons. I hasten my pace to a jog, they know I'm about to run, the guys with their panting breath echo behind me. The gap is closing. They see I'm planning to bolt. I feel sweat on my face. I'm running, they know I'm aware of them. I can almost feel their hands stretching out to grab me. I hear gasping for air as they begin to give chase. The three men behind me swiftly set me to racing at speed. I'm sober as black lead, but the liquor churns in my empty stomach. I can't slow down, not now. I can feel myself outrunning them. The black dogs that snap at my ankles through the ill-lit street I race, howling with hunger, pine to tear me to pieces if I let them catch me. I almost stumble. I wrench my spine straight feeling a rip under my shoulder, shooting pain down my spine. The pain steals my breath; I can't slow even for a second. I reach my legs out in front of me, one after the other, as far as I can, then push myself more, trusting my body to save me. Not looking back, I hear them snarling, I hear their pant and they cannot catch me, not today. I hear my heartbeat banging in my ears, almost there. Go! Run now! With all my might, I push. I move faster than I've ever moved. I don't look back. I focus on that doorway, on that glowing light. Lungs burning, the pull of over flexed muscles, a stitch knifing my side. Push harder. Legs start to shake under the strain. Only steps to go, my lead is growing.

Approaching safety, I dig into my pocket finding my last fifty-dollar note, over-extending with all I have left, I hand it to the bouncer on my arrival. Even though there isn't a line, he takes it, moving to one side instantly. There is an understanding between us. I waste no time losing myself in the hard-drinking crowd. This place was usually too violent for me. I find a group of drinkers merry enough not to notice me sitting at their table. Big hardy boys from the docks, determined to forget life for a while. I pull my hood down and wait.

I watch the front doors intently for the entry of John's men. As expected, like a pack of dogs they barge their way in, knocking the bouncer out the way. The barman sees, this votes well in my favour, they'll get no compliance from him now. It's only then I realise the trouble John is prepared to go to keep me away. Seeing the red-faced boys Johnny had sent, beefed up on steroids so their arms no longer fall straight down but bow at their sides. I have no doubt at all, John had planned to have me bashed tonight

— a warning. An example for me or anyone else who turned their mind to what was his. A cold shiver begins to snake its way down my spine. It sends a shudder of dread through me, the pain in my back is getting worse, I must have pulled something.

Still hiding behind the large group of loud brawny men, I manage to blend into the walls and furniture. After all, I've always been good at disappearing into the background. I see the three henchmen rapidly searching the place. Their eyes skim right past me and I see one questioning the barman. He points to a second exit, which leads to the other street. A conversation takes place between them. Money is offered and refused. After a second loop around the room, John's men seem to give up, leaving out the same door they came in. I'm left actively trying to breathe through my mouth in a hope to calm my heartbeat. If I had ever doubted the love was gone, Johnny had just made it very clear he loved Lilly just as much as I did.

***

I hang around in the pub until closing time, checking out the front doors. There was no sign of Johnny's men, not even having a smoke or shooting the breeze. When I was sure I was alone, I stood, banging my legs to shake the pins and needles out after sitting in one position for so long.

Getting outside I stay calm. I walk as if I don't have a problem in the world, even though my ears ring with panic. A running man draws attention and I don't need that. The second I get off Fourth Street, I race all the way to my building. I stop, hiding around the corner from my building checking for anyone shady. *They could be anywhere, inside, upstairs, in a parked car, get a grip, Adam*! I take a deep breath; steady myself, bolting across to the door of my building, yanking it open with one massive swing. My hood covers my face as I take the stairs two by two. Getting to my apartment, I put the key in the lock and turn it quickly like a psychopath is chasing me. I dash in gripping the door, slamming it behind me. A quick search from the doorway: no one's been in here. I slump down sucking in oxygen, filling my lungs with the stale apartment air. I hadn't noticed my hands were actually shaking until my face filled them. Trying desperately to come to terms with what had transpired, I ploughed through the possible ramifications, none of them with good outcomes. An unanticipated wave of fear clenches down on me quickly, transforming itself into an inflamed anger. I was just as afraid as when I was in school. Nothing has changed. I haven't grown up. I'm the same little boy running from bullies.

Before I knew what I was doing, I was on my feet. The same intense rage burning through me, just as it had been standing watching Lil pinned up against the wall. My blood boils over: no words, just an outpouring of frustration explodes in irregular movements and snarls. This anger inside me has nowhere to go, but it's building incredibly fast, doubling in size by the second. Standing, I moved forward, no reason, in no direction, just to move.

Like a nameless creature scratching its way out my chest. I can't contain it much longer.

My pants catch on the handle of the hall table, knocking me off balance. I see the small tear in my pocket as I stumble to gain balance. Furious, a blinding white-hot anger rushes through me. I turn around swinging my arms and knock the table flying. As soon as it hits the floor, I kick it with force, then again, and again and again. I lift my foot up, bringing it down hard. Stomping on its legs until they snap off. A stabbing shoots up my leg, I howl but don't stop to check the wound. I'm no longer in control. I pick up the pieces, throwing them across the room one by one. I elevate the top of the table trying to break it across my knee, more pain. It's dull and distant, my temper pushes it away. I'll regret it tomorrow, but I don't care. Noise screams around in my head. Sounds. Pictures. Slick Johnny and his fucking dirty hands all over Lil. Right now, he could be backing her into a corner, all over her. Fuck! I persisted. My hands smashed against the walls. Then, turning to the hall table I pick it up above my head and smashing it against the paintwork. The wooden top not breaking, instead, leaving a hole in the wall, plaster spreading across the floor like biscuit crumbs. With all my might I throw it as far and as hard as I can. It bounces off the mantel, knocking over a hanging clock and coming to rest on the remains of the bookcase. That pisses me off too. Its contents sent flying across the room one book at a time. I watch somehow satisfied as the smashing of glass fills the room. Objects hurled, landing outside in the alleyway.

A sudden rush of fear, what if someone is out there? I stick my head to the window to see an empty alley covered in my belongings.

The anger is still not done with me. How could I have been so stupid... dangerous? What if someone had been out there? I turn inward on myself, picking at every fault. screaming at the top of my voice. Roaring, trying to let out the animal that has taken over my insides. Filled with frustration that can no longer be named, just raw emotion. I rip at my shirt finding satisfaction in the tearing sound. My hands like claws, I pull it off my shoulders, every shred of the fabric into a million little pieces. Growling and roaring in a nonsensical language only the darkness understands, a mixture of angry tears and helplessness — exasperation beyond words or sense. A pile forms on the floor and I think about setting fire to it. I think better of it.

Finally, with exhaustion, the anger seems to leave me replaced with the familiar misery and darkness of depression. I am a pitiful mess. Shame now has me in her hands, wrenching at my intestines, twisting them in knots. Collapsing to the floor and missing the lounger completely, I place my face in my arms groaning and crying trying to let the old demons out, trying to purge the guilt. These redundant emotions must be pushed out. I feel myself coming down, every cell heavy. I'm sitting on the flipside of the high I felt sitting in the courtyard with Lilly. It was all just a big tease. She'd been in my grasp, but then John, as always, seemed to be there to take from me, to scare me off and send me running away like a child.

And what's my answer? What is my big comeback? Here I am. Sitting on the floor crying about it. Here I am hiding in the shadows. Reduced to an invisible man, carrying the rock of guilt in my guts, and unable to pass it, get rid of it or cut it out. I am unable to fully live, unable to stand up and at this very moment even unable to breathe. I look down at my shaking hands. They disgust me. I turned them into fists, useless fists, there's no power in them. Anger gripped me but not at them, the men who chased me but at me. It was me hiding! Me, who for the most part seems to bring only disappointment, me who can't stand up, and me who fails to rise! I surveyed the rubble, broken and falling apart. The outside now matched the inside. I can feel myself hovering on the edge. How could I possibly be my father's son, how is it possible for the apple to fall so far from the tree?

My father would talk about being an exceptional person. He'd speak about pride in our traditions: *A man is as good as his actions* was always his last point. These are the words of generations, passed down from father to son. These are the words that held men together while facing God knows what. It was their core, their spine. The words that they could fall back on, that they could rely upon to keep them righteous. This being an unquestionable truth, these were the words that built new cities and nations. Men like these were able to leave their homelands. To start again on the other side of the world in unfamiliar territories and countries they had never heard of, where no one they knew had walked before. They were able to keep their families safe under their wings of protection, able to weather hard times.

The magic in the words that my father spoke was a gift indeed, precious as any form of education. My father carried this deep wisdom in his every word, every movement and thought. It seemed to flow naturally like an electric current. It didn't seem to run through me, although he insisted it did. I remember him giving me those words. Each day after school a few more. They were to protect me against self-defeat as much as whatever would come onto my path. What had I done with these words, these magic words? The hours of my father's time, exhausted from a day at work, he would sit patiently explaining the virtues of being a good man, the importance of family, the importance of being brave and keeping our traditions.

I hit my fist against the wall, ape-like. The impact rippled its way along my hand, through my wrist finishing in what felt like an explosion in my elbow. Hatred burns, it simmers unsympathetically waiting for your weakness, a moment of opportunity to spring forth and demonstrate its power. I slink down till I'm lying. Lying there with the cold wooden floors against my back. Legs and arms apart as if I'm about to make snow angels in the carpet but I'm too exhausted to move, I may never get up again. My doctor warned me. He said I might experience serious panic attacks or manic outbursts. I don't know if that's what this is. I think if my mother were here, she would say I had just thrown a tantrum. Feel so lost. Just want to lay here. I'm too tired to sleep. I want to lie staring at the ceiling. My body is too heavy to move. Breathing is laboured. I feel my chest rise and fall. There's nothing left inside me.

I hear my phone. The stupid ringtone is so annoying. I must have knocked it from its cradle. It's probably my dad, nobody else calls my landline. I should get it, but I can't move. I try to move one of my legs, heavier than rock, I'm able to slide it a few inches and then it falls. It stays in an awkward position. I feel the discomfort is somehow deserved. I close my eyes. Then, in a small moment of clarity as if nothing is wrong at all, a tiny hole is torn in the paper for me to see through. A cruel reminder of sanity and the fact mine has holes. A realisation of what I am, for a mere second, I see the madness from outside myself. I claw at the floor to avoid being dragged back but before I can take a breath, I am enclosed in the darkness again. The phone rings out once again. I sigh.

'FUCKKKKK!' I drag myself up and dig around the upside-down room. I don't recognise the number. I lift it to my ear. 'WHAT!' I bawl.

'Hey… It's Lilly…'

CHAPTER 9
TIMING

New pills…
A haze has settled…
Limbo…
Mind is blank…

I held the phone to my ear, dumbfounded:

'Lilly?'

'Yes, is that Adam?'

'Oh, my God, I'm so sorry for… I was just having some trouble with my neighbour.' It was the first thing that came to me. The lie came out so easy she bought it.

'Oh, um… that's OK.' The line went quiet.

'So, what can I do for you?' I sounded like a customer service operator. My stomach started to churn with nerves.

'Oh, nothing really, I feel a bit silly. It's just that you left your phone in the bar and I wanted to return it to you, or you could come by the bar to pick it up. But that's probably not the best idea.' She must be aware of my brush with Johnny's men. Was she checking up to see if I was still alive?

'That's kind of you.' I forced my voice to sound at least a little happy as I checked my pockets.

'I hope you don't mind me calling on it. I needed to get your number.'

'No, of course not! Thank you. You want to meet me for coffee, it's the least I can do.' I surprised myself with a sudden rush of confidence for the second time.

'Sure, that would be nice.' She answered quickly. I think I picked up on a little optimism in her voice.

'How about lunch at the cafe on main at one p.m.?' To my surprise, she agreed. She said that she'd be looking forward to seeing me, then hung up. Is that just something that a person says, or could she possibly mean it? My brain ached, and I could feel a migraine coming on. Life is simply too much some days.

I put my home phone back in its cradle. It was the only thing left in its place. The room looked like a war zone. I pushed my hair back off my face with my hands. I sucked in a breath. There was blood on my jeans from a large scrape and I wondered why I hadn't felt it before. The pain in my back felt worse and a feeling of nausea prevented me from standing fully upright. Then it came to me. Every stupid joke, inappropriate video Pete had sent, texts from Mum asking me to pick up toilet roll, my brother calling me a dick for being drunk at dinner, not to mention the reply, which was simply a photo of my balls. All of it sitting on my phone saying read me and laugh. Or worse, read it and see that I'm unreliable, immature and feckless.

Fuck! What can I do? She's probably seen it all by now. I rub my eyes, then rub my whole face with a tea towel, that was really only fit for the bin, a fact I smelt too late. Tomorrow, I think to myself. I grabbed the bottle of sleeping pills from the floor, where they had rolled, and went to bed.

The second I hit the pillow; I am suddenly too tired to sleep, my eyes stare unable to fixate on anything clearly. My brain is wired to the point of a short circuit — numbness. However, my body lays motionless in a daze; my mind is in a daze too. It's not awake, not asleep, zapped of every shred of energy. I can't lock onto an idea, I can't sleep, so I stare, waiting for time to pass. Something inside me is broken and out of reach. Time-lapse, sporadic thoughts, snapshots of youth bob in and out like paper boats on a pond. My body almost separates from me. I feel a twitch of pain, here and there, a reminder that I am attached to this lump of meat. My mind is now like a muddy puddle, murky, lost, full of loneliness, of a blurry confusion like a constant dripping tap, or a restless night spent pacing. I am unsettled. There's a stirring in my being as if I'm standing in stagnant water, it gathers around me. My soul is moving, trying too; finally, it's waking and I've had enough. I must escape it. Through bafflement as thick as fog, I try to fix my mind on finding my guiding northern star but her face won't come, I am undeserving. I'm looking for a first step. Confusion, finally the relief of sleep!

CHAPTER 10
CONFESSION

__Needs work__
__Journal entry no. 38 71__
You find me,
When I can't find myself,
You see through the idea of me,
Past the walls and mask,
To the very heart of me.

Saturday rolled around quickly. I hadn't even thought about my mother's weekly present. So, in the hope that she would think I was trying to be useful, I picked up a bag of groceries on the way, instead of something wrapped or flowers. My brother was absent from our little gathering. As far as I could tell the argument between his wife, Hanna, and my mother was still ongoing. There's no way I'm bringing it up. If this is the case, as I suspect, we won't be seeing him for a while. My brother will be rallied between the two women like a ping-pong ball for weeks if history is anything to go by. Usually, it's my mother who will cave in, with the incentive of seeing her grandchildren. I'm not sure that will be the case this time.

There is an underlying tension running through the house. It's the last thing I feel like dealing with. My stomach recoils but I can't leave Dad outnumbered.

For some reason my sister, who had come early, was hanging around my mother like a fly. I could hear whispering in the kitchen. Something is going on but clearly us men were to be kept out of the loop. I have a suspicion that she has a boyfriend. She'd become the butt of the family joke, dressing in the same kind of jeans and T-shirt for a year or so. Now this? The change was remarkable: hair tidy, dresses and even a smile or two. Standing leaning against the wall in the hallway I watch as my mother and sister chat, preparing dishes together. My mother in her Saturday dress, and my sister not dressed in jeans. This is the closest I've ever seen them. It's one of those moments when you realise how much you've grown, and how much time has actually passed by since you last noticed.

Once upon a time my sister, standing in the kitchen, looked unnatural. The homeliness seemed to restrain her very being., She dressed in clothes to casual and her attitude to brash to keep her in the kitchen longer than a meal. Now without warning, she blends in with the 80s wallpaper, the vinyl chairs and the simple action of putting away the leftovers in the fridge as natural as the sun rising in the morning.

My mind starts to wonder where we'll be in five years' time. She'll be married I bet — I hope I am. I want to have children, a point to my life, a reason to get up in the morning. It's all I ever wanted to be — a father half as good as my own. I imagine conversations about the kids' weekend soccer games, school reports and house repairs. Lilly has always featured in there somewhere too. I always thought I'd have them early, like my own father, but time keeps ticking. A dark feeling comes over me, hopelessness. It's a familiar hollow feeling; I must change this strain of thought before I fall into a dark hole. Note to self: pick up a new prescription on the way home. I hear my father yell from the living room:

'All done in here!' He's scrambling on the floor with cables and a handset in his hand. My mother has had him set up the old TV for a movie night while she cooked.

'Dad that old thing needs to go, get yourself something better.' I start gathering tools and packing them in his toolbox.

'There's plenty of life left in her yet,' he says with strain as he stands. I offer my hand to pull him up, which he declines. In one dark moment, I realise that one day he will not be here, one day my life will go on without him. I feel a jolt in my core as my perception of life and time moves just an inch at a time; as though my life is sitting directly on tectonic plates.

'I'm done!' he shouts again, and my mother acknowledges by waving a wooden spoon in the middle of a chat with my sister. He'll be allowed out now I've been waiting to talk to my father all day, my head is buzzing.

I stroll out into the backyard and set up two deck chairs for us to sit on. I have also managed to smuggle into the backyard a bottle of top-shelf whisky. I want to take my time with my father tonight; I have so much on my mind. I can feel things changing and my father will know exactly what to say to steady me. This habit of coming to my father started at a very young age. He would read to me and talk about the book, going into deeper meanings. It would spill into advice and relatable myths, and tales told orally as I sat in wonder at his expressions and the life he brought to the words. Then somewhere along the line, as I grew, it just became two adults talking. Not equals, I'll never be his measure.

'There you are.' He came wandering out in his favourite around-the-house cardigan that looks a million years old. I held up the booze and he gave a little cheer, holding his arms up over his head with excitement like he'd won a soccer cup. He took a seat next to me with a groan as his back bent into the seat. 'What's the occasion?' he said with a full smile across his face. 'Did you get the girl yet?' I shook my head.

'It's just good to be alive,' I said with a smile of optimism, realising that I had.

'So, you've made a step in the right direction?'

I nodded yes, then added, 'I think so,' passing him his glass. I tried for a second to hide my grin but like holding back the tide it burst out pinning up my cheeks.

'She knows who I am at least,' he smiles and pats me on the back cheerily. His hands are weathered, not able to extend fully any longer, reminding me of knotted tree branches. I feel them settle on my back for a second.

'She'll be yours before you know it.'

'Well, I got to talk to her a little bit. I made her laugh I think unless she was laughing at me. I'm not sure.' I shook my head, slightly abashed.

'It's only a matter of time,' he said, 'she's yours believe me.' He gave me a wink.

'I hope so.' I exhale out, letting the whole week escape from me with the breath. He leaned back in his chair and unbuttoned his pants, rubbing his stomach.

'Your mother's food, I always eat too much.'

'Me too,' I said mimicking his actions. 'It's the only proper meal I eat all week.' I laughed in natural kinship.

'Did I ever tell you how I met your mother?' he said as he closed his eyes, letting the last rays of daylight touch his face.

'No.' I knew this was going to be one of his stories where I was only required to sit and listen. So, I settled into my seat.

'She was working for her father in the deli near the markets,' he began without opening his eyes, knowing I would soon be lost in his every word, 'the one with the double red doors. I think its Robins & Sons now. I had just got here, only been in the country for a matter of months. I was a fish carrier; do you know what that is?' Raising his head and looking at me for a moment, I shook my head no. I was puzzled trying to work out why I hadn't heard about this before. 'Well, as the name suggests, I would pick up fish from the boats and take it to the local restaurants and hotels. I was only eighteen. Strong legs.' He laughed patting his calves. 'I would ride my bike all day to and from. I was fit, I tell you.'

'I'll bet,' I said, endeavouring to see him as a young man.

'I didn't have arms like yours though.'

'Stacking boxes will do that to you,' I said flexing a little and raising my T-shirt sleeve.

'Well, anyway as you can imagine it was thirsty work, so I would stop at this kosher deli to get a drink mid-morning and every afternoon. Your mother would serve me. She had a pretty face and wore sundresses that allowed me to see her shoulders… that was a big deal back then.' He took a sip from his glass that he had been nursing in his lap. He then continued his story, closing his eyes as if he was trying to cast himself back in time almost forgotten. 'Her face grew on me more and more with each visit but it was more than that. When I would turn up, she'd always be struggling with something. Maybe, trouble opening a package too big, lifting a box or reaching for something on a high shelf. Even dealing with men from the docks who were trying to get something for free. It was even rougher than it is now because people were more desperate. I would offer to help.' He smiled to himself,

'Once I escorted three men out who were not behaving themselves. She looked at me with admiration, almost making me feel like some kind of a superhero. Sounds silly now but, well… I couldn't stay away.' Chuckling at the memory I saw something mysterious and private flash across his face. Almost as if he'd rediscovered treasures from a distant place. 'That and I found her perfume intoxicating.'

'Is that how you knew she was the one?' I sat up suddenly more interested. 'Because you felt like a hero around her, swooping in and saving her from a falling box or heavy-handed shoplifters?' My father looked at me a little perplexed.

'No, it's not because she makes me feel tough or manly, you're missing the point.' Taking a breath, he searched for the right words. 'She makes me feel useful, like I have a purpose. As long as I'm with her I always feel needed, wanted. I have a place to belong and to serve, a reason to be, you understand, a reason?' It was so simple, but it took me aback, I immediately saw my parents' relationship in a whole new light. She gets frazzled, he calms her down, she needs someone to take care of, he likes to be fussed over, he likes to feel useful, and she likes to rely on him. He likes to have a tick list of things to do.

'So, you knew right away, Dad?' I sat forward considering what he was suggesting.

'Not right away, it took a few months. Every time I got on my bike, all I could think of was… what can I say to her or what can I do to show her she needs me? Show her how we fit together perfectly? After we were married, your mother told me that she spent her early days of marriage thinking of jobs for me to do, so we are quite a pair.' Facing me, he said matter of factually, 'Marriage can often be a bumpy ride. But I found in our marriage, if it's my job to smooth out the bumps and her job to take care of me while I do it. It works.'

I sat back and thought about it for a moment. 'I don't think she has a use for me.'

'You have lots of good qualities,' he said, leant back with his eyes again closed, drink resting on his stomach.

'I'm not sure I could protect her.'

Dad looked at me for a moment with a puzzled expression. Then coming to the obvious conclusion, that I was lacking in confidence.' He opened his mouth, about to give me some compliment or other when I stopped him. 'Dad, I know what you're going to say, but the fact is, she's probably tougher than me.' I tried to pass it off as a joke, he didn't laugh.

'What is this stuff about you not being manly enough all the time? You think being a man is punching someone? Haven't I showed you better than that?' My upright father suddenly was miffed.

'I know in your eyes I'm perfect, but the truth is… I'm really not.' I felt the emotion starting to boil in my stomach, on a scale between calm to angry; miffed was about halfway in my dad's repertoire, the place he got most often with me. Years of guilt melt, congeal and combine, turning into a hard-boiled lump in my stomach. I feel the prickly heat of exasperation pounding behind my face, and my eyes started to itch and moisten. Dad caught a glance of my expression; his spine snaps up straight with urgent panic. Thanks to my mental health history he springs into action at any warning signs.

'What is it, Adam? Tell me what it is now!' With an arm around my shoulder and the other hand holding my arm, he shook me. 'Adam you're scaring me. You must tell me right now!' I can't, this isn't sadness, it's guilt, I don't deserve your pity, my guts twisted. Voiceless details and memories appeared in my mind's eye longing for a voice. Incidences manifested like looming ghosts, reminding me of shame long since buried. The guilt started to overwhelm me. I covered my face with my hands so he couldn't see me cry. 'Whatever you've done it will be fine, I'm sure it's not that bad.' The comforting tones washed over me like a soothing balm, easing away the last few stitches holding the walls of my heart together. Letting the wound burst open and spill forth.

'But it is. I don't deserve her. That's why I...' I couldn't go on.

'Son let me help you,' he whispered, his hands were so tense on me I could feel fear through my skin to the bone. There was a long silence as the words formulated on my tongue. He sat waiting apprehensively, finally a nudge. 'Please let me help you.'

I nodded, tried to gather myself. I wiped my face on my sleeve, digging deep I pushed out the words, 'I told you, me and Lilly went to school together.' My father listened intently without question. Making room for me to fully express myself. 'I've always liked her but in high school, it changed. I know how thirteen sounds. It's too young to say that you're in love with someone but I was... and I am. That's when it started for me. I followed her around like a lost puppy, too terrified to talk to her. She reminded me of one of those angels you see hanging in shop windows in the holidays.' I took a deep breath, hoping my words made sense. 'She was so small, Dad. I know she had it hard at home because sometimes I would follow her.' I flicked my face up for a second then looked down again shaking my head. Rubbing my eyes as I felt another wave of emotion.

'You should've seen the way she lived. Her mother used to hit her and…' I paused recalling my shock at what I'd witnessed. 'I'd never seen anything like it before. She yelled a lot too. Lil had to work. It was awful… she never talked much in school, but she would smile at me sometimes. It used to melt my heart.' My father's face was full of sorrow and concern, taking a huge breath in. He shook his head in disbelief. I wiped my eyes and nose on my sleeve.

'… And this girl has just come back to town? Bringing buried history with her?' He sighed. 'You never told me a thing about it. How could I have missed it?'

'Dad, I hid it because I didn't understand what it was… how to process it. How to raise the alarm…?' I looked at him helplessly, and then look back down at my feet. I couldn't confess my sins while looking at his face. I just couldn't, I couldn't bear to see even one shred of disappointment.

'You know Johnny Rossi was in my year, right? He would tease her continually,' swallowing hard, rubbing the palms of my hands on my jeans to take off the sweat. 'He and his gang surrounded her right in front of me. They tormented her as I stood there and I did nothing… I just stood there, from that point on, well it happened at every opportunity… and I DID NOTHING!' I waited. He didn't say a word. I couldn't look up, it felt like a weight had pinned my head down.

'You did nothing? But what could you have done…?' I shifted in my seat.

'Did you not just hear? I just stood there acting like I didn't care. How could anyone ever begin to forgive that? What if she remembers I was there… Dad?' The last words bombarded the barrier encasing my chest, and a wave of emotion broke through. His arms wrapped around me, pulling my head to his chest, squeezing my arms so tight I struggled to breathe. I could feel him trying to will the pain onto himself.

He whispered in a low pained voice, 'Let it all out, it's OK, let it out. You've held on to this too tight for too long.' On hearing those words, I cried, long and hard. It was like suddenly being granted permission to fling open doors that had been jammed shut for an eternity.

After I calmed down, we sat in the quite as evening set upon us. My father cracked open the bottle of whisky I'd brought, having finished the dregs in his. The turning of the cap sounded louder than normal, with the splash of the liquid hitting the glass I began to relax. The smell drifted, yanking my senses to attention, and I knocked it back greedily. As soon as I had one inside me, I seemed to be in a place where I could actually speak.

'Adam, you know all that happened a long time ago. We all have things we look back on and wished we had done differently.' It was more than that though and he knew it. I had been suffering from depression and anxiety since my early teens. His cure was to calmly rationalise my life and everything in it. Which for the most part worked for a while anyway until I wobbled, and I'd be back to my old ways.

As we sat in the backyard peacefully, I could see his face. He was putting two and two together. Suddenly, my bar fights, drugs, drink, anxiety, depression, all of it was being placed in context. A map is drawn, clear and precise. For a moment, I believed he registered anger. Not the anger that I knew not slightly annoyed or quietly frustrated, but a pure white-hot anger of a protector. I haven't seen its like flash across his face before.

'I worry that if we were together and something happened, I wouldn't be able to protect her, I'm a coward.' I spoke plainly with nothing left to hide. He realised this was not an isolated incident. That I had been somewhat of a third party and witness to many incidents similar to the one I described or worse. Having him know and finally understand is both a kick in the head and relief to the heart.

'That was when you were a kid. Now you are a grown man, you would handle things differently.' He spoke more matter-of-factly. There was a slight strain in his voice and I didn't recognise it. Would I though? The truth is, I don't know what I'd do faced with an angry John. I had imagined many times bumping into him and it scared me to death. I had often seen him from a distance brooding around the factory. I had always made an effort to stay out of sight. Just talking to him face to face had sent me running the other night.

'You have to give yourself a break and look at this from a new perspective,' my father stated, using his sensible voice. The one he used on my mother when she became hysterical. I agreed but I didn't mean it. 'You were a young kid faced with a whole gang. What man do you know that could take on a whole gang? You would do no worse or no better than any other man in that situation!' I let it sink in, while I nurse the whisky in my hand and take a small sip. His advice always made sense while I was sitting here. It was only when I was alone that the words seemed like an excuse for being a coward. 'Let me tell you one more thing.' He leant in forcing me to look him in the eye. 'There are not too many men that would stand up to John Rossi now, in school he must have been terrifying.' I agreed slightly squirming. It felt like a cop out, he shouldn't let me off so easily.

'I bet you would've done something Dad. There is no way you would've stood there and done nothing.' I look at him searching for answers, and I am five years old again.

'Now who's being generous with the compliments? You can beat yourself up all day and stay in this place… or you can choose to forgive yourself. This is not your burden to carry, it's his shame, what can I say to make you see that?' He refilled my glass; however, I can't help but notice it's only halfway.

'You think it's that easy?' My eyes still stung from the earlier downpour.

'It can be, if you want it to be… so my question is… what's your next move going to be?' I shrugged at his forced optimism.

'I don't know.' I knew what he said make sense, yet I felt so defeated and talk was just talk.

'You have to ask her out on a date, you still do that right. Go on dates?' He laughed trying desperately to lighten the mood. He would insist that I stay over tonight, even if that meant getting me so blind drunk, I couldn't stand.

'Well, I don't go on dates, but I've heard other men do.' I grinned in mock sarcasm. He patted me on the knee.

'So that's the plan? You think of something nice to do. You take her out. You're a better catch than you think.' When he spoke like this it was difficult not to be convinced. Tonight, however, I couldn't be so easily persuaded. The voices in my head were too loud.

'Yeah, I'm great. What do I have to offer?'

'A kind and open heart is a big deal, you shouldn't trivialise it,' he said knowingly, understanding that my anxiety was passing. I laughed a little, nodding mockingly. Though I do think that picking her up in a car is more impressive than a bus ticket. I had almost regained myself fully. Seeing the ridiculousness of it all!

CHAPTER 11
UNAPOLOGETICALLY JAKE

The bonds of friendship can be the very ropes that tie you to life.

I got to work right as the whistle blew. I was a little groggy thanks to the whisky still in my system. I rub my eyes with my palms to clear my sight. They're still sore from yesterday's upset, even though I'd used nearly half a bottle of clear-sight in order to stop the redness. It's been a long time since I cried, maybe that's unhealthy. I'm not crying as much these days. It's all still there, still right there with me, sitting under the skin. I've read books, some say hold it in, others say let it out, it seems to make no difference. The voices in my head have demanded so much attention lately. If only this darkness were skin deep instead of it swamping my soul the way it does. The feeling of falling followed by the feeling of towering walls surrounding me; until I am hidden and suffocated. Of banging my fits on the walls till they are blooded in vain. But I try. The second I seem to pull myself up, there they are to remind me who I really am. A tiny excuse for a man who can't get his shit together, the guilt of disappointing my father hits me in the chest with a thud. I reach into my pocket, pulling out the small white bottle of pills that glue me together. I read the label and laugh to myself. *One a day* clearly marked. I pour out my usual five. I swallow without water, and they leave a furry feeling in my mouth. With a deep sigh, my day begins; I won't feel the sun on my face for at least twelve hours.

I take my place at the back of the warehouse. I have eight trucks ready and waiting to be loaded, all headed somewhere out West. One has a mural painted on the side. It's a picture of a happy-looking cow standing in green fields with the sun shining high in the sky. It stands in direct opposition to my life and somehow spits in my eye even though it's beautiful. The same feeling I get looking at the picture on my fridge.

By mid-morning I worked up quite a sweat packing, stacking and filling out invoices. I search around and find a seat on an upside-down toolbox. Pete and Joe make their way over and pull a crate up next to me.

'Haven't seen you in the bar lately?' Joe says wiping his brow with a ragged handkerchief.

'I've been around,' I state plainly.

'Really? Haven't I seen you? Are you coming in at a different time?' Pete has an edge to his voice I don't like.

'I guess I'm not in every day.' I hate being made to feel like this. What? Am I accountable for helping them prop up the bar every night? Should I call in, check in, maybe write them a schedule to approve of before I make decisions? I'm in no mood for lectures but I manage to hold my tongue.

'So, if you're not in the bar… where have you been?' Pete can't help but push, it's in his makeup. I know this well enough not to be offended; it does, however, piss me off. It's the little things that tend to dig in under my skin when I'm in this kind of mood. Pete and Joe glance at each other as though they have something to say. I take a bottle of water and say nothing. The comment lingers in the air for a while but I can feel something bigger brewing. Pete looks at Joe for the nod to go ahead, which he gives, sheepishly; Joe's not big on conflict. Once in agreement, Pete starts, 'OK, so Adam, the rumour is that you have been hanging around Lilly from the bar on Fourth.'

I don't say anything. They look at each other. Joe shakes his head looking down taking my silence as an omission.

'I'm not sure if you're aware, but John has been hot for Lilly since high school.' Pete speaks low, keeping our conversation private.

'They're not together!' I fire my mouth off too quickly and it comes out abruptly.

'Any man with half a brain wouldn't go near her,' Pete snaps back cutting me off. I look over at him giving a look that suggested I was unimpressed with what he was saying.

'Well, maybe that makes me crazy,' I say in a low but firm voice.

'You've got to be kidding, right?' Pete couldn't hide his apprehension. 'So, you really have been hitting on Lilly?' he continued.

'This goes without saying, but you do know that Johnny will kill you if he finds you sniffing around Lil. You do see that right?' Joe piped in, breaking his silence.

'I know what I'm doing!' The words came out with attitude, much sharper then I would have liked. These guys were my friends, they have my back and they were just trying to help.

'I'm sorry, I'm just having some fun,' I said looking at them apologetically, hoping I sounded as sincere as I felt. I could tell what they were really thinking.

'You, poor bastard, you love her!' Joe said matter-of-factly. There was no point in denying it. My face always gave it away.

'Yeah, I think I do… and just so you know, Johnny is not the only one who loved her in high school.'

'Then good luck to you, because you gonna need it.' It wasn't that Joe was dismissive; he just had "walk away from this one" written all over him.

'I know you're not gonna wanna hear this but if you really do intend to go out with Lil then you need to leave town.' Pete seemed uncharacteristically nervous. He leaned in real close like he was about to tell me the time and place for robbing a bank.

'What do you mean, a little drastic surely?' Things were getting very real, and for the first time, I started to think about consequences.

'What... you think John is going to continue to employ you? You think he's gonna let you live in his apartment building... doesn't Lilly also work for him?' Pete was the most serious I'd ever seen him.

'You honestly think that John's not going to do anything with you rubbing it in his face every day? This town is a small place.' Joe also now looked worried. I didn't think about that. Seeing Lil had blown me sideways. Getting her was the only thing I had focused on, but the guys were right — what would happen next?

'Well, maybe you should consider a few more things before you go screwing up your life. You have a good job, a place to live, good buddies.' Joe put his arm around me in sarcastic affection, smiling from ear to ear. 'What would you do, not seeing this mug every day, you'd miss me, right?' I push him off and the mood lightens a little.

'Look there's one more thing.' I had considered not mentioning the trouble from Johnny's men but it seemed the right thing to do now they were being so supportive. My apartment, that rats' nest, this stinking job, sitting at the bar getting blind every night. In that second, I saw things clearly. I needed Lil and I needed to get us out of this place. She's worth it. They could see that I meant it my word was final.

'Jesus, what now?' Joe was at his maximum capacity. He hated high emotion or any kind of drama.

'Look it's nothing...' both Pete and Joe looked with interest. I began again, clearing the air with a sigh. 'The other night I had a drink on Fourth, there was a big crowd, so I blended in. Only…' I didn't want to exaggerate as I wanted their unbiased opinion, at the same time I didn't want to come across too blasé either.

'John saw me, I was in a staff only section talking to Lilly and he told me not to come back to the bar. It was fine. Then I left. A couple of Johnny's men happened to be walking the same way as me. It was fine. I ran into another bar and they didn't see me in the corner.'

'Fuck, you're telling me they chased you?' Pete has this look of disbelief and for once he was speechless.

'I can't be sure but I wasn't about to turn around and ask them either.' I studied their faces; Joe had turned a little white.

'Listen to me, Adam. I'm serious. Stay away. I know you like her but stop before something happens.' The urgency in Joe's voice had me rattled. Joe never raised his temper or indeed registered any emotion above moderately relaxed.

'Maybe it was a coincidence.' I don't want to blow this out of proportion. I looked up to see my brother walking across the warehouse floor. Pete immediately jumps to his feet, putting out his hand. Jake had always got along well with the boys. Joe also rose, kicking over a packing case for him to sit on.

'How's it going boys?' My brother greeted me with a punch in the arm.

'What are you doing here?' I asked a little shocked to see him.

'Mum told me to come by and bring your jacket.'

'Checking up on me I suppose,' I grump.

'Yup pretty much. I think she likes the idea of us spending time together. So, what's going on with you guys?' Jake was hoping to get some gossip. As far as I could tell, life as Superman was a little dull at times, and he needed the odd bit of news from us to keep him from going nuts. Although of course, he'd never admit to it.

'We're trying to convince Adam not to do something stupid,' Pete groaned.

'So, it's just another day.' Joe laughed.

Jake rolled his eyes, 'What now?' He put his hands on his hips.

'It's nothing, don't listen to them.' The group went silent.

'Come on, let's have it!' my brother insisted.

'It's just shit about a girl, that's all.' Joe was trying hard to kill the tension. Even Pete shuffled his feet with awkwardness.

'Adam!' My brother even more insistent raised his voice like I was a kid and he my big brother putting me into line.

'OK… there is this girl… her name is Lilly.' I purposely dragged out my speech, like it was no big deal. Of course, everyone realised how much of a big deal it was. 'She works in a bar, we used to go to school together and I wanna ask her out.' My brother scanned our faces looking for clues.

'So, what's the problem?' He looks confused.

'Someone else likes her too.'

'So, isn't everything fair in love and war? Go get her, Ad,' my brother encouraged.

'That someone else is my boss, John.' I waited for the reaction. I knew it was coming. He paused and just stared at me for a while. Pete and Joe kept their mouths shut too. This was family stuff. You don't interfere between brothers.

'Adam, I'm gonna say this once. Don't do some fucked-up shit that's going to cause more trouble. Think of Dad. Anything happens to you it would kill him.' I looked up at him, mentally taking a deep breath. I try to push away the rush of anger that I can feel flushing my face red.

'I know that.' I tried to be strong. However, the words came out in more of a seething whisper.

'You have put our family through so much crap and there is only so much I can do to fix it. For fuck's sake, I have a family of my own. What are you thinking?' His fuming words practically had him foaming at the mouth.

'All right!' I said, 'I heard you, don't have to be an asshole.' My face started to burn.

'OK Ad, that's our time gone. Time to go back to work,' Joe said standing trying to help things end before they started to get ugly. Pete got to his feet too standing between us.

'Remember what I said, Adam.' My brother's tone cut through all politeness, his finger-pointing straight at my face. I saw red. There's only so much that any man should take.

'What's your fucking problem?' Pushing past Pete, my hand landed straight on my brother's shoulder. It knocked him off balance just slightly. Pete immediately put his arms out to separate us. Joe quickly followed, trying to escort my brother towards the door. But it's too late. My brother turned, pushing me with two hands, straight in the chest. Even though I was braced I fell backwards onto the floor. Knocking over the toolbox I'd been sitting on.

'Boys, boys! That's enough!' Joe insisted, throwing his arms around my brother's middle before he could go after me. By this time, I was on my feet. Pete cut me off, lashing my arms to my sides with his. I try to get myself free however Pete is a much bigger man than I am.

'Get him out of here!' Pete yells over to Joe. I watch as Joe assists my brother to the door. The other men working around the factory floor make their way down to see what the excitement is about. The foreman starts walking towards us. Pete still holds my arms as I seethe.

'It's all good,' Pete calls out, 'it's fine, nothing happened.'

'You sure?' the foreman replies, looking for damage around stacked boxes. The foreman is a good guy and he ushers the others back to work, playing down the excitement.

'I'm gonna let you go. You're not gonna do anything stupid… are you?' Pete speaks in a low voice only I can hear. I shake myself free like it's my choice and kick one of the empty packing cases so hard it goes spilling across the room. I see Pete in my perennial vision. He has his hands on his hips and is waiting to see if I calm down.

'I'm fine… just need a drink,' I bawl, kicking another crate.

CHAPTER 12
ADDICTION

<u>Note to self:</u>
Like! Put in journal (highlight page)
Also number all journals so entries read in progression
<u>Entry no. 3888</u>
Drown in oblivion
Empty it
Starve it
Purge it until it's gone

In the depths of my eighth whisky, I bow my head over the bar, making the most of my drunken mutterings with anyone who will listen.

'Enough! The world should hear!' I stand with drunken self-importance. Turning to face my audience with passion. I bellow the songs of my heart, the poetry I keep buried. Verse after verse of hidden words spill out, then as quickly as I start, I am spent, I collapse myself down. A swamp full of poison and I'm sick of it all. I am defeated. I complain to the equally intoxicated witnesses sitting beside me, confessing their own secrets to the amber liquid. Like a soothsayer, whisky pulls the truth from me, whether I like it or not. I need to forget. Total blackout. But the words keep spilling out, like a tap I can't turn off. So, I mutter under my breath...

Drown me in a cascading river of piss.
Let all my thoughts be flushed away along with my body.
No more than cheap versions of the original,
Tonight, I am a poet.
My words are the words of truth.
The words that cut and scatter you,
The words you both loathe and love.
Freeing you from all,
Turn my water into wine.
Turn my blood into whisky.
I see life clearly even with my eyes shut,
I speak for the broken and savaged.'

I lifted my voice higher as I heard shouts of 'shut-up, sit down, I can't hear the game!' coming from the blur of faces and bodies filling this place I barely recognise. I contemplate life in all its exasperation in my seat waiting for a reason to pick a fight. For something or someone to blame or be angry at. Do they not realise, I am a poet speaking the truth and this bum sitting next to me knows it? He bows his back to stretch further into his drink. The animal is just about inhaling it off the counter. I roll the liquor around in my glass. I watch it. Its slow delicate movement. It consumes all. It flows through pain, anger, and happiness, wiping it all away as it slides down the back of my throat.

'What are you saying, Adam?' says a familiar voice.

I lift my head an inch or two, struggling to focus. The room spins into blurriness. The crack of my head hitting the counter and a dull ache quickly follows. My hand lifts to the spot that hurts but I have trouble locating the exacted place.

'It's OK mate, I'm calling his brother.' A hand is laid on my back.

'No!' I mutter. I go unheard, pushing and shoving starts around me. I seem to be at the centre of things.

'I want him out. He's upsetting people!' the barman?

'He'll be out real soon. There's no need to call the cops.'

'Try holding it together, Ad. Come on, stand up.' Two strong arms are under my armpits, heaving my body. I have no control. Legs limp. I can't feel my legs. They're being yanked, someone's pinning me to the bar.

Blackness.

I'm being propped up with a stool. I wrench my back, twisting to hold on. I try to fight it off, open my eyes. Nothing is making sense...

'Hey buddy,' comes another familiar voice.

'Jake...' The word only half leaves my mouth and I attempt to say it again. This try is worse than the first. Balance escapes me, and I grip the edge of the bar. I slide down my stool. I melt over the floor. A conversation goes on around me, something about taking me home. It's my brother, I think, yes, he's taking charge, I knew he'd come.

'We found him like this. I thought it was a good idea to call you.' Laughing? Jovial? A light kick in my side doesn't hurt.

'You did the right thing, thanks,' says a mature voice. Pissed off this time. That's Jake.

'Has he taken anything?' Concerned, but angry.

'Just whisky as far as I know.' My head is yanked back. I feel a slap on my cheek, my neck overstretched.

'Ad, are you just pissed or do I get a doctor?'

'His eyes don't look dilated, he should be fine.' Pete's voice… I think.

'You, stupid fucker! This is going to kill our father.' Definitely my brother! He's getting worked up. Jake has always had a low tolerance for this kind of thing.

'I'll give you a hand getting him upstairs.' I'm being picked up. Held either side. Marched.

The cold night air.

Pain like a punch in the guts.

I'm retching.

'Let him go for a second.'

The bricks are rough against my hands.

I'm slipping down.

The smell of garbage.

The ground is like ice.

My jacket being yanked upwards.

My brother, he's there — shouting,

'Oh, for fuck's sake… not on me Ad.'

Retching.

Heaving.

The splash of something wet.

Coughing.

I'm hot but cold.

Vision-impaired.

Lights, bright lights forcing my eyes to shut tight.

Steps, the echo of a hallway.

'Foot up, Ad,' says Pete's voice, it sounds strained.

Hand on my back, pushing me upwards.

The door swings open and slamming against the wall.

The stink of my apartment, stumbling.

'I love her, Jake. You hear me, for real.'

'I know buddy,' says Pete again.

Swaying, falling onto the bed.

Shoes and jacket yanked from my body.

'Stay there! … Sleep it off you, selfish bastard.'

'Jake?' The word shoots out with a cough.

I lay on my back, my neck crooked; am I here, am I not.

Pete?

His name echoes around my mind, I'm not sure if I said it out loud.

Heavy footsteps.

Click of a light switch.

Darkness.

Stomach pain.

My whole body convulsing.

I feel the wet stickiness but can't move.

Nothing...

Awoken by a dream in the middle of the night, I am rigid in the blackness, frozen as if I am stapled to the bed. Beads of sweat on my forehead begin to puddle. The darkness is an entity, it breathes into my face heavily. It's staring inside of me like it's waiting for me to make a move. It knows what I'm thinking. I screw up my eyes recalling the night terror. The nightmare began with a Moses-style scroll unravelling. The parchment pours down from the sky, seemingly never-ending. As I look at the words in the ancient script, I see it's a list of names. As I look closer still and my eyes begin to focus, I see it's a list of names that are familiar to me. My father's name, trailing behind him, his father's name, and behind that, his father's name and his father's, father's name and so on, all reaching back to the dawn of time. I look for where my name should be... I find it. On history's page, my name is nothing more than a dirty smudge, which once was, as if an attempt has been made to remove it or erase me completely. My name does not seem worthy, it does not continue with the others. No name appears after it, I am the end. I have ended it.

I lay there in my bed, breathless, awake, alone and restless. The darkness speaks to me, whispering things I already know: worthless, useless, no good, failure. Why don't you get your shit together, Adam?

There's a line, a thin white line, I see it on my ceiling at night. It's the joint between two panels that meet, nothing more than a cheap way of fixing a bigger problem in the roof. To me, lying there alone in almost darkness it's the line between good and evil. No grey area, one side good and one side bad. I use that line to make decisions. It makes things simple and cuts through the crap. Like watching two warring factions, I line up *'the for and against'*.

CHAPTER 13
THE VISITOR

<u>**Journal this**</u>
Entry no. 3890
Will Mother know?
A portion of unknown parts
A gathering by night
The sight of the hysteria
The mouthpiece for the perceived
To toy and push and win.

The lightest of taps at my front door gave me a start, yanking me from my daydream. I drag myself up off the lounge, my legs like bricks and my arms like concrete from a day's work. I stood for a second, lightheaded, then plodded towards the front door. I never have visitors, in fact, I'm not sure that even my mother knows where I live, or at least, I avoid the question whenever it comes up. I wouldn't dare let her come to this place. She would try to move me out and take me home again.

I looked through the peephole, assuming someone has the wrong address or Mrs Vagon had let another salesman in the building. My father stood there a little damp, dressed in the same brown raincoat he has worn since I was young. He didn't tell me he was coming. For a second, I turn cold. I pray Jake didn't say anything to him about the other day and he's here to sort me out with his version of an intervention. I fumble to unlock the door, my eyes a touch blurry. He greets me with a warm smile and a hug, which ends in him patting my back as always.

'Adam,' he says, with a more jubilant smile than chocolate cake.

'This is a surprise. Come in, come in.' I stand back against the wall, out of his way, letting him enter.

'Finally, I get to see your place.' Looking around as if impressed. I laugh in response.

'Let me give you the grand tour. As you can see there's this and well that's about it.' I signal with my hands like an airhostess. I move shirts and a pair of pants off the armchair for him to sit down.

'It's pretty nice…' My dad shakes his head as though he's impressed. I stand for a second shaking my head right back.

'Dad, if I could, I would burn it to the ground.' Tickling us both, we laugh at this tragic space. Self-mockery is a trait we share.

'OK, so it's a starting point. You're only twenty-six.' He admitted to his over-generosity with the compliments. I notice his eyes settle for a split second on the prescription bottle on the coffee table. Neither of us acknowledges it. He's never liked me taking pills, he doesn't have much confidence in doctors and he worries.

'Didn't you have a house and three kids by twenty-six, Dad?' I pick up the free newspaper and junk mail, strewn all over the floor. Quickly I screw it all up tightly and stuff it in the bin, becoming more aware of the way I live.

'Don't ever compare your journey to another person's. It can only ever end in tears,' he answers, making his way to the couch.

'You are wise as always, Dad.' Affirming I am indeed listening as I grab a couple of cold beers from the fridge, I join him on the couch. Trying to relax in this situation, that seems odd. I assume he has something to tell me, but he seems hell bent on small talk. Reluctance often means a message from Mother.

'How long have you been here now?' he asks with interest. He's sitting too straight-backed in his chair; I relax back hoping that will make him more comfortable too.

'Just on eight months,' I said, putting my feet on the coffee table.

'You've been out of home a whole eight months?' I shake my head and roll my eyes.

'Dad, I hardly left home early,' I state sarcastically, thinking of both my brother and sister who had left home by twenty-two. I put a beer in his hand after I had flipped the cap with a small metal bottle opener I keep on my key ring.

'What's the picture on the fridge?' He peered into the kitchen looking at the poster-sized picture covering the door.

'Oh that?' I laugh. 'Nothing, just a dream that will probably never happen.' The truth is I was a little embarrassed about it. It was the kind of thing you'd read about in women's magazines. I could just imagine the headline: Visualise where you want to be and you'll be there. I felt my cheeks burning red.

'Tell me about it anyway,' he prompted.

'So, I promised myself this year I would finally make it to the beach. It's not gonna happen now.' I swig half the bottle knowing realistically that with doctor's bills, rent and my bar-tab, the money wouldn't be there for anything extra.

'You never know, you shouldn't say that,' he says with a wink.

'What do I have, a fairy godmother I don't know about?' I joke.

'So, is there a particular place you wanna visit or just any beach?' He completely overrides my last comment. He seemed curious as he asked, as though he had an ulterior motive.

'Well, if it's a place with a palm tree, a big blue sky and I could see that girl with a drink in her hand... I'd be happy! Even happier if it was Lilly of course.' I tried not to convey my disappointment in my realisation that yet again I would be stuck in the city for this summer.

147

Everyone I knew was going away, the whole city would become a ghost town.

'I remember when you were a little boy there was an advert on TV, it looked just like that picture. I think it was for family holidays to Whitehead Point or some little holiday resort. Your mother and I were going to take you away. It just never happened, even with our best intentions.' He looked down at his hands as he spoke. The beer still half full, I could see it cause him genuine pain, as though he had let me down in some way. He started to reason under his breath for his own benefit as well as mine. 'I worried about getting laid off, Ad, all those men out of work. I don't suppose you remember but there were strikes on the docks back then, men being laid off and the never-ending recession. I went the extra mile. I didn't take holidays, saved as much as I could, and always limited what we bought. Now when I look back, the only memories I seem to have — involves my work and paying bills. Sometimes, I think you have to take a risk.' I couldn't believe that my father would be anything but proud of his life. I only ever saw him steadfast and strong, I didn't like the sound of this self-doubt, it scared me. My rock can't show any signs of cracking, I couldn't handle it.

'You always kept a roof over our heads, not everyone was able to do that. Besides we had some good times. When I think of my childhood, I always feel lucky.' He put one hand on mine; it was cold from holding the beer bottle. He wrinkled up as he clutched with meaning, tapping it a couple of times then squeezing tight. His age was beginning to show. For the first time, I saw an older man looking back at me. There was something about his eyes more than tiredness, more than worry, wiriness behind just needing sleep. I turned my head knowing, in part at least, I am responsible for causing at least some of his present state. I could see by his face he was starting to get emotional.

'So,' he said clearing his throat, 'do you have a picture of this, Lil?' I shook my head no.

'I'm too afraid to use my phone to take one. She may think I'm a stalker; it would be weird if she caught me. I really don't have that much going for me in the first place. I think if she caught me taking a picture of her, I would definitely be put on the "make sure you avoid" pile.'

'I didn't think of that,' he said over the bout of emotion. He cleared his throat, 'What do you want from life, Adam?' Although he said it casually it had a sharp edge to it.

'Nothing.' It was an easy answer, and I knew he wouldn't be content with it.

'Nothing? So, you want to pack boxes for the rest of your life?' He sat forward in a more demanding pose.

'And what's wrong with manual labour? You told me it was a good honest job.' I regretted mocking him soon as the words left my mouth. 'And you know what I meant it.'

He took a deep breath and rubbed his hands over his eyes for a second, as if clear his thoughts or at least rubbing out my taunting attitude. 'If the warehouse makes you happy, then I would be happy, but as you're taking medication to stop you from diving off the docks and ending it all, I don't think it does.' He looked at me sternly taking a swift look at the pile of medication receipts I had meant to move. The merry-go-round of my unhappiness had been played out for nearly three years. Even before I had reached this point, I had been unstable, although he had tried to convince me it was just teenage angst that would pass. And even a man as patient as my father was drawing close to breaking point. I shuffle around trying to be causal.

'I don't know... normal stuff I guess.' My answer came out with even less enthusiasm then the answer had in my head. It's not what I intended. My father cared for me immensely. I was surprised however that he broached the subject at all. He was well aware that my mental state had been dangerously fragile for months. I had the sudden need to kick the prescription antidepressant tablets off the table. I don't however, I stare at my glass, the dark brown sap-coloured whisky circling with its sugar ring trailing as I turned the glass gently my hand. I can't recall a time when I didn't have a glass in my hand. It used to be a beer after work, a social drink with mates. Now it starts with a double that doesn't touch the sides I don't even count the beers. I owe my father a response so glancing up with a sigh. I shrug my shoulders. 'I want a family, of course, it's what I've always wanted, but you do need to have a date first.' I heard my own agony. I no longer bothered to truly hide from my father, especially when we were alone. There was no point, he knew me too well. I was well aware that he was concerned about my stagnation. For that matter, I was concerned about it too. Lately, most days I rose with dread, knowing ahead of me was only the exact carbon copy of yesterday. When I was younger, I would try to think of a way out these days, however, there is little point, that's when everything seems to grow dark and heavy. That's the feeling I can't shake. 'So, Dad, is this a social call, or have you come for a reason? It's a bit out of the blue, not that I don't love having you of course.' It was an awkward thing to say and the words fell out of my mouth jagged, almost discombobulated.

'Well, I do have a reason.' I sat waiting. I couldn't think of a single reason why he would possibly be here. It's not like he regularly came to town, and if he did, I tended to meet him at a coffee shop. 'OK, so here it is son, I've been thinking about you all week…' he looked at me seriously.

'Dad let me stop you there. If it's about my meltdown last Saturday I'm fine now, honestly, there's no need to worry.' Feeling a little guilty for letting go the way I did. I had phoned twice since that day, concerned that he would be dwelling on it.

'… Don't interrupt me when you don't know what I'm going to say.' I shut up signalling him to continue with my hand holding a beer. 'Thank you, now you know I'm not a rich man. However, I do all right, so I want to give you a little something.' He held out a set of keys. 'Now don't get excited it's an old thing, but it works.' I sat in shock.

'Dad, what is this? Are these car keys?' I stared at the shiny silver keys now lying in my hand.

'It's second hand, but it will take you where you need to go.'

'I can't take this,' I gasped, trying to place the keys back in his hands. My father would have none of it, withdrawing his hands and putting them in his pockets.

'You're going to take the car and it's going to make me happy. Do you understand?' He grabbed my face into his hands, looking deep into my eyes. His stare locked in on my face. 'Then you are going to take this girl out and you're going to have a nice time, do you understand?' He used his hands to shake my head *yes*. He was determined to help me, and I realised how truly worried he must be to go this far out of his comfort zone. 'Then, you're going to tell me all about it and while you're on this date, you're not going to say one negative thing about yourself.' He shook my head *yes* again.

'OK, Dad. Yes, I'll do it. You can let go of my head now.' He looked at me not convinced. He released his hands slowly and sat back down. 'Yes, I'll take her out on a date,' I said more firmly, trying to put him at ease. 'However, if you see me on the news for kidnapping her,' I said sarcastically, 'you only have yourself to blame… Thank you, Dad.' In order to rip the emotion out of the moment, he tells me to stuff the keys in my pocket. I start to tear up. Although this time I have enough control to halt.

'After you finish your beer we'll go downstairs and I'll show you the car. It's parked on the street.' He pretends not to notice the tears. We both get a little excited clinking our glasses.

'I can't believe you bought me a car. Why did you do it?' I shake my head feeling the keys wedge into the side of my leg, forcing me to adjust myself.

'Because you're missing your life!' My father's words were serious enough to cut me deep.

'I don't want to. I just don't know how to get out. I don't know how to get out of my head and it just doesn't stop. I can't turn it off.' My fluctuating emotions push me to and fro. I gulp down the last of my drink.

'I know that. What you need is a catalyst. Lilly could be that catalyst for you if you let her or maybe it's another girl, or something else. Regardless, what I want from you is a phone call.'

'I don't understand?'

'I just want to get a phone call. You say you're never coming back, that's what I want from you.'

'Thanks, good to know you'll miss me.' Of course, I was joking, but with my severe emotions circling above us, my father didn't risk not taking it seriously.

'Being alive is not the same as living — I want you to live. It's not about if I'll miss you or not. It's about you claiming your life. The day I get that phone call, I know you've grabbed your life with both hands. That's what I want for you.' There was urgency in his voice. Although at the same time I could see by his furrowed brow he was exhausted. This was the last big push to finally get off an ongoing merry-go-round and downward spiral. He had been there for all of it. The night calls from hospitals, finding me lying unconscious and unresponsive in the backyard. The meltdowns, the panic attacks and tantrums, none of it was fair on him. I hated myself doing it to him, yet seemingly not enough to stop. I knew things had to change. For what it was worth I hated living in limbo. Getting out of limbo is another thing though. I have a million excuses. At this moment as I watch my father rub his brow, not one of them seems to jump forward as being honest. For some reason, it was at that moment that Lilly's face came to the front of my mind. I don't really understand why. Only at that moment, I wanted to hold her. No, that's a lie, I wanted her to hold me.

CHAPTER 14
OPPORTUNITY KNOCKS

__Journal Entry no.3895__
Nothing else matters in the sight of you,
Beholden, my duty is to you only,
Shackled at the wrists,
Heart tethered,
Soul bound,
A promise,
In only a wink.

Thirty minutes after the end of my shift, my feet started to drag. My arms felt so weak it felt like I'd been carrying bricks. For me, this was a sign that it was nearly beer o'clock. The siren (a post-War remnant) would sound any second, allowing me to leave. I counted the last hour down every day, just as I had in school. I had half a truckload to go, a simple stack and pack job. It was computer parts from Japan on their way to a private school in the West somewhere. I didn't spend much time reading the details. It wasn't my job to know where the stuff was going. I only needed to get the load into the truck and off to its destination in the time given.

My blood went cold as I saw Johnny enter the warehouse with a face like a pit bull. He had a handful of what looked like businessmen with him. All engrossed in conversation, they headed towards my end of the warehouse but took a sharp turn left at the stairs. Johnny looked eager to take them off the dirty ground floor and up to the boardroom. I heard these business meetings went on into the night, but this was the first time I'd seen them arriving. Although he owned many factories and clubs, he didn't like to be seen that way. In his mind, he was an executive, not working class. I watched them like a long line of penguins, smartly dressed and smelling of money. It's not something I'm used to. It reminds me of how "us *versus* them" life can be. Shaking my head, I get back to work.

I went back to pushing crates around with the help of a rusted trolley. It had one annoying wheel that refused to move forward and been giving me grief all day. The crates were small, yet difficult to move. It was my last load for the day. I glanced at my watch: five p.m. Lilly gets off her shift at five thirty today. I knew her timetable as I knew my own. A thought started to develop. If Johnny is upstairs, then Lil is entirely alone. I tidy my stuff away as quick as I can. If I leave right now, I could probably catch her before she leaves.

A conversation is well underway between the foreman and a couple of the guys when I sneak off the floor. I had managed to get away easily thanks to Joe turning a blind eye. When he sees me slink out the back emergency door,

I notice he gets into a truck and backs it close to my area, covering it from view. *Now that's a buddy!*

Standing out on the windy dock I am surrounded by men hard at work. The clinking, clanging sounds of industry and the coming and going of ships offer me perfect cover. No one gives me so much as a sideward glance.

I knew that the day bouncers (mostly older guys acting as a deterrent) would change their shift at the same time as Lilly. Which gives me a few minutes when there would be no one on the door. Of course, if I waited too long the muscle-enhanced guys from the night shift would be there, ready for when the docks empty and close for the day. A chain reaction began, setting all the workers to lose for the evening. This meant I simply had to wait up the street until I saw the day shift guys move inside.

I parked my car out of view, getting out; double-checking it was locked, I yanked on the handle. I took a step back, it gleamed red with its silver chrome trim shining in the sun. I began to walk up to the doors of the bar, taking stock of who is around. The docks still blared with noise, so I am safe for a while. The bouncers, eager to get to the end of their shifts and go home, are already starting to move inside. I watch the door for an opportunity to make a move. Trying to walk as slow as possible without looking conspicuous, my eyes scale the front of the building to figure out the best way to get inside.

I notice someone coming through the back gates, which lead out on the main street. They creak loudly under strain. I hear the sound of the lock and chain being wrapped around and re-locked. A woman holds her phone in her mouth while she fiddles to get it right, a job made entirely harder with the wind blowing her hair in her face. The small-framed woman has to be Lil. I would recognise her in the dark. I jog over to where she is, hoping that no one's seen.

'Lilly,' I call out loud enough to be heard, but not loud enough to raise suspicion.

'Hey Adam,' she says, turning and smiling as she yanks on the lock checking it holds in place.

'Lilly, I'm so glad I caught you. I wanted to ask you something.' I pushed the words out quickly and purposefully before I had a chance to get nervous again, 'I was wondering if I could take you to the markets. They're having a late-night thing, a festival. You know if you're free…?'

'Sure, I have your phone… not on me,' she said before I had time to finish my sentence. 'That would be great; I haven't been out in ages. With moving back here on my own, I don't really have any friends yet. Well, not good ones… you know what I mean.' Her face flushed a little pink as she rambled.

'You'll come? That's great,' I wasn't sure if I was taking her on a date or we were going out as buddies so she could return the phone. It felt too awkward to ask so I was content with the yes; I didn't want to rock the boat. 'I don't suppose you're doing anything now?' I continued pushing my luck. 'I was going to get coffee if you wanted to come.' As the words left my mouth one of the day bouncers leaving his shift walked past, giving me a stern look, stern enough to send me a sufficient warning. Lilly saw it too. She stared at the ground.

'No. I don't think so, Adam,' she said looking at me, then subtly shifting her eyes to the bouncer.

'Of course not,' I said trying to let her know with my eyes, I got it. 'No Lilly, I understand.' I took a step back with clear space between us. He may have thought he was out of sight but I could see him hanging around on the corner on his phone watching us. I knew it would lead to trouble and by Lil's expression, so did she. Lilly took a step back messing with the lock, softly whispering so only I could hear:

'I'll meet you at the night markets. Seven thirty p.m. by the honey stand. Now walk away.' I took two paces back, my arms in the air like I'd been shot down.

'No, no, I won't bother you again,' I said loudly, giving her a wink. We then parted ways, and I cursed Johnny all the way home.

CHAPTER 15
THE NIGHT MARKETS

Journal Entry no. 3897

Walking to the edge,
Heart in my throat,
Is it worth jumping?
Or should I stay remote?

Twinkling lights dotted the edge of each stall like a thin pencil has drawn outlines. Although late in the evening, there was a feeling of community and safety that may have been due to the large police presence. Some stood on corners in full uniform, others were patrolling, others tried to blend in in plain clothes. Of course, they stuck out like sore thumbs. Rumour had it that there was a big drug deal going down tonight somewhere. Joe and Pete had told me while we ate lunch together. It put me at ease to think that some of Johnny's men could get caught. I was too high on what I imagined would happen when I saw Lil to care, or even take in the information.

Lilly had promised to meet me at the honey stall. It was somewhere that we both knew. I slowly make my way through the busy lanes between stalls, as I was a little early. I approached my destination expecting to wait but I could see Lilly leaning against a lamp post, bunting flying over her head and with her phone in her hand. Illuminated by a halo of lights, her delicate features stood out against the humdrum faces all around her. To me, she was an angel gracing this mundane place like royalty. My insides did their normal acrobatics seeing her face.

'Hey,' I shouted across the busy market walkway. She smiled seeing me jogging over to her. I could be reading it wrong, but she looked more than pleased to see me. She gave me a wave and a grin as I approached. 'Hey, you're here.' I couldn't quite believe it.

'Of course, where else would I be?' Her laugh was bright as she reached out and touched my arm as she inched closer, sending shivers down my spine.

'So, are you hungry?' came an automatic question. My mother always told me that food brought people together, and so my hope was that we would bond over a hot dog.

'I'm starving,' she said, leading the way to the food court. A girl that eats well is a good sign. At least that's what I'd heard.

The market was full of energy, even though the evening was damp from the earlier rain. People seemed to be relaxed and having fun, walking around smiling and laughing. The stalls held all kinds of things in the countdown to summer — bright Hawaiian shirts hung from coat hangers, along with equally bright shorts and swimming costumes. Another store was full of fruit, using desk lamps to shine down on the boxes, emphasising the colours and shapes. Next to that a store sold toys, then on the corner books and jewels, candles and coffee. Each with brightly coloured signs. I recognised most the faces of the vendors, most of them gave me a smile or a wave in acknowledgement. They did the same with Lil as we pushed and shuffled our way through the people, some with prams, in couples or with walking sticks. The aisles were jammed with families, old and young. Kids looked excited to be outside and up so late with ice cream dripping down their hands. The smell of hamburgers and frying onions filled the air entering the food court. Music came from a corner, fenced off by rope, where a small band was set up. A middle-aged man with a guitar, a long-haired girl about thirteen on some kind of keyboard, another guy on drums and speakers as tall as they were, gave the market an optimistic, upbeat vibe.

I watched Lilly walk past the tables taking in their wares. I pushed myself to get closer to her, but I didn't want her to feel suffocated or nervous of me either. She had to feel perfectly comfortable in my presence if I had a shot with her. She turned to me.

'How about burgers?' She grabbed my hand and pulling me into the line. A young man with shoulder-length hair at the front counter waved her forward. They clearly knew each other. She reached up against the side of the food van and he smiled and kissed her on the cheek.

'Two with the lot,' she shouted up to him over the music. I rush forward to pay, offering a twenty.

'On the house buddy.' He waved away the money, moving out of reach.

'This is my little brother, Mark.' She stepped in close to speak. Virtually touching my ear to make sure I could hear over the noise. It sent tingles down my spine.

'Brother!' I nodded, acknowledging I heard. I put my hand up to shake his hand.

'Please to meet you, I remember you when you were a kid. You came up to my waist then, now I think you're taller than me?'

'I'm twenty-one now — a man,' he smirked at Lil.

'Oh whatever,' she beamed back. I liked him. He seemed to have '*personality*'. You could tell he had a gift with banter and was clearly witty, maybe it was working in the markets. I'm always a little jealous of confident and clever men; it all comes so easy. Not with Mark though, he's too decent to have ill feeling towards me. Lilly passes me a burger. 'OK, Mark, we are out of here, don't work too hard.' He nodded, then kissed her on the cheek again. I saw him whisper something in her ear, which made her smile and then went back to work.

'Thanks for the burger, it was nice to meet you,' I shouted up to the platform where he stood. We walked over to a small table with a clean white tablecloth. It was laid with homemade sauces and napkins.

'These are really good,' she said, 'He's been making them since he was young, his secret recipe.' She took a massive bite, smiling. She was right, they were good.

I get a couple of colas from the next store over. 'Here,' I handed it to her and I pointed over to a small corner with recycled plant pots and boxes hanging off the wall full of flowers and herbs. She followed me and the ease of it all made me smile. We sat in the small courtyard made of benches with plaques on them. They made up the edge of the adjoining parkland. I began to read one out:

'Donated by Mr and Mrs Lang.' I watch her drink through a straw as she reviews the people passing us. It's wildly fascinating to watch her lips sucking and I feel a heat starting to rise in me. So, I look out in the same direction as her, trying to cool down. I can't believe we're just hanging out like two regular people. She seemed comfortable with me, and I loved it. Even if she never agrees to come out with me ever again, I would die a happy man knowing that I had taken her out at least once. No, I wouldn't be happy with that at all, I'm greedy. I want her and her alone, all the time. How could I ever get enough? She turned to me stopping my thought.

'What do you want to do next?'

'Whatever you want,' I said, with a mouthful of burger.

'OK, so I was hoping to get a dress, do you wanna look with me or does that sound like agony?'

'No, sounds great,' I said, stuffing the last piece of burger in my mouth.

***

The evening had been amazing, but by eleven p.m., people were starting to pack away and leave. In an effort to end on a happy note, I thought I'd do the gentlemanly thing, 'OK, so can I walk you home?' Then quickly realising how it might sound, I continued, 'I don't want anything, I just wanna make sure you get home safe.'

'I trust you.' She threaded her arm through mine. 'We're friends now, right?

'Yeah...' I said, taken aback. Friends? That's got to be a breakthrough. I feel a surge of happiness — I could explode.

'So, do you think you might want to do this again with me sometime?' I couldn't look at her as I said the words, knowing I'd be crushed if the answer were anything but yes.

'Sure,' she said, 'I love hanging out with you.' This is great, I tried to hide the smile on my face, but she caught me and laughed. 'You look awfully happy,' she giggled.

'I had a good time,' I replied, trying not to focus on the fact she was touching me by choice. The moment I finish the sentence, I felt a drop of rain on my head, then in quick succession half a dozen more. Before I knew what was happening, it started to pour.

'Quick.' Grabbing her hand, I race across the road, pulling her under the shelter of the awnings. We stood there. The rain lashed down heavier and heavier, louder and louder. 'My building is right there, literally.' I pointed to the two large doors. 'Do you wanna come up for a little while, until the rain stops, and I can get you a taxi later?' I looked around. 'I would get you one right now but I don't think there's any left.' She looked up at me, then at the rain that was now coming down like a sheet. 'I swear I'm not trying anything, if you like we can wait here until a taxi comes, it's just getting cold and you're wet.' I shrugged.

'You're right. It seems silly to stand here getting wet.' She pulled the hood of her jacket up over her head getting ready to run.

'OK, I'll go first and open the doors.' Then I added, 'But I hope you're not expecting too much, my place is shit.' I turned.

'We'll go together.'

'One, two, three...' I grabbed her hand as the rain lashed on our faces. She screamed and laughed at the same time. I could feel her trembling with the cold. I put the code into the keypad, opening the big front doors. Finally, out of the rain, we walked up the stairs.

'Sorry, there's no elevator in this building. I'm on the fifth floor. I hope that's OK?' she nods politely, visibly nervous, I led the way up the stairs to my place. As I got to the door, I had a sudden rush of embarrassment. I put the key in the door. 'Look, my place, I wasn't lying... it's pretty shit.' I sighed. Oh God, what would she think of me? I pushed the door open.

'You're a bachelor, I expect it to be shit.' I flicked the light switch and walked in holding the door, inviting her in. 'Well, that's... what I was expecting, it is shit!' We both laugh. There was something easy about us being together, no judgement, I didn't feel as ashamed as I thought I would. I watch her wander around the apartment. I offered to take Lil's wet jacket. It was soaked through. I hung it over the back of the chair to dry.

'Why are there only three chairs?'

We are comfortable, but I didn't feel ready to tell her about my tantrum yet. 'Because I picked it up off the side of the road.' I wasn't lying, just conveniently missing bits of the story. She still lingered around the door. 'Come in. Can I get you a drink?' I opened the fridge as if I'm expecting something to be in it. 'Well, I have juice.' I pick up a carton and shake it. Has about half a glass in it. 'I hope you're not too thirsty?' I sigh.

She laughs. 'You know what, I'm fine.'

Surveying every inch of the apartment, she touches odd objects, stopping to pick up this and that. I stood watching her silently. I still had a sense of wonder at her even being in my place. I hovered as she paused at the window, 'Don't you love my view?' I shrugged sarcastically in an attempt to seem humorous.

'It's not so bad; at least this is your own place.'

'It's nothing special. Less than that even.' I shook my head, wishing I could offer her the world.

'It's something.' She smiled, and all nerves were gone. A calm came over me.

She wanders off into the kitchen. 'You want to sit down?' I say, but she walks straight past the lounger and looks at the picture on the fridge, pushing on the fridge door so it closes.

'Why do you have this…?' She looks at me, waiting for an answer. That's the second time that fucking picture has forced me into an embarrassing explanation I think to myself.

'It's nothing,' I said, hoping to get off the subject quickly.

'Why don't you tell me anyway?' she said. For a second, I think of my father and him telling me to live and take more risks.

'Well, I was gonna take a holiday this year… I wanted to find a place just like the picture. You know, spend a week or two lying on the beach, but I'll probably end up spending the time I get off for Christmas at my folks' house.'

She smiled and nodded, and then she walked straight past me. 'Do you ever use this kitchen?'

'Sometimes, I guess, when I'm here.'

'Can you cook?' She paid deep attention to my expression. I had the feeling I was being summed up.

'Sometimes, I used to cook with my mum, so I can make family recipes.' I shifted, suddenly aware of myself.

'Very impressive.' She nods, which makes me smile, and then she continues on to the lounge, perching on the edge of the seat. She smoothed her skirt down over her knees. I notice her legs pushed closely together. I followed her into the room but choose to sit on the far side.

'Would you like me to try and call you a taxi?'

'No. Do you want me to leave? Am I keeping you up?'

'It's not that at all. I promised I would and I don't want you thinking I was just trying to get you up here.' She let out a small laugh and seemed to relax a little.

She looked at me for a while and each and every cell in my body snapped to attention. She rose slowly and walked over to where I sat. She seated herself so our knees slightly touched.

'I had a really nice time tonight.' Her hand brushed my leg settling on my knee and all I could do was stare at it.

'I really did too, you're so easy to be with.' However, the words didn't flow easily with her being so close, my heart pumped like a racehorse at top speed. Does she want me to kiss her? I'm so bad at this stuff. I put my hand on hers to test the water. I lean forward; I pause, waiting for her to lean in. Quick, she pecks me on the cheek and pulls back. I'm so stupid, she said friends.

Taking a deep breath, she turns to me. 'I'm sorry it's not you. It's just happening a bit quick and my head needs to catch up.' She covers her face from me a little, pushing her hair behind her ear. I nod in an effort to show I understand.

'Why don't we just talk a little bit?' I try to suggest gently, moving back in my seat to give her room. She scanned the room searching for a topic of conversation.

'You must read a lot of books.' Moving her knees a little, in my direction, she closes the gap I'd just made. I swallowed hard, smelling her perfume.

'I read.' I swallow, trying to act normal, whatever that is. I'm sure other men would have pounced on her by now.

'I've only read one book: *Dracula*. My brother dared me. He said I was a baby because I was scared of the dark. I was scared of everything actually.' She laughed at the thought of it. Shrugging, then continuing, 'So I read it and it gave me nightmares for a month.' She was looking at her hands as she spoke, and although she laughed it off, the memory had an uneasy edge to it. I felt compelled to hug her, but I fought hard not to enter her space.

'Why do you like me, Adam? You do like me, right? That's why I'm here?' All the ease, the small amount I had tried to find disappeared. I sat up straight.

'Because you're perfect...' I stammered out, 'You're the most perfect person I know. You don't belong here.'

'You're wrong. I'm not what you think. I'm not...' she stopped, hands twisting in her lap, she tried to force out the words as I listened. 'I'm not this innocent little Catholic girl. I've done things... Adam, please don't look at me like that. You make me feel like a lie.' She cast her eyes away from me.

'How am I looking at you?' Wanting her pain to stop, she sat not saying anything. 'You can talk to me.' The gap between what she felt hindered to say, and my will to get her to say something, got too big for the room.

'Maybe I should call that taxi.' Excusing herself, she reached inside her bag for her phone.

'You don't have to do that…' But her light had turned off, and even though she still sat on my couch; I knew she had already gone.

CHAPTER 16
FIXING BROKEN THINGS

Stick into journal
Entry no: 9002

Raining,

Hard, in need of relief!

Thinking of Lilly,

Taking bus to work.

Written on the back of a bus ticket, coupled with an Ikea pencil I found stuffed down between the seat and the armrest. The 'route thirty-nine last call bus' window has 'Fuck You' scratched into it and I agree. The world can fuck off!

Today's Total:

- ❖ *Seven whiskies,*
- ❖ *Seven beers,*
- ❖ *Bombay Sapphire Gin — some, mug full?*
- ❖ *A handful of pills,*
- ❖ *Weak legs, blurry eyes, stomach pains,*

The world at dizzying speed, too fast,

A blur of noise, overcrowded and congestion

Rain in streaks hitting the square metal-rimmed window.

It's delicate, sad and hypnotic,

Each drop powerful enough to make a leaf bow down
as it passes as if a lord walks by
Subtlety,
Seemingly without effort,
Power beyond muscle,
Like Lilly.

I thought I'd give my father a break from my ongoing neediness of late. Instead, I called my brother. I had calmed down, now feeling bad about our misunderstanding. I asked him to meet me for a drink after work on Thursday. I knew I'd be there first and half expected to get a call saying he couldn't make it. When we were younger, we had been close but since he left home it had been hard to find the time, what with one thing or another. The few times I saw him now, I was off my head or there was a family crisis.

I didn't recognise him at first. My brother's hair had been cropped short since I'd last seen him. These days he showed no signs of boyhood. No youthful bounce to his walk but rather a heavy step like the stride of a man. On seeing me, he came over and took a stool owning his space fully. He moved in a way only a father could. There are only two years between us in age, yet a million miles on our life paths. I push a drink his way and greet him with a slap on the back; he returns it with a punch in the arm as we always have.

'So, you called me down here, something up?' His tone was friendly but there was now an essence of management about him. His manner carried authority, while not rude there was an unfamiliar weight to it.

'Not really, just wanted to catch up… and apologise for the other night.' I looked straight ahead, biting my tongue. In my head, it had been far easier to apologise.

'We're brothers, forget it. Promise you'll try not to do anything stupid for at least a while.' He was letting me off with a warning. I had expected much worse and to be honest knew I deserved it.

'Well, I'm sorry I haven't seen you much, what with the whole Mum thing going on,' Swigging my beer I tried to open up a conversation.

'Ah yeah that, I don't know what's going on there. I'm sick of hearing about it.' He gulped at his glass. 'I think I need something stronger.' He ordered Scotch with no ice.

'Trouble in paradise?' I didn't mean to smirk. He saw but ignored it.

'Kids. Mum on the phone every five minutes, which starts Hanna off. Don't even ask about work…'

'Wow, that good…' I couldn't help but raise my eyes. I hadn't heard him speak about his 'wonderful' life this way before.

'Things are worse if I'm honest.' He looked straight ahead using one arm to lean on rather than sitting.

'So, what are you going to do?' A spark of panic seemed to ignite in my stomach, quickly followed by guilt thinking of my dad. He couldn't cope with both of us losing it.

'Nothing, it's a time thing… it should all sort itself out.' I noticed stress lines on his forehead.

'Do you ever regret it… the whole marriage thing?' I needed to hear the words but remained as candid as possible, hoping it would induce honesty.

'About twenty times a day but then in between, I couldn't be happier.'

'So, it's fifty-fifty then?' I joked trying to lighten his mood. He looked at me straight in the eye.

'It's more complicated than that.' He began to speak of his children, day-to-day things, new additions to the house. At first, the words were more of a rant than a conversation. I let him empty the stress out of his head. Within a short time, his speech changed, it softened into the brother I recognised. He now tried to hide his pride with sensible comments. I wouldn't if it were me, and I told him so.

'It's the pressure mostly, Hanna has it worse. Any move she makes is scrutinised down to the last breath, not just from Mum but from her mother too. Thank God I'm not a woman, the kids have been sick and crying day and night.' He clinks my glass with sarcasm. 'Have I put you off marriage yet?' I chuckle conceding the point.

Although I agreed, I kept the truth inside. The things he spoke of didn't scare me. What he described gave me a sense of optimism. He had a refuge, a place to shelter from every day even though I could see right at this moment, he couldn't see it. Some people run from commitment; it's scary to think that the person right in front of you will be the same person for the rest of your life. That's not the way I think at all. I have been ready for that 'till the end of time partnership' my whole life. In fact, I'm shocked it hasn't happened yet. I expected to marry young, start a family and all that comes with it from about the age of twenty. I recall thinking, 'OK, I'm not a teenager any more — so let's get started already'. All I felt while my brother spoke was: This is what I want.

Lilly, even her name is enough to drive me crazy. I'm hard again; I stand and adjust as inconspicuously as I can. It has been like this since she sat on my couch since I got close enough to smell her hair. The pills should stop this; one of the side effects but they don't.

'Ad, are you listening?' Jake's annoyance is a sharp pain of guilt.

'Yes, course I am!' I focus on his face giving him a sheepish smile but it's Lil's face I see.

CHAPTER 17
NOW OR NEVER

Journal Entry no. 9004
Note to self: do something with this?
Heavenly song of a siren
Her sigh is enough to raise me,
The way her hand circles the tip of her teacup,
Fingers twisting in her skirt (why do I love that,
venerability.)
Oh my God, so fucking beautiful!

My night out with Lilly had ended pretty abruptly. Which had kept me up all night, but despite myself, I had managed to lock in another… I hesitate to say… a date, today. I think it's a friendly catch-up. I don't know. We are meeting for coffee. Friends, I think. I don't know if that's what we are. It had been driving me crazy. I hadn't slept all week. The more I think about it, the more I checked my phone, and the more I'm certain she was going to cancel. What am I saying? Of course, we're just friends, she's too good for me. Yet again I'm fooling myself. She could have anyone. I have to stop talking to myself, a bad habit I've acquired since living alone.

I look in the window of the Perk-u-up coffee shop just off main. It was hidden enough to be safe. I had seen a couple of guys looking my way at work. Ever since, I had been checking over my shoulder, expecting guys to fly around a corner and force me into a blacked-out car. It occurs to me I may watch too many movies as I enter the friendly little place. It's hard to believe that this place coincides so peacefully with Johnny's Street. This stylish hang-out is run by two girls I knew from high school. They are a little older than I am, and both are now mothers. They felt homely in a fashionable way, somehow in a different age bracket to me. As if overnight they had joined my brother's club. A little clan I am getting more desperate to access.

Lil isn't inside, so I find a quiet table in the back and order a cup of coffee. I check my phone half expecting to see a letdown message. There is an internal sigh of relief when the screen shows no new messages. Sitting back, I get comfortable and watch customers reflected in the bay windows. I watch them talk, laugh, gossip and drink coffee. It all seems so easy… so normal. Sitting here, like this, I don't know why I find this everyday stuff so hard. I look down at my hands. I tried to clean them up best I could but the orange industrial strength disinfectant stain from the factory never really goes away. It sinks into the lines and wrinkles on my knuckles making them look more worn than they are. The nicks and cuts from punching the door mixed with drunkenly falling from the bar with my brother the other night litter my skin. My hands suddenly seem like a history book on my past transgressions. Every stupid thing I've done is written there with a bruise or a cut. My knuckles are swollen, slightly blue and there's a tremor from alcohol I assume. I squeeze my fist tight to stop the shaking. As soon as I release the tension it starts again.

It's then I see Lil from the corner of my eye. She halts in the doorway searching, casting her eyes over the bustling room. I stand to give her a quick wave. The smile I receive in return is like turning on the sun. My stomach drops a little as she approaches, it is a quick reminder of how much I want her. She bounds up and kisses my cheek automatically. My cheek buzzes with her touch. I signal for the waitress who proceeded to take our orders.

'I'm so glad we decided to do this,' she said, fixing her hair to the side.

'Me too.' Things felt a little awkward or maybe that's just me. Was this a date? It felt like one. I'm paying, she's dressed up, I'm nervous but then there's the cheek kiss. That was definitely a friendly gesture, how friendly? She's sitting opposite me when there's plenty of room on the bench seat next to me, is that what a person does? Shit, we're sitting in silence; think of something to say quick. 'So, Lilly, what's it like working in the Black Dragon?' How did that sound? Is it more weather and elevator music? I have to stop thinking. Brain shut up. This incessant internal rambling triggers the beginning of a headache. My shoulders pinch the nerves in my back tight. My stomach flips over.

'Well, it's a job,' she says stirring sugar into her coffee. She continues, 'No, I'm lucky to be employed but you know… there's John.' She glances up almost apologetically.

'Yeah, I work for him too. He can be a real dick.' She snickers with agreement.

'When I first started at the bar, I never used to see him, but now he's always buzzing around, pissing people off… like in school.'

'So, you don't like working for him?' I say sarcastically

'I don't think anyone chooses to work for him — do they?' The comment was loaded but I didn't quite get what she was trying to say, so I left it. 'Did you know John at school?' She looked up as she sipped.

'Everyone did,' I answer.

'No, I mean, did you hang out with him?' Her question seemed to be leading somewhere.

'No, I used to avoid him like everyone else,' I said. She was quiet for a second contemplating my answer.

'Did you hang out with him, Lil?' It was a stupid question bordering on hurtful, it was meant to be funny. Stupid, stupid, stupid me! She saw straight through my deflection. I suddenly realised she had remembered something from school, maybe that day, maybe how I didn't help her. My hands shook more prominently so I folded them in my lap as subtly as possible. A headache, not a headache! The tension began to rise as the symptoms line up. The shaking, pain across my forehead, tight muscles — I knew where this was going. I try to calm myself down, breathing deeper. Think of the picture on the fridge, calm blue ocean.

'No, I didn't, but he knew me.' She gathered herself for a second then continued, 'Adam it's OK. I know, you know, everyone knew.'

'What did they know?' I knew exactly what she was referring too, however, I tried to sound oblivious, shrugging my shoulders.

'Adam, seriously, it's OK. I don't mind talking about anything with you.' I didn't say anything waiting for her lead. 'We are friends aren't we, Ad?'

'Yes, absolutely,' I fired the words out like a car backfiring.

She smiled at my outburst and nodding, 'I know you're being polite but it's common knowledge, don't worry, I'm not going to moan about it too much.' She nudged closer, leaning over the table. I resisted the urge to stare down her top. Being close to her still had such a strong effect on me that I constantly tried to appraise my behaviour. Hopefully, it was unnoticeable and not like a drunk who over-articulates his words so much the drunkenness becomes even more obvious. '… I don't like playing the victim.' She paused waiting for my move. 'I just want it out…' she encouraged. I put my head down in order to try and hide my sheepish expression. She reached out a hand and placed it on top of mine. My whole arm pulled stiff as I fight to control the tremor. It was now empty, and I wished it were full in order that I could use it as a prop. 'Adam, if we're going to be friends, I need to say these things. I don't want anything between us.' I lifted my head in acknowledgement. And nodded slightly. 'Most people think it started — Johnny's attention I mean — when I was fourteen but the fact is, it started a lot earlier. I was playing in the street with my brothers when I was about nine. He stole my brother's ball. I ran after him, following him down an alleyway to retrieve it, he grabbed me. I try to scream out, but he put his hand over my mouth so only the merest of sounds escaped.' She stopped, turning off the emotion in her voice as if she were turning off a tap. She continued in a plain-speaking voice. 'I didn't really know what he was doing, I knew it was wrong because he threatened to hurt my brothers if I told anyone.' She paused flushing a delicate shade of pink. 'The fact is I would never have told anyone anyway; actually, there was no one to tell. It's not like I could have told my mother — she was very strict.' I noticed how hard it was for her to make eye contact. 'He used any opportunity he could to get me alone so from that point on I only played in the hall outside our apartment. I never played on the street and ran to the shop and back. I don't want to blow it out of proportion, it's not like he raped me or anything just, groped me a bit.' She looked down and shrugged it off. Even tried to put a smile on it, like it wasn't worth talking about.

My stomach turned over. A mixture of anger, revulsion and pity light up a million fireworks in my brain, the images too big to cope with. I focused on my arm, focused on keeping it still. I looked up at her, I needed to say something, to bare my soul or show understanding, compassion, and love even. The words didn't come. Instead I smiled weakly. 'It's OK, we all have a past.' The words were not close to the churning ocean inside me. What I wanted to say... what I was actually thinking was: Is there anything sadder than when abuse gets so normal, so commonplace its harshness becomes reduced to everyday drama? Not the shocking truth it should be but another daily thing, like going to the dentist or doing overtime or an ex you have to put up with! I wanted to tell her I knew, I saw it — I wanted to stop it. I wanted to hold her, to tell her we shared this experience in some strange way. I too feel the burden, the pain, it followed me around like a black cloud too. She smiled back, quickly diverting her glance to the counter, a telling sign she was nervous, making sure no one had overheard. I gripped her hand loosely.

'It's OK, really.'

She smiled back. 'I know. I just don't like talking about...' She sipped at her cup to avoid finishing the sentence.

I always knew deep down there was some truth to the gossip still I refused to listen to shit people said back then. There were always rumours about Lilly and her family. Apparently, her mother was a whore and her father was in jail. Once I heard that the police had raided her apartment because her mother had helped a couple of guys escape from a cop car park outside their building. I heard that a

183

truant officer used to go regularly because her mother didn't send the kids to school. I heard that Lilly and her brothers got a warning from some street cops for stealing clothes from the charity bins. Also, this rumour went around that a market vendor had broken her brother's arm when he tried to steal fruit from his cart. There were so many, I lost track. Every week there seemed to be a new one. I was lost for words, I hope she didn't feel I was passing judgement with my silence, but I got the impression that maybe she did.

'All the rumours at school, only a handful of them are true. I never agreed to anything, Ad, you must know that that's important to me, I never agreed to anything.' She hid her face behind a coffee; I admire her strength and not crying, I wanted to grab hold of her, make it all go away. A churning in the pit of my stomach started, I felt so inadequate, so useless. 'I dread to think what you must think of me,' she blurted out dramatically.

I squeezed her hand, looking deeply at her face holding back my own emotion. 'You never have to apologise for anything. You need to know that.' I hope to sound sincere.

'Feels good to let out to someone actually.' A smile began to appear on her face.

'I'm glad you chose me.' And I was glad. As upsetting as this was, I felt blessed that she chose me. I felt renewed with the feeling of hope.

'Can I tell you something else?'

'Of course, anything.' I couldn't believe she was confiding in me, I ate up every word.

'I mean we can… we can really talk then?'

'Of course.' I was filled with a sort of nervous excitement.

'I'm just going to say it. I've remembered who you were at school.' Stunned into silence, my mood suddenly swings. I feel my hands clammy and hot. The excitement quickly shifting to stinging pain: I've been found out. 'Actually, that's kind of a lie, I knew who you were straightaway. It's just that…' She's holding back. What is it that she wants to say but can't?

'Just what?' The words came out too direct, defensive almost. I was trying to put my shields up and let them down at the same time. The panicked feelings in my stomach start to take effect.

'What I mean is, when guys from school come into the bar, they would see me in a certain light. Look at the surroundings and because of what they heard or thought they knew, they thought I was a whore. I just thought that's what you wanted.' My hand grabbed at my temples, rubbing for a second at an irrational pain that simultaneously spread across the front of my head and down the back of my neck. I knew this pain was a fierce warning sign, if I choose to continue; well, I know what's coming. I ignore it.

'You know that's not what I want by now or are you asking?' My words are hanging in the air, I know, I shouldn't have said it the second it left my mouth. The words were cutting, far too sharp.

'Yes, of course, I wouldn't have come here unless I thought you were nice a guy.' She looked bewildered. I'd embarrassed her.

'Sorry, sorry, I know that. I'm just shocked that you could think that I… that's not what I want.' The wrong answer I should have left it as sorry.

'What do you want?' she asked firmly.

Although my head screamed; to hold you, to make you feel better, to marry you, all I said was, 'I just want to get to know you better. That's all…' She can see through me, she knows what I am really here for; she sees my longing. A small smile appeared on her face. The atmosphere calmed.

'I wanna get to know you too.' She leans in, so her words stay between us. 'I know John bullied you too…' she whispers. I can't say anything. I feel my face burn and I know I've turned scarlet. 'Oh, I didn't mean to make you feel uncomfortable, I'm so sorry.' She reaches out touching my arm, which serves to intensify the tension in my face. It's coming, I can feel it, there's nowhere to run, she's going to see, a thought that starts to set off fireworks in my brain once again. I wasn't going to say anything… As if there were magnets on my face I couldn't look up. Well, now there's proof she has bigger balls than me… as if I didn't already know. I piss around hiding shit and she just comes out with it.

'What do you remember?' I manage to let out as I focus on the grains in the wooden table top. I can feel her eyes on me.

'Enough...'

My eyes begin to burn, and I stare at the wood varnish. I analyse how uneven it is and how it follows the natural lines and pools in pitted dark rings. I cannot cry here, not in front of her. Suddenly, the room becomes too full, too many people sucking the same oxygen. I breathe in, trying not to let go, keep it all locked down and bottled in. I breathe in, sucking in, trying not to look out of place. I'm suddenly aware of every single person in the room. I feel their eyes on me, none more than Lilly. I inhale air through my nose, and concentrate on the air flowing into my lungs. Suddenly, my whole body is alert with sensitivity, every detail of the room from the women talking to the cups in the saucers clinking, line up and form an imagery wall of overwhelming information. It's too much — claustrophobic, I feel my breathing change. I'm on the brink of a full-blown panic attack. My heart is pounding, forcing the walls of my veins to expand with the gush of adrenaline, burning my throat as though it's trying to find a way out. Under the table, my finger and thumb tap briskly together as my therapist showed me to ward off an escalation. Focus on your fingers tapping together, feel the pressure on the tips of my fingers. I said it over and over again in my head. I was far beyond hiding it from Lil. I could feel the sweat on the back of my neck and pearling droplets across my forehead. Her eyes covering me, I don't have to look up to know it.

'Ad, it's OK, we don't have to talk about it if you don't want to.' I couldn't speak, it was like my voice box had seized up, there was so much noise in my head, white noise, black noise, barking dogs and sirens. My heart pounded up past my chest and throat, into the back of my face, as though trying to push itself to freedom through the back of my eyeballs.

'Adam!' she demanded. 'Adam, don't be upset. Do you need something? Water?' She tried to pass me a glass, but I shook my head and she moved away. This is when I would swig whisky straight from the bottle with a handful of pills. Why did I leave them home, why didn't I take them this morning? 'Ad, do you want to get out of here?' I hear the alarm in her voice. She stands, picking up her bag. I get to my feet... barely; I stumble forward as I see her heading out the door. My feet will hardly move, the room suddenly feels overfilled, like each and every person is sucking the air straight out of my lungs. The walls bow over my head. My vision slants to one side, the door seems to shift... suddenly, Lilly is in front of me, grabbing my hand and pulling me forward towards the door.

'Slow down.' I seem to fly up the street behind her. 'Lilly, not so fast.' She's pulling me along.

'Which one's your car?' she demands, with a hint of fear. I pull out my keys, pointing. She runs around to the passenger side, pulling on the handle. 'Get in,' she demands, putting her hand on my head so I don't hit it. It's almost as though I'm outside my body. As though I'm trying to scream myself awake. I try desperately to shake it off. She hates me now, she hates me, and I've blown it. Behind the wheel, she turns over the engine and I hear it roar to life.

Without making eye contact I ask her, 'Where?' I'm trying to control my shaking voice.

Lil swings out onto the busy street. 'I'm just getting us out of here, Ad. I'm so sorry to do that to you it was thoughtless.' There are tears in her eyes.

'You didn't do anything. It's me, go straight.' Panting, I pointed, aware that my voice was quivering. I squeeze down on the palms of my hands until I can feel my nails cut into the skin. I focus on the pain, it's the only way I can get order in my head. 'I know a place.' She breaks the speed limit, taking us out of town and along the coast.

I direct us to a small car park. As she pulls up, I open the door before she's fully stopped. Jumping out, I run over to the fence overlooking the docks, nothing comes up. This is normal, the empty retching — the dizziness. I'm down on my knees. She stays in the car, I'm glad. I know she's watching without looking. I am living my nightmare. I fall back onto my ass and cover my face.

After a while, I look at the darkening shadow of the factory sprawl and disregarded industrial waste left behind. Pausing for a second, I rub at the now gathering sweat on my forehead, preparing to face whatever is coming. I think about rising. As she approaches, she turns her head away from me, looking at the view. I stand slightly to the side, giving her room.

'Sorry for the drama,' I say, 'I just need a minute.' Embarrassment doesn't cover it.

'I'm the one who's sorry. I'm so stupid.' She puts her hand on the centre of my back, it's warm and she rubs in circles. I begin to calm down a little, the broken feeling inside me stays. 'That was a panic attack, right? My brother used to get them…' Her voice is soft and warm.

I so wanted this to go well. My eyes meet the ground, sighing with futility. Why did I expect any more than this? I knew I'd fuck up. As she turns, I see she's tearing up. My stomach drops and true to form I freeze. Without warning she throws herself at me, wrapping her arms around me, forcing me to swallow. The warmth of her body surrounds my being, and I slowly lift my own arms and watch as they curve to the shape of her.

After a few minutes, she releases me. She looks up at me.

'Adam, we have to talk about it and clear the air. I know it's awkward now.' She puts her hands on her hips. 'If we don't talk about this then we'll stop hanging out, and I'm not letting that happen. No one can hear us, it's only me so that's what we're doing OK?' Her body was resolute and defiant, all an act. However, I agreed.

I launch into a speech with nothing to lose. 'Johnny was always in my class, right from my first day he was a pain in my ass.' I swallowed hard trying to make things right, this had to come out. 'He pulled my hair and made me cry in first grade. When the teacher saw, she told him off, he kicked her. That kind of sums things up for me.' Saying it out loud, standing there in her presence, my whole life suddenly seemed so ridiculous. 'I didn't really know about him, you know his family and stuff, until high school. He didn't like me because…' She cut me off.

'Because you're a Jew, I heard him calling you stuff like that. I went home and asked my mum what it meant, after that, I thought *Jew* was a swear word for years. She told me the Jews killed Jesus and wouldn't say anything else on the subject, but she was like that.'

I looked to the horizon for some kind of comfort. The humiliation I had suffered at the hands of Johnny was bad enough, now knowing there had been a witness was so much worse. Keeping it to myself had made it nonexistent as far as the rest of the world was concerned. Knowing Lilly had seen was unbearable. I have to keep going and finish what I started. It was like trying to throw up barbed wire, it burns, cuts and scrapes, but I knew it was better out than in.

'There was this one time near the start of school.' I stop and look at her. This is difficult; I've not spoken about this before, not even with my dad. I turn back around and fix my eyes on the horizon. I draw an invisible line using an invisible pencil along the line that separates heaven and earth. Focus on the line, I tell myself, steady. I draw breath and begin to speak. 'My father decided not to send his kids to Hebrew school. Instead, he wanted us to make our own way. It was his way of giving us the freedom to choose, and he knew my mother would educate us in our faith just fine at home.'

'Is that why you couldn't tell him about what happened?' She's gentle in her approach, her words tiptoeing across mine.

'Yes, I think so…' I cleared my throat. 'Yes, but also letting him down,' I said more clearly. 'He would blame himself.'

'Do you blame…?'

'No, he's the greatest man I know. He would do anything for me, anything.' I realised I was yelling. 'Sorry, sorry.' I pushed the hair back from my face. 'This is hard.'

'Take your time, it's OK.' She stands quietly, stroking my arm till I'm ready.

'I don't really know where to start. There isn't one incident, there's a million. Each of them took little pieces of me. I can tell you that he stuck me in lockers and pissed on me in the showers with his mates. If I ever scored well in tests they would be waiting outside the classroom, but you learn to keep your head down, just stay out of their way. By my second year of high school, I knew how to avoid it… mostly.' My hands still trembled. 'It's just that it…' Taking a huge sigh, the words like razors on my tongue became almost impossible to spit out. Now is the time to say it, come clean, Adam, the voice booms loud as a canon in my head. Her eyes focused on me intently. 'The hardest part was feeling helpless.' I sucked in a deep breath, and then let it out. 'Watching people that you care about being hurt and standing there, who does that make me?' My hands gripped the rails; I felt my face screw up. 'Standing there, watching like a fucking coward.' I panted for breath at the unplanned words, which flew from my mouth, not daring to look at her. 'I'm sorry. I'm so sorry.' I couldn't hold back. The words cut and bit my tongue as I tried to spit them out. 'Lil, I saw him pin you against the wall. I did nothing, I didn't even try, I was too scared, I'm sorry, I'm so sorry. I swear if it ever happened again, even though he would probably kill me, I will try to do something.' It was out — the truth now set free. I started with my eyes locked forward. How could I meet her eye to eye now?

 She handed me a tissue from her bag. Only saying, 'Here, take this.' She put her hand on top of mine as I gripped the rail overlooking the drop to the water. She let me catch my breath not saying anything at all. I appreciated the pause, my heart still beating rapidity. 'Adam, there was a whole classroom full of kids standing around that day. All of us were too scared to move, including me. Why would I single you out, or blame you? Besides I wouldn't want you to fight back. John would've really hurt you, and I would have blamed myself…' She turned to me inviting me in, and I grabbed hold of her. Years of grappling with it, layers of shame peeled back and laid raw in only a few sentences. My perspective re-arranged.

***

We talked for hours on the hood of my car. The evening drew closer and it became too cold. Seeing her shivering, we continued, sitting in the backseat. Nothing dirty as I imagined it would be if I ever got her in the back of my car. I watched her lips move as she spoke. As I watched, I realised she was making room for me in her life. There was an openness to her, a freedom of expression. Lil wasn't the kind of person to put up walls like me. Unfortunately, the situation she had found herself in had isolated her, so she put her feelings in a locked room. I could see it was a place only she visited. This was the first step, she was handing me a key. A chance to unlock a life together — an invitation. Her eyes began to grow heavy, her face finding a resting place on my chest. I listen closely to her breathing, rising and falling in her smooth rhythm. My mouth began to move, and my words fell freely in the still.

'Sometimes, late at night when I dream, I see our town made of building blocks. It's like someone has placed a rope around our whole city, an invisible line keeping us all in our place. In my dream, I push against it, but I can never get through.' I stroke her hair.

'What do you think it means?' she mumbled, half asleep.

'I don't know. The night after I went to the markets with you, I dreamt I took a long saw from work. Then I hacked into the rope until the rope was no more than a string, then I woke up.' I could feel her smiling under me. I kissed her forehead, feeling her grow heavy and still. I turn the volume of my voice down. 'I think for the most part, or for most people, life is pretty shit with a sprinkling of joy. Those moments of pure joy are so powerful, so overwhelming, that we spend the rest of our lives trying to find them again. To relive them for a second time, somehow to taste them for one more incredible rush. Like you're standing next to God, like the universe is running through you. In those moments, we are privileged to see another person's soul, see kindness, sacrifice, love... real love, that's more than yourself. That's what life is about, those moments.'

'That was beautiful, did you make that up yourself?' She seemed to be impressed.

'Yeah,' I said a little taken back. 'It's nothing.'

'Yes, it's something, Adam, A gift.'

Finally, as the night blacked everything but the red and yellow aeroplane warning lights on the top of the factories, she slept soundly. I covered her with my jacket, sucking in the natural, sweet smell of her hair, feeling her soft skin on mine. It still felt unreal to me. I didn't move, scared to break the moment. I lay there, soul bare, open to ridicule, ready to be picked over. It's like a string of hope hanging from the ceiling, like an obscure spider's web so delicate that a tiny breath could blow it away out of sight. This is what you trust someone not to break. The flimsy string that your life comes down too in the end. The threads of hopes and dreams hidden inside the essence of you.

CHAPTER 18
WARNING

Add somewhere!

Lifeline, unmeasurable,
Loyalty, unfathomable,
In a handshake, a beer and a smile.

Fifteen minutes from the end of my shift and my arms are dragging like lead. The siren would blare across the yard echoing off the walls soon, allowing me to leave. I had half a truckload to go, a simple stack and pack job, not complex at all, but no part of my job was taxing. Any lug could do it. The boxes consisted of the last of the computer parts from Japan on their way to a private school in the affluent suburbs out West. I didn't spend much time reading or taking notice of the details on the invoice papers. That would only serve to make me pine more for the world outside this squalid truck bay. It wasn't in my job description or indeed my concern to know the exact details of the job at hand. It was made clear, my only job was to get the truck loaded and off to its destination.

Sweat gathered at the top of my neck causing a trickle of liberal-sized droplets to roll down my spine. I fanned my T-shirt out from my body to stop it from sticking and enjoyed the waft of air chilling my damp back. The shuffling of feet took my attention away from my work and to the small gathering of men across the factory floor. It was an unwritten rule that every couple of hours you could take a break. Most men around here need a cigarette every couple of hours. However, cigarettes being one of the few addictions I am not drawn to, left me a few moments of time to swig at my water bottle, wishing it was vodka. I take a breath to alleviate the pressure from my feet by parking my ass on some packing boxes.

The warehouse gets incredibly hot and stuffy. Even in winter with so many bodies sweating and heaving heavy loads, the temperature soon rises incredibly. The doors are locked down after the morning siren. One: to stop latecomers claiming time they haven't worked, and two: to stop boxes falling off the trucks and into the hands of would-be scavengers or businessmen.

Taking a minute to appreciate the rest, I wiped my mouth with the back of my hand, out of habit, tasting the dust and grime from my dirty skin. I spit it out, so it made an arched shape puddle on the floor. The box compacter, which would continue to crush cardboard through a nuclear bomb, competed with the constant certainty of the clock. It all joins with a cacophony of obscure clunks, dings and shuffles which form an industrial symphony behind me. I release a sigh from deep inside me. Focusing my eyes on the ridges of the bottle top, the drip of water making its way down off the label and onto my hand. The edges of my mind are blackened; facing the indistinguishable pattern of my daily drag is best blocked out. In moments of clarity like now, I am fully aware that alcohol serves as scaffolding that holds up my sky. I loathe it. I am wretched. Ironically, this makes me wish I could turn my water, not into wine but vodka.

Knocking the dust off one boot onto the other, a shadow falls across me. An instinctive shiver darted wildly across my skin, like hunted buffalo. So lost in thought was I, I hadn't noticed them striding over my way. I recognised them instantly. The same guys who had chased me a couple of nights ago, John's men. My heart instantly rose to the back of my throat, seemingly cutting off my air supply. It took me a few minutes to comprehend the magnitude of what was happening. Frantic! The factory floor cleared and became silent and empty, all noise ceasing with the exception of the continuous clunk of the air conditioner grappling to work, its grate thick with filth. Instantly, everyone had something important to do somewhere else. Hiding out of sight.

I watched them as they stride over. The first guy was tall with exaggerated mannerisms and a long face that reminded me of a horse. His front teeth moderately stuck out beyond his top lip. He chomped on nicotine gum like it was grass. With a Mediterranean look, a deep golden tan and dark features, he looked slightly unkempt with greased back hair. The second was wide and roundish in the middle. Light, with a tinge of red in his hair and beard, he had an Irish glare with fixed blue eyes, hard looking, with powerful arms, like concrete couldn't smash him. Unusual though, John was rather strict on the appearance of his men. Who, apart from these exceptions, all were clean, tidy and well turned out, is that they were somewhat extensions of Johnny himself?

The two figures, an enormous sight up close, now stood over me, blocking out my view of Pete's work bay. I forced my neck back as far as possible before it snapped, making a transparently courageous effort to look them in the face, which only made them grin. My heart stopped beating for a second. Then, cranking back on, it increased to double speed, like I'd stuck my finger in a socket. My stomach drops as every part of my body paused in fright, but I desperately struggled to force my face into a stoic pose. Anxiety had trained me to smell fear, I'm aware I'm not fooling anyone. Mindful of my surroundings and my place within them, I wanted to cast my eyes around freely, to take note of who was watching the unfolding humiliation. I knew instinctively the whole factory crew would be transfixed, whether I could see them or not. This was nothing short of an event, not one I sought to be a part of. A top-billed news scandal right here in the open which would be picked over for months, blow by blow. Beckoning a bit of nerve, I look up at a slight angle, unable to swallow under the glare of the first man's physique. A smirk spread across his face with his clear superiority. The other guy moves a touch to the left, creating a semicircle of terror around me. He proceeded to kick my stool with such sudden force it sent my head snapping back with a start. I grabbed the back of my neck with the shot of pain; he leaned over trying to further intimidate me, saying nothing.

I shifted suddenly, flushing with humiliation and anger; I tried to sit up straight taking ownership of my small amount of space. They edged closer to my face for pure effect until I was gagging on their combined cheap colognes. With a snort, they stood upright once more. A towering shadow cast downwards. One lit a cigarette that he pulled from his back pocket, lighting it in slow motion.

'I don't believe it's rest time... the whistle hasn't blown yet; on your feet!' the taller one barked the order as if he had a right to. The other nodded, backing him up completely. Their bodies standing over me forced me to stay perched where I was. The sight of me squirming caused them to laugh, it echoed off the factory walls, drawing attention. However, not one man in the entire place made an objection or even made it known they were observing.

'Nope, he's not getting up,' they concurred in a low tone, forcing me to strain to hear.

'I do have to get up actually? There's a truck that needs filling before the siren, so if you don't mind.' Attempting to rise, I tried to sound confident and unafraid. My stomach was doing backflips and my balls had taken up residence somewhere behind my kidneys.

'It's OK, you don't have to panic, boxes can wait,' the darker, greasy one said, flipping his head around to check out the wall of invoiced packages. Clearly enjoying the power of it, they were centre-stage and knew it.

'We just came over to say hello,' the Irish guy said, knowing I was terrified, now showing the power in his full chest. Talking a step forward in the limited space, again their presence pushed down on me. I could feel his hot breath at the top of my head.

'You see... the other night we thought we recognised you on Fourth,' Irish continues, the leader out of the two.

Not to be left out, the darker one piped in. 'We came over to say hello, but you were in a hurry.' Dropping his remarkably heavy hand firmly on my shoulder, he squeezes the joint uncomfortably.

'You disappeared into thin air, that's not very friendly.' Irish again,

'No, it's not... anyone would think you were avoiding us.' Their words overlap, one another, woven together as though one were person speaking. Well-practised in intimidation, the act is seamless, even able to anticipate movements, synchronising their body language perfectly.

'Sorry, I don't suppose I saw you.' The words came out slightly quivering. I forced my chin up, making eye contact while feeling sweat breakout across my brow. 'I was meeting someone,' I managed to say, '... anyway like I said, I've gotta get on with my work, boys.' I edged my way up, only to have two hands push me back down on the crate with a thud.

'What's the hurry? We got a few things to say before you run off.'

I seemed to lose my voice; I felt my voice box contract and shrink. Sweat dampened my temples; my heart pounded ferociously. I hadn't been this scared since school.

'We heard you've been sniffing around a young barmaid.' They acted so smug; I want to bang their heads together. That is if I hadn't been concentrating on trying not to choke on my own vomit.

'We like to protect our employees against people that might want to take advantage…' At this, the Irish guy then put his hands on his hips. It was almost comical; as if they had morphed into a couple of caricature school bullies or watched too many movies. I would have laughed it off if I hadn't been so shit scared.

'She's a sweet girl with a good job so in a brotherly kind of a way,' the greasy looking guy continued, his voice was thick and low as he spoke alongside my ear still holding my place while the larger of the two lit a cigarette.

'What my mate is trying to say is… it's best if you don't come down onto Fourth anymore,' the Irish interrupted, receiving an eyeballing from his partner.

'We've noticed that you like to frequent another bar on Market Street with your buddies… Pete and Joe, right?' Maybe I hadn't been paranoid after all, had I been followed?

'Why don't you stay at that little place you like, you know the one in your building.' As I sat unable to move, I almost choke on my own vomit. My stomach swished from side to side, the crate creaking, buckling under the extra weight of their hands on my shoulders. This was clearly a warning; I'd be lucky to get out of this without blood in my urine and all my teeth intact. I nodded in agreement purely out of being utterly petrified. The two men looked at each other seemingly happy with their intimidation tactics.

'I don't think you want to come back to the Black Dragon, right? You're much happier frequenting the bar on Market Street. Your friends go there; it's close to home. It's a better fit, right?'

I nodded, petrified.

'OK, so we have an understanding. Everyone's happy; that's all we need to know.' The larger guy draws deeply on his cigarette, exhaling the smoke out just above my face. I held my breath, not wanting to breathe in the second-hand smoke from his mouth.

'He's got the message.' The taller one patted his mate on the shoulder. As my eyes followed his hand, waiting for something to happen now, the speech was over. Semi bracing for the first hit.

'So, I'm glad we had this talk.' He pats me on the back in mock friendship. The taller guy then kicked the back of my stool hard, sending my body lurching forward with fright, scaring the shit out of me. I cry out with shock, stumble, almost fall, and even though I don't hit the ground. I feel like I have. The shorter guy flicked his lit butt, singeing my shirt with hot ash. He then let out an unabashed laugh, stuck his hands in his pockets and began starting whistling. Proud as punch the taller guy joined him, strolling away like nothing had happened.

I checked myself; my legs were shaking like jelly. I can't stand yet. I suck in air. The sound of the exit door, slamming with the breeze jolted me. I truly believed they were going to kill me. I push the hair back out of my eyes, aware that my co-workers are watching me. My face boiling hot with embarrassment, I pushed down every emotion. They will not make me cry at work. Even though my hands tremble I try to continue as though nothing has happened. A few of the other office employees have gathered around, I hear them whisper. The whole factory has seen me cowardly break under their attack, this will be the topic of conversation for months. I muster up enough energy to stand; even though I can barely walk. I pad slowly with jelly legs, over to where the truck is parked. I lean for a second out of sight, wiping my brow with the back of my sleeve. I have to summon a brave face, or at least try. I gather myself, standing up straight; trying to carry on like nothing happened. A few employees exchange looks, whispers and pretend not to notice. I can't believe the whole factory saw me shit myself. A rush of humiliation clouds my whole being. I have to walk back out there and hold my head up. I check my watch only a little while to go; I can last.

I finish loading the truck, although I dropped about half a dozen boxes. Each time a box fell, the sound echoed off the floors and walls. An alert to remind everyone I am still here, like a giant red arrow has appeared from the sky pointing straight at my head; signalling me out from the pack. My hands continue to shake, shaking so much I can't seem to muster my normal strength. Not one person approaches me, not even the foreman. I guess they're scared of being placed on John's bad list by association. No doubt, I'm on that list for life now. Where were Pete and Joe? This wasn't their problem, they warned me, I know; but it was odd that even now it had concluded, they hadn't materialised for a drink offer. I glance over to the spot where Pete usually stands but there's only an empty space, odd, Joe too seems to be out of sight.

After what feels like an eternity, the siren rings out. The end of my workday has come at last. I shut and lock the truck's heavy bolted doors. The last job for the day done, I mentally tick off. The locks clang together sending an electric shiver back, the sound seems piercing, metal on metal grinds together, my skin reacts instantly becoming covered in goose bumps, I rub my arms vigorously aiming to escape the feeling. My hands still trembling, legs a little shaky under my own weight. I grab my jacket and water bottle. Then wait a minute or two for the bulk of the crowd to leave so I can get away without confrontation. I see a couple of guys hanging around the entrance, tilting their heads; they won't look at me directly.

With a flash of fear, my heart kicks up; beating double time as I come to the realisation these guys could be here on John's behalf. It's too late to turn back. The warehouse is now empty. I push in my time card, keeping to myself, getting ready to run at the first sign of trouble. Keep walking; just keep walking, I tell myself. My eyes dart around, realising he could have men anywhere. So, this is where it will happen, out here, away from the security cameras? Makes sense. Why didn't I think of this early? I should have sneaked out with the crowd, not hidden away.

Examining the extended line for the shuttle bus into town, I know I will be vulnerable standing there alone at the end of the line. No one would help me if there is trouble, not today. More than anything else, it would be getting to the line in the first place that would prove difficult. Crossing the yard was fought with danger. There were too many parked cars; too many trucks with swinging open back doors, packing cases piled up to the sky, creating alleyways, reels of plastic packing. I could be shrink-wrapped and thrown in the docs in seconds, no one would see. I have a hunch if there were witnesses, no one would report it.

I have to be smart, be unpredictable. I made the decision not to get on the bus back to Market Street. I'll walk it instead; my legs are still a little shaky, but now more filled with adrenaline than fear. Inhaling deeply, walking is the last thing I feel like doing. I've never needed to drink more. I checked over my shoulder yet again. It felt like I was developing a nervous twitch. The last bus pulled away, choking up the place with diesel fumes. My muscles twitch with anticipation, now or never.

***

I almost tumble down the little stone steps to the bar below my apartment, exhausted from both the jog home and today's ordeal. It might be my imagination, but the bar hushed to a weak silence as I wander through the door. With a complete cross-section of punters, I knew, I had to be paranoid in thinking that they're whispering about me. Nonetheless, I felt people's eyes on me. Having John's men threatening you is big news. It will be all over the warehouse and dock by now.

I saw Pete and Joe drinking in our usual spot. I trudged over but was careful to leave a couple of stools between myself and where they sat. Leaving them an out, in case they didn't want to hang out with me right now. Pete glimpses me from the corner of his eye, shooting a cockeyed look my way.

'What are you doing all the way over there?'

Equally as perplexed, Joe pushed out a stool with his foot, shaking his head grinning.

'Get your ass over here!' Pete yells over the noise. I stood and proceed over in their direction. I felt a ridiculously wide smile spread across my face, the kind you can't hide if you wanted to, the kind that props up your cheeks.

'So, Ad, another quiet day at the factory for you, I just heard.' I laughed with relief. Emotion boiling up, using the palms of my hands to rub my eyes and forehead I realise I'm sweating. I sigh. I felt safe in their presence, almost overwhelmingly so. It was then I noticed Joe has a slightly blackish, purple eye and a bandage around his wrist. His hands also looked pretty bruised up. I look at him for an answer.

'It's nothing, Ad,' he said, staring at his hands then shaking it off.

I look at Pete, knowing he can't keep his mouth shut. He comes in close. 'It seems, that our friend, Joe, is a bit of a sly one. A couple of John's men came to see us today. They sent us on an errand to the west dock, the empty bit. When we arrived I smelt trouble.'

'Yeah, he smelt trouble, Ad. More like the hamburger he was eating,' Joe interjected, laughing.

'Hey, who's telling this story? So, four guys were waiting in a parked car, big guys, Ad, scary as all shit. One had a baseball bat.'

Joe's laughing into his beer, 'I don't remember any bat, Pete.'

'There was a bat,' Pete continues. 'They got a little pushy, a few fists were thrown, and you know what I mean.' He winks, standing for impact.

'Seriously Ad, don't go fishing with this guy, he'll have you catching a shark with your bare hands.' Joe takes another swig from his beer, chuckling at the recent memory.

'Don't leave me hanging, what happened?' I asked, feeling Pete's excitement rubbing off on me.

'I'll tell you what happened, *Mr I don't like confrontation* over there went off like a frog in a sock. Head-butting one of them straight in the nose — blood everywhere Ad! Another tries to grab him from behind;

Joe knocks him off like he's nothing. A third guy joins in, blow to the stomach, that's when Joe gets mad, left-right combinations.' Pete picks up a bar stool acting out moves, dancing around like a prize fighter. Joe and me kick back and enjoy the show. 'It was a scene, Ad,' he went on, demonstrating a chokehold with his hands. He'd clearly been dying to tell me.

'And where were you, Pete?' I press, encouraging the display.

'Me? Well, I took on the guy with the bat.' With that Joe spits his beer across the bar with a huge barrel-like convulsive howl.

Nearly splitting with laughter and disbelief at Pete's tale, I pat my usually calm and placid friend on the back. Joe was a big man, fists like bulldozers. I've known him since school but not once have I ever seen him be aggressive. He was the guy who would get you in a bear hug. He'd pin you down, hold you back, or get in there and break the fight up. Or more commonly, stop fights from starting in the first place, he was known for it. This was a surprise, to say the least. Pete, in his typical form, regaled me with the highlights, low lights and every other detail of the fight he could remember, unabated until late. Joe humbly sat there shaking his head. I hadn't noticed my heart calm down or myself relax, but here it feels like nothing can touch me.

After a couple of hours into drinking, when the alcohol had mellowed us all to a dull stupor and we'd listened to a multitude of conspiracy theories of what, who and why the fight had taken place, Joe turned to me.

'Adam, you're one of my oldest mates, my brother, you're family, truly.' He placed his hand on his heart as he spoke. 'So, don't get me wrong when I say… you need to start taking this seriously. You need to get your shit together and get out of town.' Pete looked over at Joe, he nodded in total agreement, calming down for the first time all evening.

'I hate to say it, I think it's time.' He paused for a moment. 'Have you got family you can go and stay with somewhere?'

I let out a slow, long breath, facing the inevitable outcome, nodding with agreement.

'I know what you're saying is right…' I raised my voice a touch, in frustration and gritted my teeth. 'I detest the thought of leaving, it makes me feel like a coward.' In my heart, I knew that didn't change the fact they were right. Joe takes a moment, pausing on the edge of saying something as if shuffling the words around to put them in the right order so as not to offend me.

'A coward is someone who hides from what is right, that's not you, Ad. Remove yourself from what is unhealthy in order to be healthy,' Joe utters in a low and strong tone.

'Where the fuck did that come from?' Pete chokes out, mouth full of beer. 'Who are you? First, you turn into Jackie Chan on the docks, now you're Confucius?' Pete is more animated than I'd seen in a while.

Joe smugly drinks his beer. 'What? I read!' Joe says, giving me a wink. His eyes signalling to a drink smart poster on the wall. The exact slogan is written in bold, along the bottom. Indeed, Joe is a sly one.

Sisters, like blisters,
Are better taken care of, right away!

CHAPTER 19
SHE'S NOT SO BAD

Most of the time my sister Rachel does a good impersonation of a tramp. Old torn jeans, baggy T-shirts and her hair scraped into a ponytail so tight it looks like she's giving herself a brain squeeze. This is mainly due to the fact she works in a florist. Not the lavish art deco kind you see on high street corners, but a mail order company. She works among plants grown in peat bags in extended lines of budding stems. Her time is mostly spent hauling tools, dirt and insecticide around on her back, up to her neck in manure. The few times I've seen her go to the effort she has actually looked OK, not glamorous, but pleasant. So, with that in mind, coupled with the fact there isn't really anyone else to ask, I arranged for her to meet me at the south-side shopping centre. She had said *no* repeatedly when I called her. Until I reluctantly told her, I hoped to take Lilly out on a proper date with candles, wine and food that didn't come in paper boxes. Unfortunately, I have fuck all to wear. I guess I must have plucked at a tender heartstring because she agreed, with her only condition being that it doesn't take all day.

I only brave this artificial haven when I absolutely have to. It has packed walkways full of pensioners and crying kids in prams. The unnatural lighting bothers me continually, it's suffocating. I hate the phoney ultraviolet light signs flashing hysterically, it reminds me of ambulances and police cars. I don't wanna know about specials or sales, please let me get in — let me get out. This rant began running through my mind long before I chose my sister. However, I was careful to pack it at the back of my mind, along with all the other things I don't care for. If Rachel had even sniffed my complaints, she would have taken the first bus home. She hates moaning, particularly about things you can't change.

'So, we're here for date clothes. Is that right?' my sister yells across the first store, purposely to embarrass me. I roll my eyes in response. If I reply with anything more the banter will start; with us two that could go on for hours.

'You and Mum, what's that about?' I question her as she holds a pair of pale grey pants up to me with the look of indecision.

'What do you mean?' she says plainly.

'You know… suddenly BFFs. You never hang out with Mum!'

'Ahhh, you're jealous I'm getting all Mummy's attention?' She laughs in reply avoiding a real answer.

'So, there's something going on but you're not going to tell me what it is? That's fine.' Dismissively I turn to pick through shirts, pulling a few out and musing over them. I know how to get under her skin. She stares at her brightly coloured drink with the little paper straw floating in it, trying to block me out. I wait. If the silence is long enough maybe she'll feel the pressure to talk. Just a little more prodding, 'It's OK if you don't wanna tell me…' I let it hang in the air.

'Come on, it's not like that. I'm not telling anyone,' she said, shifting from one foot to the other. I say nothing, shrugging my shoulders. 'Fine, you wanna know? OK, I'll tell you. But you repeat this to anyone I'm killing you,' she says, giving in.

I shrug smiling in victory. 'Well if you can't hold it in, I'll listen.' She punches me in the arm. There's a pause, a long one as she gets herself together. This must be bigger than I thought it was going to be. She looks at me and I don't recognise the expression.

'I'm pregnant…'

'What?'

'I'm about three and a half months.'

'I didn't even know you had a boyfriend. Do you have a boyfriend? I mean who's gonna take care of you?'

'Me, I'm going to take care of me. Just as I have since I left home,' she said defiantly.

'So… How did this happen? Are you happy about it? You're happy about it, right?' The information flew into my brain so quickly I was processing and trying to reassure Rachel at the same time. A combination which wasn't working for either of us.

She nodded. 'Yeah, I think so. It's still sinking in.'

'Of course, it is, sorry. I'm not saying the right things, am I? But it's kind of a shock. Fuck… no wonder Mum's going nuts.' I sink back into the bench seat near the changing rooms. 'And Dad? What did he say?'

'I haven't told him yet. I don't know how.'

'And the father?' I watched my sister squirm, but she couldn't lie to me.

'The father is… was… just a… how do I put this? … a passing interest. He won't be in the picture. I'm not sure I'm even going to tell him.' She struggled to look me in the eye.

'You have to tell Dad. He'll be hurt.'

'I know. I don't have what you have with him though. You can tell him for me if you want!' Her expression contorted into a pout, her bottom lip pushed out. An impression of a baby about to cry, a remnant from our childhood. The same face she had taunted me with when I lost board games. Putting her hands together begging, she let out an invariable: pleeeeeeease.

'Na, I don't think so.' I take a deep breath. I focus on my to-go cup of coffee to get my bearings. She intensified her stare in hopes to sway me. 'He'll be fine… excited, I bet.' I let out a sigh, shaking my head. Putting my hand on hers. She leans forward grabbing me in a bear hug. I lift my arms and hug back. She squeezes tighter, so I reciprocate.

'This is new. Hugging my stinky-ass brother,' she jokes, her face muffled in my shirt.

'I love you too,' I replied playfully. I didn't realise her face was wet; the relief of letting it out had brought with it some emotion she hadn't expected. 'It's OK to be a bit scared,' I whispered, my arms still around her shoulders. She nods, letting me see her soft underbelly, something that she always kept hidden. A sudden rush of protection for the sister that never needed anything hit me. 'And you're not alone, don't ever think that you're alone. Mum lives for moments like this... something real to worry about, she'll be in her element!' She nods her head, yes.

'Yeah, I know. But it wasn't exactly planned, Adam — what if I'm no good at it?'

'You never see the best things coming till they get here.'

'That sounds like advice Dad would give.' She wipes her eyes on my shirt, half laughing as she did so. I smirk.

'I wish.'

'Don't say anything to anyone.' She taps my shoulder playfully with a soft fist.

'Mum's the word.' I wink. That was almost clever. She laughs.

I pull a tissue from my pocket and offer it to her. Automatically she screws up her nose. 'I wouldn't touch that if you paid me.' She turned her back to me, looking in a dressing room mirror. Then wiping her face with the back of her hands she attempted to fix the slight dark shadows under her eyes from mascara. 'OK, enough of this, let's get you an outfit.' I roll my eyes and follow her to the next store.

I peer back over my shoulder to make sure John's friends aren't in the vicinity; a habit that seems to have taken hold.

CHAPTER 20
ALMOST NORMAL

Note to self: so close, yet so far, story of my life.
A vista from a mountain,
God's word present in every touch,
Magnificent, yet untouchable,
It envelops every sense,
Become one with it,
All is yours,
Although,
None of it belongs to you,

A week after our second official date, two days after our third, Lil dropped by after work for no reason at all. I'm shocked to see her standing quite innocently at the door. With her work shirt on, the logo clearly printed across her chest in old-school cursive. There was such a normalcy to it, yet I was still shocked to see this person I had coveted for perpetuity, thrilled to see me.

Dirty and reeking, I had been in the house for ten minutes. I felt myself blush, leaving her standing at the threshold. I ran to put on a hoodie knowing it wouldn't erase the smell. Fumbling with the can, I sprayed a cloud of deodorant, racing back as quick as possible. Red-faced,

I asked her in. She chuckled, it was too obvious to be polite, and she was laughing at me. Not in a mean way, in a very Lil way, almost as if she was a naughty child trying to get away with taking the last cookie. That made me smile inside, bringing with it a homely feeling. That's when I noticed she was carrying Asian food in a substantial white bag and what looked like cokes in a plastic bag. The smell made my mouth water. I hadn't eaten for a while, maybe my mother is right, I don't eat as I should. I stood to one side letting her walk past me. Following her in, I assumed we'd eat at the table. I pulled out a chair for her. Shaking her head pointing to the rug, she continues past me to the lounge room. Pushing the coffee table to one side, she signals for me to join her.

'A rug picnic… really?' I tease sarcastically.

She giggles:

'Yes,' continuing to set up the food in the centre of the space.

Soon we are settled on the floor, Lilly's legs crossed and me sprawled amongst the open boxes. We eat without too many words, they're not needed. A comfortable silence, envelopes the room; a space that doesn't need to be filled with chatter. Both of us are lost in peaceful thoughts, scooping sweet and sour greasy food with plastic forks. I wonder what she was thinking. Could she possibly be as happy, as contented as I felt in her company? Almost smug, the thought hits me, look at me having dinner with Lilly like it's a normal thing to do. Like this is what I do now, have dinner with Lilly. I'm a grown-up. Lil has turned me into a grown-assed man.

With a tap on the leg, Lilly passes me something in a white box with a little wire handle. I attacked the meat inside with chopsticks, trying to grab a piece. She grins, which turned into a laugh. Then handed me my plastic fork from the bottom of the bag.

Smirking, she said:

'Some of us are just plastic fork kind of guys, even if we don't admit it!' bating me to do better, laughing to herself as she expertly took her chopsticks, picking up the piece of meat I was trying to get and dropped it into her mouth.

'Amazing,' I said pulling a face. 'How was work?' I continued as if I didn't know.

'Fine,' she nodded, and then pulled a face demonstrating her true feelings. I laughed then we went back to eating. So, this is normal? This is what it's like to live a regular life? I closed my eyes as I felt a sudden thud of anxiety, *No, shut up, and don't ruin this moment.* An internal voice that badgers me anytime I sense contentment can be put in its place if I try, I can master it, if my will is strong enough.

When we were finished, we were so stuffed full we lay back on the floor. Her head lay on my chest but I couldn't tell you what was on TV, it didn't matter. The sounds blocked out the street noise, and the odd clattering from the apartment above which somehow acted to reassure me that all is well. I stroked her hair out of her face, listening to the slight sound of her breathing. I looked down at our bodies so close together. Entwined legs, coiled fingers, the fabric of me joined to the fabric of her.

Lifting my hand up and taking hers with it, I compared them. My hand is a broken wreck with nicks and cuts, an abandoned ship on the docks, weathered and worn. Then there was the delicate beauty before I could finish my thought her hand left the cradle of my palm. I now began to watch Lilly's fingers dance with the lightest of touches as I started to doze. She made the tiniest of circles on my palm, so gratifying to watch, it's almost torture. Slowly, drawing larger and larger rings, until inevitably, there's a shot like a bolt of electricity up my arm, when finally, the sensation reaches the sensitive part of my wrist. It shoots straight to my heart and to my groin. I have no inclination to open my eyes but every part of me stirs, tries to summon the strength to grab her, while my mind insists I do nothing. She knows it, she feels the battle inside, my defiant will and want pinned against my self-controlled. I think she feels it, does she? I look for signs, more than kindness or pity, a sign of wanting me; a hint of an invitation to take her — right here in this moment. Yet there are no signs of lust or wanting, only peace. Drifting lightly on the edge of sleep is this brotherly love she feels for me? We're good friends, maybe we're only ever going to be friends. I watch every move closely. A glimpse of breast when she turns toward me, the thrill of her inner thigh brushing mine, and it goes on... I become drunker on her love.

CHAPTER 21
THE GOLDEN CHILD

Note to self:
Do I put Mother in the journal or is she best left out?
The dread of spiders' webs fills my head,
Tangled in long sticking threads,
The undoable,
The unsayable,
It all fills my head.

I am determined to be optimistic. I can't deny the feeling of it being another drawn-out Saturday and another fatigued dinner. I can swallow these feelings down. I put a smile on my face, lock my back up straight, tuck in my shirt and walk through the front door. Today I am not Adam, he needs a drink in his hand. I am not Adam who struggles through the day. I am the new improved Adam. The positive Adam, whom has a girlfriend and a job. Who will stop taking pills and pour his whiskey down the sink? This new Adam will be a family man within the year. This new Adam will be able to look his father in the eye. This new Adam will make his brother jealous just by walking in the room…

I wonder if anyone will notice that I am in fact the new Adam if they will see the changing me if it's obvious yet? The table is laid with the good lace cloth and silver. The smell of traditional food tells me I'm home. The radio is on in the back room keeping my father company. My sister's feet twitch as she talks on her phone, possibly to the father of her baby, I wonder. I'm somewhat a little taken aback to see her here. I thought she'd be lying low, getting a few phone mother/daughter calls under her belt before showing up. I wave hello, then kiss her on the cheek and continue into the next room leaving her to chat in peace when I see Jake sitting at the table. I smile. peeling off my jacket and draping it over the dining seat next to him. Mum doesn't truly acknowledge my presence, rather smiles at Jake resting a can of beer with a frosted glass in front of him. Her way of letting us all know she is happy with him and consequently unhappy with me. I find these stunts ridiculous. With her back to me, I pretend not to notice, knowing that I'm driving her crazy. I wish I could say otherwise. My mother's actions do tend to bring out the defiant in me. Reorganising my legs, I try to stretch out and suppress all the thoughts of mischief now running through my head. I must be in her bad books for something, although I'm not entirely sure for what. Maybe for existing, staining her perfect family photographs with my insanity.

'I'll get you a drink too, Adam.' She takes the open newspapers from the end of the table and places them on a pile of magazines, which were filling up half the sideboard.

Mum gave me a look, which suggested I shouldn't bother asking for alcohol as Jake had. Understandable I suppose… She marches to the kitchen, a woman on a mission. My mother clings to her martyrdom like a kitten on a twig high above the ground. When I was a child, she had genuine concerns for our family's financial health, with the strikes on the docks, my sister's extra tutorage and specialists for her dyslexia, burglaries in our apartment building. These were real plight to get her teeth stuck into, to call the neighbours about, to pace the kitchen over and over. Nowadays, I am the source of her internal pacing with Jake's wife a way's behind me. In those early years, she had to cope with it all, largely alone. My father worked every hour that God sent to cover an ever-increasing cost of living. With time her issues reduced, leaving a void where her purpose had once been. Breaking from my thoughts, I could see my mother in the kitchen working away, turning the latest catastrophe into a Broadway musical with my unwilling sister.

Rachel sat nodding in agreement, eyes pinned to the screen of her phone. Another mess for my father to clean up. It would blow over quick enough; he was well versed in event control. I noticed the table was only half set.

'Mum must be truly upset,' I said under my breath, walking back into the normally polished dining room where my jacket sat holding my spot. 'How are you, Jakey-boy?' I whooped in a stupid accent next to his ear and begin tapping the back of his chair to incite a reaction. He hardly flinched.

'Fine,' my brother mumbles, not looking up from his small bowl of nuts he is less than impressed with.

'Something wrong, Jake?' I pull out the chair next to his and sit facing him, annoyingly close. A habit from childhood, which at this moment is not having the desired effect.

'No, everything's fine.' Clearly, it was not.

I pushed down on the prongs of my fork, then dropping it, letting the heavy end tap the table. I repeat this in quick succession. Jake shot me a look of annoyance. It had worked far quicker than I planned.

'You could just tell me, what it is?' I said shrugging.

'I'm just a bit short this week.' he said cutting me off.

'Well, I'd love to give you some cash… if I had it.' He nods, however, doesn't look up. I realise it's a much more serious problem than I had anticipated. Something is actually upsetting him. I lean in. 'Jake, we both know I'm gonna keep pestering you until you tell me what's wrong. It's our annoying family trait, persistence!' He gave me a half smirk, conceding to me.

'OK, just keep it to yourself.'

'Of course,' I nod, not quite believing he was about to put a chink in his own armour.

'The other day, some out-of-town clients were in my office. I needed them to sign a contract. To put them in a good mood, to seal the deal as it were, I thought I would take them to the races. Last time they were in town, that's all they talked about. We ran out of time so I thought it would be a good idea to show them a good time. They had money to blow, I didn't.' He pauses for a second, 'Ads, Alderman's is a small company. I don't have a wine and dine credit account. I tried to put a brave face on, using my own money. I badly need some work to come my way. I haven't signed business in months. I kept up with them at first, few wins, and few losses. Then the wheels kind of fell off, if you know what I mean?'

'How much did you lose?' I checked in the direction of the doorway to see my mother wasn't eavesdropping.

'Two months' mortgage repayments.' The look of shame on my brother's face was almost too much for me. Understanding he was genuinely worried for good reason, I tried to think of a way I could come up with money. The only thing I had of any value was the car and I couldn't sell that. So instead I shook my head in sympathy. He reached up, putting both hands over his face.

'How do I tell Hannah?' There was true fear and his voice. He began rubbing at his temples with the onset of a headache. 'Marriage is a delicate thing. Things haven't been going well at home, she could leave me over this… my kids, Ad!' He pushed his body back into the chair, sitting upright. 'What have I done…?'

'Blame me,' I said with a sudden rush of compassion. He said nothing in reply. I leaned over the table and smoothed the corner of my placemat down.

'I'm your only option,' I went on, turning back around in my seat.

'What are you talking about?' My brother's indignation grew from two branches, firstly because he didn't consider me the answer to any problems, more the cause. And secondly, because I had dared to suggest something with less than a five-star morality rating, i.e., *lying*.

'I'm serious, blame me, you've taken enough bullets for me. I can pay you in small payments, believable right?'

'I can't it's not…' he hissed.

'What's not right? Since when is half the stupid stuff I do right? It's not like you haven't spent a fortune in taxis rescuing me.' Shockingly, I meant it with more resolve than I first thought. The weight of financial pressure became evident in the heavy wrinkles of his forehead.

'Hannah will find out—' he hissed.

'Ahh great,' I cut him off mid-sentence to shut him up. My mother frowning positioned a huge pot of kugel in the middle of the table. I shot my brother a look, letting him know, I'm doing it whether he likes it or not. Jake put his head down. Jake loathed conflict. His meagre attempt at hiding his shame was almost embarrassing. He could barely lift his head to meet my mother's eye line. At this rate, he'd give the game away before I could even utter a word. Poor bastard! When we were kids, he'd hide under the bed at the first signs of an argument. My mother sat down shooting me a sharp look, that woman can smell bullshit a mile away.

'What have you done?' she says under her breath in a stern tone, sitting so straight her spine was in danger of snapping. She pulled her napkin onto her lap, letting the fabric snap loudly in the air.

'I haven't done anything.' I see my brother's forehead screwing up tightly.

'What have you done Adam? If there's going to be trouble, tell me now,' my mother demanded without raising her voice, although the accusation was sharp enough to cut the air itself.

I said nothing, shrugging and beginning to fill up my bowl.

'Don't get Jake into trouble,' she said to me but staring at Jake to get answers. She gave a low sigh.

'He's not going to get in any trouble, don't worry.' Any time my mother was even a little angry at me, it felt as though she was physically prodding me. I tell myself repeatedly, I'm not going to react, and I'm good Adam today.

My sister, entering the room, pulls out a chair and looks over at me. I realise she's overheard the tail end of our conversation.

'Mum, it's nothing... he hasn't...' Jake began but before he could utter another word.

'Jake lent me some money. I will pay him back, it's fine,' I blurted out before Jake could betray himself.

'What did you need money for?' she said reeking of disappointment, picking up her spoon. She looked at my sister for support but got none.

'Nothing much, it's fine, I'll take care of it.' Sighing calmly, trying to sweep it under the carpet, my mother was having none of it. She had her teeth in, with no plans to let go.

'Where did I go wrong?' She shakes her head passive aggressively. There was a short-lived silence apart from the sounds of spoons dragging against bowls.

'Well, don't ask your father to bail you out again.' The *again* stuck in my side like a nail. I replied with an eye roll, continuing to shovel food into my mouth. I don't make eye contact with the others at the table, although I feel their eyes on me. There was a lull for a minute or two, but I sensed my mother's blood boiling. I knew it couldn't be contained for long.

'Adam, I don't want to be angry with you and I hate fighting at the dining table, however, this childish behaviour must stop. I would like to sit at this table for once and rejoice in us coming together. Why don't we just forget it?' She takes a deep breath in an effort to steady herself. 'Whatever it is that you've done let's just forget it and not be angry.' I don't respond. 'OK Adam, we're just going to forget and move on.' That's exactly what I should've done that I couldn't help myself, I have to answer back.

'I'm not the one that's angry, Mum!' I shovel more food in.

'OK Adam, I'm not mad either.' She has to have the last word.

I swallowed my food, feeling my hands beginning to shake. Breathe, I told myself. Not upset with her, but with myself. After all, although wrong about this incident, any

228

other day she would have been correct. Yet the automatic assumption that I was in the wrong tapped at my brain. I'm ready to take accountability for the stupid shit I've done, but my brother and sister are no saints either. She doesn't jump the gun on them. Am I truly that bad? It's not over, she is simmering, waiting for me to give her details. I grin to myself and I realise I look smug. However, the smirk stays there.

'You can wipe the smile off your face, you've done nothing to be proud of.' I glare in her direction, now she's the one that looks smug. My sister tries to break the tension in the room by offering my mother bread. It's too late, there's a chasm between my mother and me that I fear is too wide to cross. She has to say something. She can't bear silence or tolerate things unsaid.

'Your brother has a family and mortgage. He works hard! Don't take his money, your father and I give you enough!' Banging the end of her finger hard on the tablecloth, she makes it wrinkle. I stuff the emotion in with a fork full of meat; I chew it up and swallow it down. I say nothing; instead, I concentrate on the food on my plate.

Jake opens his mouth to say something. I give him a swift kick under the table to shut him up.

'It won't happen again, I thought the horse was a sure thing.' I don't look up. I know if I lock eyes with Jake, he'll come clean.

'Sure thing?' my mother scoffs.

I'm sorry, I'm such a fuc... disaster,' it takes everything I have to hold in the curse words dying to spill from me...

'Well, that's another meal ruined,' she complains, placing her spoon down.

I raise my voice to meet hers, pushing the chair out from behind me. I throw my napkin onto the table. 'I've suddenly remembered I have to be somewhere. I'll be going.' It takes everything I have to stay calm.

'Ad, come back.' My sister stands up, trying to coax me back.

My dad comes in from outside.

'Are you going?' he grabs my arm warmly. I shake him off, rougher than I'm proud of. He stumbles back, regaining his balance with the aid of the wall. Seeing his expression, I realise I've even managed to shock him today. I reach out to his arm, giving him a quick passing assistance.

'I'm sorry, I've gotta go.' I yank the door shut behind me.

As I unlock the car parked on the street. I can hear the sound of raised voices coming from the hallway. At a guess I would say Mother is telling my father not to come after me, which I'm glad of. *If only I was more like Jakey*, I say to myself, brimming with frustration. I adjust the mirror; my reflection is rough *and everything I touch turns to shit*, I tell myself as the knotted guilt builds inside. Catastrophe achieved, now Jake can openly borrow money from my parents without losing face with Hanna.

That homespun anguish starts twisting in my gut. My body demands Lilly, I need to talk to her... to touch her... to...

CHAPTER 22
UNTIL NOW

To angry for words!
Words will only expose the darkness that lies inside
me.

A glaring light bounces off the dashboard's chrome trim hitting my face, forcing me to screw up my eyes. I shield my profile from the stabbing rays, feeling the onset of a headache. Irritable and itchy from the heat, I search the glove box for some aspirin. Finding a couple in a mangled packet, I knock them back with the last dribble of cola from the now warm can. It wasn't enough to lubricate my mouth and I feel the hard pills weld themselves to the soft pallet at the back of my throat. Fizzling unpleasantly, I try to swallow them down, leaving my whole mouth furry.

Ten minutes later, I'm still slumped in the parked car. She's late and it's unlike her. I unconsciously tap the dashboard. It makes the same hollow plastic sound that I used to make when I was a kid waiting for my father outside the corner shop. I start to think about my father, then my mother. Then from nowhere, I try to imagine taking Lilly home to meet the family. Would my sister be kind? I don't know. She wouldn't be able to hold her tongue when Lil's job comes up; she's protective that way. But then lately, she's met with so many opportunities to have a dig at me and let them drift past. Maybe motherhood is setting in.

Fifteen minutes drag past. Should I go in? She's probably just catching up on end of day stuff. I adjust myself and I try to relax into the seat. I watch a guy across the street. He struggles with a ladder and bucket cleaning the second-storey window. The sun is still piercing. I've moved enough to be out of the direct sun, I can settle my hand away from my eyes without going blind. I put the shake down and lean back in my seat. Is she my girlfriend? I haven't asked her. We hang out, we don't kiss though… only hello. I should ask her, no, that's lame! Maybe she'd stay over. Fuck, I'd cum before she was even in my room. Jeans suddenly too tight, I adjust.

Twenty-five minutes I've waited. She's forgotten. Should I go in? I should really go in, says the needy boyfriend. She'll be here soon. Maybe she said half past and not o'clock?

Thirty minutes. The mature guards are twitching around, looks like they're about to change shift. I don't recognise them. They must be new. I could probably walk straight past them; they wouldn't know I've been barred. One guard's hovering, someone's late, or not turned up. OK, here it goes. If I'm doing it, I just need to do it. Walk up naturally, head up, straight back, walk right past him. I approach fists tight at my side, ready to swing if I need to.

The doorman barely looked up from his phone. Feeling a smirk developing on my face, I almost skipped down the stairs with relief.

After the dizzying afternoon sun in the car, the club was cool and dark. My eyes took a while to adapt to dimmed light. The unassuming outline of Lilly against the artificial lights looks wrong somehow, like a perfect rose with a plastic stem. Her true essence returned when my sun-spotted sight recovered. It took a moment to understand her stillness. She was nodding yes to someone; I couldn't quite work out whom. Then I saw it was John. Both, staring at the timetable; he underlined the changes in shifts with his thick fingers. Broad shouldered, his mammoth frame towered over her. I felt my heart start to pick up its tempo, feeling each individual beat. Oxygen sped into my lungs then out through my nose, filling my ears and inciting the growth of my rage. His body was too close; he was taking liberties yet again, leaning over her. He moved a wisp of hair off her cheek. She smiled, not quite humouring him, more like complying out of habit. It was maddening. Lil, detecting my presence from the corner of her eye, wanders over nonchalant, picking up a glass and starts pulling a beer for a guy next to me.

'You need to leave,' she half lips under her breath, 'Now.' Her face remands serious — careful not to alert John.

'I'll just wait…' The jealous acidly burning inside me making me braver than I had right to be.

'It's not safe. Go now, please.' Her blue eyes begged me.

'I'm not scared, Lil.' My whole body was starting to seethe.

'Please, Ad. I'll get away as quick as I can and meet you at your place.' She rushes out back as the shadow of John begins to appear in the doorway. I stand there, quite aware she's not coming back out for a while.

'Fuck this shit,' I fume to no one in particular. Leaving the way I came, I knock shoulders with some bloke on the stairs. I hear him collide with the wall.

'What the fuck!' he calls after me in a shocked tone. I don't care, I don't care, and I'm over this shit!

CHAPTER 23
MATES WARNING

Journal this:

Time is a hook,
Time is pressure,
A push,
Time is a force,
A change,
Time is unstoppable,
A present,
Master of us all.

*(Counted Journals, **43**. Fills two shelves on my bookcase. I feel oddly proud)*

A new company had opened its doors on the very site where Joe had given some of John's boys something to think about. Most likely from overseas or out of town; no one from here would be that stupid. This is what was running through my head entering the bar. From the second I entered, it felt off. It didn't look quite right. Then it hit me. As a consequence of the new company, many new faces occupied the bar. The whole dynamic had changed overnight. It was no longer segregated into two parts, the dockers on one side and the market folk on the other; instead, there is a complete cross-section of locals. It struck me as peculiar to see the bar changed. It's the one place that should stay the same no matter what.

With a stomach flip and knees a tad weak, I tried to get over the expectation of the old place and get my head around its slight variation. New people. I felt an irritated growl in my chest. Intentionally, I had stayed away from this place, mainly due to the fact that each second apart from Lilly felt like time wasted. However, true to form, Joe and Pete resided on their stools laughing and joking. To see them felt comfortable, like a staple in my life's diet. A good feeling; like something dependable. I lifted one hand in a sociable wave and Pete hailed me over.

'Well hello stranger, what brings you to these parts?' Pete mocked me, dripping with sarcasm.

'Don't be like that, Pete,' I shrugged, straddling a stool. Joe didn't look too fazed by my reappearance. 'Can't a man just come for a beer because he misses his buddies?' I asked, returning the mock tone. Joe downplays it with a hand gesture toward the TV, and instantly it's over. I sit. It hadn't been that long, maybe a week.

'It's good to see you guys. What's new with you? How's the game?'

Joe shook his head. 'That's not a good topic to talk about right now'

I burst out laughing.

'So, how's life?' he asked me, getting us off the topic of sports.

'Nothing much, taking Lil out later.' I feel the warm gladness in my bones as I say the words. Pete and Joe look at each other, their expressions; of a serious nature.

'Look, it's not my business,' Joe starts, '… I think this thing is starting to get out of hand. I heard a couple of John's men talking the other day.' Joe makes a circular pattern with the bottom of his glass, not affording me eye contact. This is not how things worked here, the unspoken rule to stay out of family business was being broken. After all, girlfriends were family. His awkwardness was rebounded onto me. I stared at the TV, nodding, not agreeing or disagreeing.

'He's not happy about the way things are going. They can only end in tears for you,' Pete interrupts, who by all accounts still can't read a room.

'Thanks for the heads up, I'm gonna be OK.' The drop in my stomach told me otherwise.

'I wouldn't be so sure about that.' He pauses for a second to get some eye contact from me, 'They don't mess around, take the warning.' Looking into his face I saw my true feelings being mirrored back to me.

'You're gonna end up at the bottom of the sea if you're not careful.'

Joe pushed in between us grabbing at the nuts on the bar. His hands dwarfing the glass bowl, I felt palpitations in my chest as my heart rate rose.

'Guys, it's fine, really.'

I shook off their words lightly. Deep down, however, I knew I needed a plan.

Before they could tell me I was an idiot, a goal scored by Brazil in the soccer game on the big screen, snapped their heads around. Clearly, both invested in the winner. I only glanced at the game, mulling over what they had said. I feel like I'm playing hopscotch through landmines. I look at my mates and time stopped for a second. They hadn't changed. This could be my basement ten years ago, with cola instead of booze being the only real difference. I couldn't put my finger on it, but something was happening, a transition I had no control over. Like I saw my life taking a new path, whether I wanted it to or not. Its real and alive, I'm hungry for a new level. I hope the boys will be part of it, deep down I know probably not. I'm being tested, or at least that's how it feels. I can feel the day fast approaching when standing up will be my only option. Hopefully, I can be the man that my father sees in me.

CHAPTER 24
OPENING UP

__Note to Self,__

Add This To Back Page (Buy New Note Book, Nearly Full):

Truth can be a mental slap.

It can barrel toward you screaming out of the blue.

It can be a sharp backhand, like someone has suddenly ripped the sheets from you in the middle of winter.

It can leave you completely vulnerable and stupefied.

Or it could be subtle, seeping through the cracks over time.

A steady realisation, like someone is whispering in your ear.

You stop.

You think.

You piece the puzzle together slowly.

Lilly stretched out on the lounge in her work T-shirt and a pair of jeans, her kicked-off shoes lay under the coffee table. I put a drink in her hand, less booze and more ice than in my triple. She takes a teensy sip gazing at me over the top of her whisky glass. It was the first time I had seen her drink anything other than water from a plastic bottle. Intrigued, I let my eyes focus on her without blinking until my vision blurred and she morphed into crystal rain in the reflection of her glass. She pulled a face wrinkling her nose, she looked cute and she knew it. I got the distinct impression, for the first time, she could see just what she does to me or maybe she'd always known. Shuffling back into the low-backed lounger, she got comfortable.

'I like it here,' she said, 'I can just be myself.' She closed her eyes, tasting the whisky held in her mouth. A boozy smile spread across her face. I want to be that whisky. I want to be held in her mouth, I want to sit on her tongue. Her limbs loosened, unwinding into a calm sprawl. I stretched out on the other end of the lounge trying to mirror her relaxation; worried that getting to close would disturb her. I stop myself from crawling over her. There was a risk of seeming like there was an expectation. I settle my feet on the coffee table. She opens her eyes, propping her feet next to my own, gradually, edging them off with her toes, playfully giggling. That giggle, it stirs the animal in me. I lift them back to their original spot, faking a grumpy face that makes her grin. This time, she uses the bottom of her foot to rub the top of mine. Her feet look delicate next to my size thirteens, what with her pale pink polish and toe ring; like dancer's feet. Lil's skin against mine felt exquisite.

'So how did you end up here?' I had to take my mind away from the path it was starting to explore. Lilly had still made no indication that she wanted to take things further. If things progressed on this path, I'm likely to lose control and pounce, pinning her down. I'm so hard it's difficult to contain and I cover my lap with a cushion, trying not to be obvious.

'You don't wanna know.' Although jovial, there was something about the way she said it that made me curious, and a little nervous.

'Oh, but I do, Lil.' I'm not entirely sure what we were talking about. Wait, were we talking about today or life? Letting it hang in the air always worked with my sister…

'It's not a nice thing to talk about.' Suddenly serious, I noticed she swallowed harder than normal and she looked away deflecting my question.

'Friends talk about all kinds of things…' I lowered my tone watching the ice in my glass, floating in a sea of treacle-brown whisky.

'But what if the things I say upset you, what if you don't like…?" she sighed with a deflated spirit. 'What if the things I say change the way you see me and you don't want to hang out anymore, Adam?' There it was. The same furrowed brow from school. My heart dropped into the depths of my stomach. A spark of unhappiness I must put out before it escalates.

'Impossible! I don't care what you've done. We all have secrets. Isn't that the point of friends, someone to hide in the closet with you so you're not scared in the dark?' Friends, I hated using the term. If I said it enough in all likelihood, that's where I would stay, in the friends' box. The expression she tried hard to suppress told me the truth she keeps hidden was hard for her to speak about. I didn't want to push, yet I fought to stop yelling; just tell me. Then, in that second, I realised I probably already knew. The phone sex! I could kick myself.

'You say that now, but...' The words halted quite suddenly, she was unsteady for a moment. I had to think swiftly before she shut down completely.

'Lil, I'm not exactly an angel myself. I've done things that I'm not proud of, things I regret, things I wish I could take back or undo... Life's not a pretty postcard.' I kept my voice slow and steady. It was my best impersonation of my father. She nodded. 'Lilly, wasn't it you that convinced me that in order to love yourself you have to accept yourself?' Again, I let it hang. I understood I was being moderately manipulative, however, I have her best interests at heart, I thought to myself, letting myself off the hook. I have to show her she can trust me.

A prolonged minute passes. A thought begins to resonate; Lil has no idea that I know about her after-hours work on the phone. Is this the reason for the standstill, is this why handholding never continues further, why kisses remained on the cheek with only a few exceptions? It would be stupid to risk upsetting her. Should I change the subject? It's plain to see the topic is uncomfortable.

'It doesn't matter, Lil. You'll tell me if you need to, right?' She nodded, sitting up, taking her feet off the coffee table. The moment of sweetness passed, and I had a terrible feeling she was going to leave. Deep down, I had a horrible feeling that I had blown it. Her back stiffened. She took a gulp of alcohol, adding a second in quick concession. She surveyed the room nervously, backing into the chair. Finally, she arrived at a place where she felt equipped to talk; scanning my face for objection. I didn't shy away: my father never did, it was his steady presences that strengthen me.

'It's just my mum, that's all. It's not a big deal.' Her voice was serene and she was locked but composed. However, her eyes told a different story. Everything inside me advised me to come clean. It said *fess up to following her home, to watching her sitting on the rooftop, to telling her how I really knew about the abuse, both at home and in school.* Lil was about to confess her sins, about to break herself in two in front of me and open up. But I needed her to say the words first. If I could convey to her that I didn't care about that shit. If she could confide in me, if she could trust me, then we had a shot at being sincere, long life friends, more even.

'My mum died two years ago.' The words filled the gap between us, suddenly, savagely stealing my breath. Not having time to think about how to respond, I froze, locking eyes, trying to gain understanding, if indeed I had heard right. Lilly scarcely blinked, flinching under my heavy expression; yet now obligated to speak, she cleared her throat shyly. 'I hadn't seen her for a while before she passed on.' Her head tilted back in an effort to transcend this dreary apartment. Letting out a huge breath then scanning the ceiling to find the immunity from the hurt she needed to continue. 'It was my aunty that told me she'd gone.'

Composed again, she searched my face for judgement. I was careful, not an ounce reflected outward. She began so softly I strained to hear. 'Only half my brothers attended the funeral. I don't blame the others for staying away.' Pausing to navigate my reaction to the information, she herself found shocking, she searched my face one last time. Not finding anything displeasing, she went on with more rhythm, although a little hesitant still. 'I discovered my mother was sick when I was seventeen, still in high school,' her voice halting again. Then, resting her head back in order to avoid eye contact, she was able to speak plainly. 'My youngest brother, Ben, was still very young. We don't really know who Ben's father is, my mother never hid that he was different, but it was never talked about either. My mum started seeing men. A handful of regulars at first...' She stopping to calculate a time frame, she counted on her fingers, then went on when it made sense in her head. 'I think I was about ten when it started. We would get pushed into the hall to wait. Although we never understood really what was going on, we knew enough not to talk about it openly at school. That, coupled with the laundry, enabled us to get by on the bones of our ass.' She laughed to herself without humour. 'My mother once said that punishment for her sins had come to her in this life and were probably waiting in the next too; I never understood what that meant.' Quickly switching topic, as though the facts were simply too painful to dwell on, she physically pulled herself up straight, using the arm of the lounge. 'She'd known that her cancer was terminal for five months before she said anything to me.' I didn't know if I should stop her from talking but she kept going. 'I'm not sure how long she thought she had or why she kept it a secret. I stayed with her through the first round of chemo, managing the boys, house, high school and my mum's care. At that point, I don't think she'd considered actually dying. Mentally she believed there would be a time of sickness, and then she'd recover. To be honest, it wasn't that different to normal. I'd always taken control of the house and kids.'

'Mother suffered moods as she put it and would lock herself in her room for days.' Lil sighed with exhaustion, dwelling for a moment, taking stock of the situation she'd escaped from. 'I wish I had been closer to my mum, but she wasn't the kind of person that needed anyone. Sometimes, I hated her...' I didn't respond, the anguish had pushed its way to the surface. It felt inappropriate to stop its flow. Every muscle in Lil's body seemed clenched and tightened with pain, violently wrenching the spectre out from under her skin.

'When the treatment wasn't successful, my mum called her sister. She repeatedly told us her family was dead. What she actually meant was, dead to her. I found out there was so much about my mother I didn't know. I remember the day my aunt arrived. She looked just like my mum but thinner, more upright, same fierceness though. She genuinely looked horrified at where and how we were living. My mother refused to acknowledge her, apart from spitting a few cross words her way. 'Aunt Eve is very religious, pious, taking my brothers as her cross to bear.' A half smile turns up one side of her face. 'She's cheerful in her martyrdom I think, even now... She lectures about it enough... I am grateful to her, don't get me wrong, but sometimes it gets a bit much... *oh, those poor children.*' Lil does her best impression of her Irish aunt and crosses herself. I chuckle, understanding it is simply a break to catch her breath before she goes on.

'We didn't take much with us, when she came to fetch us. She said everything we had was only fit for burning. Which was probably true but to be honest it felt like our old skin was being torn off and left in the apartment. In some ways, it was good, a fresh start. In other ways not, there was nothing left to remember our mother,' she adjusted and looks at me. 'She was still my mother,' she spoke softly, almost apologising for defending her.

I looked at her sympathetically, hoping that the pity I felt hasn't reached my face. 'It's OK, I totally understand,' was the only thing I can think to say.

'I helped Aunt Eve with the boys on the train. She doesn't own a car. It took a while to get to her house and I ended up staying about a week to get everyone settled. My aunt was straight with us, no-nonsense, strict, but fair, quite the opposite of my mother. She wanted me to stay longer, for good, but the guilt over my mother's illness was too much. I felt bad; her being alone, it was too great for my conscience. My aunt said I was doing a good thing, but sometimes it's good to think of *you* too. She wanted me to finish school. I chose to go back to my mother until… well until the end. Then I planned to return, going to community college or something.' Lilly shook her head.

'Adam, it just seems so long ago now. So, I got a job at a deli and did my best to take care of Mother. She was an awful patient. After a year or so, without the catalyst of my brothers to keep me home, I'd had enough. At this point I didn't know she only had five months till the end or I would have stayed. One morning, I made up a breakfast tray before work. I tiptoed into her, positioning her breakfast near her on the bed. I always tried to make the tray look appetising because I knew she struggled to eat. Her eyes were blackened by this time; her skin was like tissue paper. Blue-black veins popped out all over her arms, from drips and the drugs that constantly were being pumped into her system. Although she still was large in size, it was more to do with swelling from the medication and not being able to get out of bed. The strength seemed to have disappeared from her. She leaned, slightly slumped. For weeks she'd had terrible insomnia, not sleeping at all for days. The second I put that breakfast tray down; I knew she was in a bad mood. Nothing to do with the drugs or cancer, or sleep, she scowled, it was the same mother from my childhood. Without warning, she lurched forward, grabbed hold of the closest end of the full tray throwing it and its entire contents, as hard as she could, my way. The food covered my work T-shirt. Although she couldn't get out of bed, she tried hard, pulling and ripping at the sheets. If she could have gotten her hands around my neck, she would've strangled me for sure. But as she couldn't, it was followed by the normal barrage of foul language, screaming *Get out!* at the top of her lungs. I'd always been terrified of her, this day, however, looking at my work shirt covered with egg and tea, I snapped. I told her I was leaving through the door, not brave enough to go in just in case she'd managed to get herself up. She yelled back at me to *get out and not come back!* She was sick of the sight of me. And so, I did. I left that day.'

Lilly tried desperately to finish what she'd started. Words tumbling out, then correcting herself when they sounded too harsh. 'After I packed everything, as I was leaving, I passed her door. I put my cardboard box down, didn't own a suitcase. She shrugged, she bellowed, demanded I come into her room. I was too scared not to do what she asked. I entered the room like a timid kitten, virtually sticking to the walls. She didn't invite me to stay like I thought she would. She was calmer than I think I'd ever seen her. Blank-faced with a drug-induced trance, arms folded across her chest, determined not to be a victim.

'*So, you're going?* was all she said!' Lilly looked tortured with guilt. I watched a pang of regret wash through her. '*Well, I've had enough of looking at you.* That's what she said, as I stood in the corner of the room. I remember the feeling of my stomach dropping. I thought… even though I had no reason to, that she might pull some words of affection from somewhere. She didn't.

My mother didn't ask me to sit or didn't ask me to stay. She just left me standing at the end of her bed like, like I was being reprimanded in a principal's office.' Lil became almost wistful. 'It was so still, I could see light pouring from the gap in the curtains, with waves of dust spinning in circles. It was silent. Odd in a place that had never known peace.' Lilly drew a long breath. 'My mother just gazed toward the window, no focus in her eyes. I wasn't sure what to do, leave or stay, but that silence felt like drums building to a finale. So, my feet stuck to the floor as if they were glued. As though at any second the walls would cave in on us or the whole building would fall taking us with it.

'Without warning, she snapped to life like a magician had clicked his fingers. She pointed, with a look that shot straight through me, ordering me to sit down with a low growl that grated along my spine. So, I did perch on the furthermost edge of the bed, automatically I began to apologise. She cut off my words with a raised hand. She needed me to know a few things before I left. That's how she started the only real conversation my mother and I had, in my entire life. Looking back, she knew it would be our last. She went on to enlighten me about my real father. I have a different dad to my brothers. I'd always just assumed that... you know we were all the same. She showed me a little photograph of him, in black and white. I wasn't allowed to keep it or take a copy. My aunt mentioned she was buried with it... he looks like me, or should I say I look like him. I don't know his name, or where he is now. He could be dead for all I know.' She put her face in her hands, in an effort to hide her tears from me. A weak quivering smile exposed.

'I'm fine, I'm fine…' I wanted desperately to comfort her, to cradle her in my arms. Even so, I stayed where I sat, aware that this waterfall of pent-up emotion shouldn't be stopped but encouraged.

'I think she always hated me, purely based on the fact I reminded her of my father.' Her eyes screamed, searching my body for ill assumptions. 'When my mother was sixteen, she ran off with a man who promised to marry her. After she got pregnant with me, he left, leaving her alone and frightened. She couldn't return to her family with a baby, so it forced her into a life that was extremely difficult. Later on that year, she met my brothers' father. He married her but drank a lot. He worked as a truck driver, his absences became longer and longer periods, and he wasn't at all reliable. I don't think she ever really loved him. In the end, when I was eleven, he left one morning for cigarettes and never came back.'

Another sigh. 'Like I said, she asked me to watch over my brothers, which I would have done whether she asked me to or not. My aunt's name is Eva by the way. Did I say that already, sorry?' Pausing for a second to make sure I was keeping up she turned her eyes on me. It was piercing, a thousand unsaid things passed between us, and then she quickly launched back into her story.

'Aunt Eve never married but still taking on so many boys was really too much to ask anyone. There's just so many of us. My aunt did her best; she only has a small house. We were crammed in, but we had regular meals and clean clothes; it was the best we'd ever known it.'

'After leaving my mother, I got a job working in another deli on the meat counter with a couple of nice women. Then, when that came to an end, I worked as a waitress in a late-night café, and a handful of other jobs. That's when I saw this job, which I have now. It was advertised as a barman, I just thought they meant a regular bar. When I interviewed with Michael. He seemed OK and put me on straightaway. When I realised it was a strip joint, well there was nothing else. I'd been working for about two months before I realised Johnny owned it; naïve, I know.' She stopped. 'I'm such a dumb-ass, how didn't I know?' She let out a sarcastic laugh.

'My whole life is based on dumb-ass-ery,' I say, tilting my glass her way.

'I couldn't believe my eyes. John came waltzing down the steps, girl on his arm, all puffed up. I hadn't set eyes on him in years. One of the other girls working behind the bar nudged me, telling me that he owned the whole street, pretty much. If I could have found another job, if there had been another option, I would've taken it. But there wasn't. My aunt depends on the money I send. I still keep my eye out for other jobs, but right now, I'm kinda stuck.'

The emotion, the misgivings, the dread had spilt forth, cleansing Lilly of her pain, for a while at lease. I moved to little closer placing my hand on hers,

'How are you not more angry, Lil? Don't you just want to scream?' I got up, sitting next to her. My internal workings flipped and wondered if the move suggested I expected something.

'You're so nice to me Adam, too nice. The bar job, it's not only bar work… Now you're going to hate me.' Her whole being bowed like the inevitable end was in process, and she couldn't stop it. 'Ad, I can't even say it.' I had to help her release this pain, pull it from her, I couldn't stand to watch her suffer.

'What? Do you mean the sex lines?' I said it for her; it was out, saving her from the humiliation of saying it herself. She glared up at me, still, too still.

'Don't all the girls at your work do it?' I just assumed. I shrugged, in an effort to make it casual.

'And you don't mind?' Her voice almost non-existent.

'It's not about me minding or not. It's that I understand.' I dare to weave my arm around her, pulling her head into the nook between my chest and my shoulder.

'I don't like it if you're wondering. It wasn't exactly a choice. I felt stuck like I had no choice, I had nightmares for weeks afterwards. I thought I was going to hell. My brother, Mark, came into me one night. I woke him with my crying, he asked me what was wrong, and so I told him what I had been doing, how I was damned. He laughed, he said not to worry about it because we were already in hell.'

'I don't think any less of you, I don't. We've all done shit we're not proud of, all of us. Those things that stick in your heart like thorns, as painful as they are, it's even more

253

painful to remove them and forgive yourself. Because granting yourself forgiveness somehow suggests that you don't understand the seriousness of what you've done. Almost like letting yourself off the hook. Lil, I've done shit. Things I'm not proud of, things I can't tell anyone about. I feel them sitting there poking me. They nudge me when I get too happy, particularly when I'm proud of myself, reminding me who I really am. Don't think I don't understand, because I understand far more than you know. I don't want you to look at me like I'm some kinda hero or Prince Charming, because I'm selfish. You're saving me, that's the truth, Lilly, you are. If I can pull the thorn from your heart, then maybe you can do the same for me, so at best we're equals.'

She lifted her head from her hands. Every inch of her face wet, her eyes red, deep set. Her agony was so prevalent that I felt it harpoon my own heart. She tried to speak, but the words came out as a sob. Slowly I edged towards her again, not trying to impose myself on her. She pushed her cheek into my neck and shoulder. This time, her arms snaked around me until I felt her hands grabbed my shirt tightly in fists, as though I was a rope hanging off the side of a mountain's edge and she dangled off the cliff face. She was crossing a great divide between us, allowing the opening, tiny though it is, to let me in, the otherwise safeguarded fortress that is her heart. I gently put my arms around her. The rest of her body followed, pushing so tight up against me I could feel the blood in her veins. Lilly's life was slowly unfolding, tiny piece, by tiny piece.

'You must hate me now?' Lil twisted her fingers in my shirt.

'Nope,' I smiled. There was a prolonged silence; I knew I should endeavour to speak. Nonetheless, this quiet space, between her words and our future was healthy. I had to find the right words; this was critical. Trust, of the most intimate value, was being established.

'I only see love in front of me, when I look at you Lil.' It was then I noticed the hands screwing tightly in my T-shirt loosening, the fear is making its exit, I thought, glad her pain was easing.

I leant down so my cheek touches hers, whispering, 'Self-sacrifice lives in grey areas, it's never clear cut, but it's always born of love.' She looked at me with something so pure and honest in her eyes, it humbles me beyond words. 'I wish, I could claim those words as my own, but they belong to my father.' They seem to fit, and I mean them. I hope I've sounded sincere; I hope that she could see they came straight from my heart because they did. I squeeze her hand, in an attempt to prove I'm sincere.

A small smile appeared, vanquishing her teary eyes. 'I told my brothers that love is all that matters growing up because we had nothing else. But sitting here in this exquisite apartment, pausing for a second with sarcasm, I know it to be true, Adam. Family is everything.' Honesty beamed from her. I tried to find the same calm place within me that my father did when he was seeking to soothe me. She tried her best to shrug it off. Of course, I realised the scars on the inside, like my own, would probably never

255

heal completely, it was evident to me, solace could be found within us.

I close my eyes, resting my chin, gently on her head. Words, like my own personal music, drifted through my mind. *There she is, my little sparrow, free falling for me to catch. So, I put out my arms as the twig broke under her, and she fell into me.* Her sobs were hushed at first, and then the rain came. I became the hands that caught her, saving her from the storm.

Later, after she was calm, she managed to say, 'What about you? What's a nice boy like you doing here?' She laughed. I smiled under the weight of sleep, us both edging close to nodding off.

'Well, it's complicated,' I muttered out.

'I think we're beyond awkward now. I've snotted up your shirt,' Lil said, drained but lighter. After the truths that Lil had purged, cleansing her past so truthfully, I knew it was my turn, to come clean.

'A couple of years ago, I let things get on top of me. It's hard to talk about; it feels like I'm talking about another person. Life just seemed too hard. I didn't want to be here anymore, so I took pills and I left it in the hands of the gods. My dad found me. My mother has never really forgiven me for doing it to him. I don't really remember it, but I wandered to his house and lay down in his backyard. He got me help, and I woke up in hospital, that's why he panics so much, I really didn't mean to worry him. I wasn't thinking. They told me I have an environmental depression and gave me some more pills. I still take them, more than

I should.' My voice dropped low with shame. 'I drink too much, as you probably noticed. I wish I didn't need them. I've tried to flush them a few times, the next day I get more. If I'm lucky I can go a day without taking something. Without them, life seems unbearable. It's like they are a tint on the lens I'm looking at life through. You don't have to worry, I'm not crazy or anything, and I don't feel unstable that way anymore. I think I'm getting better. I only take pills when I need them, mostly. You help.'

'Me?' Lilly questioned.

'Just being around you makes me feel better, you're something to look forward to.' She reached over and took my other hand, she just held it for a while calmly and that was enough.

Time seemed to lapse from moments to hours. Sleep took both of us at some point. When I finally opened my eyes, the apartment was dark. A cat I didn't recognise strolled along my windowsill looking for a way in. It's scratching confused me for a second and it took me a moment to get my bearings. Lil was curled into a ball on my lap. She seemed to be drowning in her own hair. I pushed it to one side. I watched her breathing in and out. There was a crumpled line between her eyes. A line of held pain and I wanted to iron it out.

Stirring, blinking, then pulling my arm around her for warmth, she clears her throat realising I was awake too.

'So here we are,' she whispered with a finality that suggested we had just reached a new level.

'A couple of offcuts used up and thrown out of the sawmill, do you think society has any use for us, Adam?'

I shook my head, 'Nope.' Although it pained me, I set my glass down still half full. My alcohol levels were more obvious when I was around her.

She let out a laugh, devoid of humour.

'We can look at it two ways. One we're the biggest loser's on earth and should hoe into those pills you have on the coffee table, doing the world a favour. Or Two, we can set ourselves completely free… because if we are no use to anyone, we should be useful to ourselves. We could go anywhere. Adam look at the picture on the fridge, we could do anything.'

'We?' I asked.

'Yes, we can do anything,'

'We, like as in us, together?'

'Yes us!'

'Do you mean that you would come somewhere with me. You would travel with me. You trust me that much?' I struggled to comprehend the words she was saying.

'Course I do, Adam, you're like a giant teddy bear, you couldn't hurt me if you wanted to.'

'Why do your compliments always sound like insults,' I said sarcastically.

She laughed, sticking out her tongue at me. 'Because you're such an easy mark and you're a good sport too.'

'Would you seriously come away with me, if I asked you to?'

'I'll have to consult my social diary, it's jam-packed you know… You know I would, Adam.' No matter how many times she said my name it never gets old.

'If you're serious, I'll look into it and make arrangements.'

CHAPTER 25
UNEXPECTED TURN

<u>NOTE TO SELF:</u>
IMPORTANT, Not Many pages Left in Notebook —
MUST BUY NEW ONE!
Life is hard,
We all struggle,
Some situations we see coming,
Some situations we don't.

Standing at the mouth of the warehouse I try to busy my mind with thoughts of Lilly's legs curled around mine. Then what it would feel like to run my hands the full length of them. This seemed better than continuing to think about the dust, dirt and grime that covers everything, and the damage it's doing to my lungs.

The sun pierced through tiny holes in the stacks of boxes, revealing the almost choking thick air. As the temperature climbs higher and the light brighter, the dust becomes visible, sitting on the air like a sparkling crystal mist. Boxes and crates are always piled precariously at the end of the week. Men in a hurry to rush off home dump their loads without a second thought. Falls are common, it happens, it doesn't bother me… mostly. I'm quick enough to move out of the way, if I had too. However, twice they have tumbled and fallen today making me jump out of my skin… I'm jumpy.

The tide has changed on the floor, there's a pulling of rank. Nothing I can put my finger on exactly. A self-protection that wasn't there before, men standing in huddles, rumours are flying around that I'm not privy too. It could be my anxiety playing up. I'm tired, stretched thin by work. Although earlier this week when I left my post to use the toilet, I was shoulder barged twice. At first, I wasn't sure; I thought maybe it was an accident. Nevertheless, when I tried to return you could have cut the air with a knife. It was almost like the walls were talking. It sounded crazy when I tried to resign it in my head like paranoia had set in, but I'm sure I'm not imagining the dirty looks.

I try to busy myself with invoices and pay as little attention to what's going on around me as possible. Holding my breath so I don't breathe in the thick air that springs from open boxes, pulling my shirt over my mouth like a filter. I'll probably die of lung cancer at forty with the amount of shit I'm breathing in. God only knows what country it comes from. Some poor bastard with leprosy, rabies or some other godawful disease has probably packed these at the other end and now I'm breathing in what's left of them.

Something caught the corner of my eye. Arthur, who had been standing in as a timekeeper, on top of his foreman position, came walking over my way. He didn't have his normal expression on his face. A cold shiver shot through me. I automatically put down the case I was holding, waiting for him to catch up to me. I put out my hand on his approach. He didn't take it in his normal manner. Instead, his grip was light, inconsequential and he looked passed me rather than meeting me eye to eye.

'Adam, we need to talk.' He put one hand on his hip and spoke as if he was reading from his clipboard; he didn't want to say whatever was coming. I felt myself pull back a little. Feeling myself flinch, Arthur glanced up for a second, choosing not to say whatever came to mind. After a minute to re-think, 'Adam, I have some news for you… It comes from above. There was nothing I could do. We're looking to cut down on staff numbers. The board feels your position is unnecessary…'

Dumbfounded. The wind rushed out of my mouth with no sound attached. 'What! I haven't done anything wrong… you can't…?' Breathlessly, I reached out for his shoulder, forcing him to engage with me.

'Yes, they can. Read your contract, my suggestion to you is to go quietly. I'll make sure you get severance pay… if you make a complaint, you'll walk away with nothing.'

'What's happening? Be straight with me, Arthur.' He looked at his watch stalling. Taking his clipboard and staring at it is so hard it was as though he was willing new information to be there so he can take back what he just said.

'To be honest, Adam, I don't like this any more than you do. I've been working here twenty years and, in that time, I've never had to do anything like this before.' He looked around, putting one hand across his forehead.

'Off the record… and I mean off the record. There are certain things you just can't do in this town and expect to get away with them, Adam. You crossed the line. It may not be a fair line, but you still crossed it. The consequences… I can't fight them, I can't bend them; the only reason I can get you severance pay is I'm friends with your dad. Be smart and walk away; if not for yourself, then for him, I'm sorry.' With that, he patted me on the shoulder and mumbled, 'No hard feelings.' My eyes followed him in disbelief as he walked away with his clipboard. I felt the urge to scream. To knock down boxes and cases, scatter them like paper to the wind. I stared at the crowbar near the truck, picking it up, cold and heavy in my hands.

Directly in front of me, the panel of one of the biggest trucks in the fleet sat there with its thick black paint and yellow logo. One scratch would send it to the panel beaters for a month; the whole cab would have to be re-painted. The crowbar sat growing heavier, the iron biting into the skin on my palms. Men gathered together like flocks of crows, the whispering was definitely not paranoia this time. Feeling the eyes on me was enough to make me think twice about doing anything I would regret. Yet, my temper was up and I could feel it burning my face from the inside out. An exasperated irritation — a gut reaction with no direction and no place to go. I began to run hot, a

263

scratching inside my skin, smouldering away at my insides. I'm nothing more than a dangling spider.

Lifting the bar, I saw my hands as they travelled past my face, my mind disconnected from my body. Everything was so loud, the workshop, the docks, the men and the trucks. A sound that blocked out all rhyme and reason. The shadow of my arm blocked the sun from my eyes. Arms shaking from holding the iron, without warning I simply let go. In slow motion I watched without emotion as one end of the rod ripped through the panel like butter. The almost deafening sound brought the whole place to a standstill. Again, the bar moved past my face. The sound was deafening as it echoed off the walls and concrete floors. Full of rage and far beyond control my arms came plummeting down, smashing the mirror clean off, then repeatedly against the window. Watched without feeling as the glass turned from clear to opaque, to a crushed web barely hanging in its frame. Firm hands from behind yanked at both my arms, shoulders, pulling at my shirt. I lost my grip on the handle as it was pulled back over my shoulder and into someone else's hands. A blurring of the ceiling with concrete floor, followed by the slapping of my back hitting the floor, the wind rushing out of my lungs forcing me into the foetal position with pain. I roll and stumble to find my feet. A dull thud struck the back of my head, then another hit in my side, speeding up, in quick succession, so I fling myself this way and that way punching out at anything I can reach. Harder blows come from a frontal attack, over and over, to each side of my rib cage.

'Take him down, boys,' Arthur's voice.

There's a scuffling of feet as I'm blinded with my shirt reefed over my face. Spinning around, I break free only to see Joe and Pete with sweated brows. Joe clutching his forehead as blood spilt from his temple. Was that me — did I hit Joe, Pete, even Arthur?

CHAPTER 26
TAKING LILLY HOME

__Note to self:__
Don't lose this parking docket, as I must remember this day!
My soul has screamed out for you since I was twelve years old.
Now, let it be known!

Am I nervous about taking her home? Maybe a little? A lot rides on it. She grabbed my hand tightly, as I'm driving. Lilly was uncharacteristically quiet.

'It means a lot to me that you brought me here, Adam. I will try not to mess up.' She rechecked her bag, doing some kind of mental list in her head.

'You are perfect!' I smile across at her. A new blouse I'd never seen her wear before made her look slightly older, I guessed it was her, *good girl, impress the parent's, outfit*. 'Really, you look lovely Lil.' She smiled and smoothed her skirt down, an action that told me this meant a lot to her and was uneasy — a fact that touched me.

The house was quiet when we arrived; like no one was home. It hits me; I could have planned this better. Should

I have said something to Dad? I curse inside my head carefully, not to show Lil. When I take her through the front door and into the adjoining hall, the smell of home surrounds me. I smile at her, trying to act like it's the most natural thing in the world — me bringing a girl home. Not letting on for a second it's the first time. My stomach drops a little bit with the sureness of a dream finally happening, rather than nervousness or worry. My father is likely to be in his shed until he is called in, Mum will be cooking. I thought it best not to let her know about bringing Lilly home. The tension would have built to an explosive point. The moment I walked through the door a barrage of questions would have hit us, like a chat show host gone crazy. As it stood, I was sneaking Lilly in without her realising she was unannounced. It should be fine. I reassure myself as a sudden uneasiness snakes through me.

'May I?' A gold heart necklace was hanging over the corner of the mirror, Lil seemed intrigued reaching out to touch it.

She had asked me what to expect in the car, I had answered, '*pure madness*' and laughed. She had screwed her face up. She looked adorable.

'Just be yourself,' was my standard answer to her self-doubt, but she was perfect, and they would see that. The necklace now sat in her hand and I showed her the initials on the back.

'It's my mother's. She puts it on when she leaves the house.' I encourage her to look around more. I can tell she wants to. She became surprisingly confident. Picking up this or that to investigate it further. She stopped, picking up a framed photograph. I realise it's me, aged five. A smile spreads across her face.

'Oh my God… Look at that, it's you, right?' I walked over trying to prise it from her hands. She is so amused she wiggles around so I can't quite reach. 'I like it, I want to see what your kids might look like one day.' Focusing her eyes on the tiny version of me.

'It's just embarrassing the way my mum used to cut my hair.' She releases the frame to me and I swiftly put it back.

'I can't believe you were blond as a kid, you're so dark now.' I nodded, trying to move on quickly.

'What is this?' Lil was pointing to a framed cross-stitched poem on the wall.

'My mother stitched it. It reminds us to remember where we came from, our roots.' I scanned the room realising there are a million things to explain in this house, with a million stories attached. Unexpectedly I felt proud to be woven into its narrative. 'My mum goes through fads you see; like there was a knitting club, jam making and calligraphy. This was from her cross-stitch phase, she used to recite this poem to us before bed.'

'Read it to me. It will sound better in your voice.' She touched the frame and ran her fingers over the linen lovingly.

'I don't think so.' I snorted bashfully and pushed my hands in my pockets.

'Come on, pleaseeee…' She had her head on one side and leaned, nudging me lightly with her shoulder.

'No,' I laughed shaking my head.

'Please,' she said again in her angelic voice.

'Fine, but you'd sound better than me I'm sure.' I began to read, not needing to look at the words, knowing it by heart. I could feel her eyes watching my face as I recited, hands in my pockets looking at my shoelaces. As I turned my head to catch her staring, she quickly looked back at the poem. I wished I knew what she was thinking. I hadn't quite figured her out.

'Read it again.' She smiled.

'*Silver and Gold*
Make new friends, but keep the old;
Those are silver and these are gold.
New-made friendships, like new wine,
Age will mellow and refine.
Friendships that have stood the test of
time and change are surely best;
Brow may wrinkle, hair grow grey;
Friendship never knows decay.
For 'mid old friends, tried and true,
Once more our youth renew.
But old friends, alas! may die;
New friends must their place supply.
Cherish friendship in your breast
New is good, but old is best;
Make new friends, but keep the old;

Those are silver, these are gold.'
By Joseph Parry (May 1841 to February 1903)

I tried to read slow and clear, the way my father did. I could feel her eyes on my face as I read. This time, as I caught her, she looked back unashamed.

'That was really beautiful,' she said, pausing for a second, drawing in a huge breath. She leant over and lightly touched her lips to mine. It sent a shockwave through my entire body. Before I return the gesture, she pulled away, smiling.

I persisted to watch her fascination as she daintily continues on a tour around the front rooms. Stopping only to query me about objects of significance, asking thoughtful questions. She is weighing up my past and putting my life in perspective. She was taking me in, recording each mannerism, all my reactions and responses. I already know her like the back of my hand, apart from that tiny piece she keeps for herself. I long for her to let me into that part of her. If only for the fact that no one else has ever ventured there. I would be the first to get invited in.

She stopped. 'It's called a menorah. I've seen these before.' She looks at candelabra inquisitively. 'I thought there were nine candles.'

'No, that's something different for Hanukkah; we're not that religious really. We just keep a few traditions.'

'Like?'

'We try to get together on Saturdays… We celebrate Hanukkah… I had a bar-mitzvah… but that's about it.'

'What about Christmas and Easter?'

'No, we don't celebrate Christian stuff. Does that bother you?'

'No not at all, I'm interested in what you do, besides our Christmases weren't that great. I spent most of it wishing I was part of other families. Like the ones on TV.' Before the conversation could get any deeper my father came down the hall.

'At last, he's brought you.' My father's arms spread wide, embracing Lil like one of us. She turns, springing forward to do the same.

'I'm so glad to meet you,' Lil replies excitedly smiling wide.

'So, you'll stay for dinner, right?' Father's face was full of optimism.

'I'd love to,' said Lilly, jumping at the chance. 'You have a beautiful home,' she added.

'You are welcome anytime.'

'I'm not spoiling plans, am I? Is it just family?' she said quietly.

'Do you want to stay? I want you to stay,' he urged, nudging her towards the lounge room door. He turned only to look at me, making sure he'd not overstepped.

'I guess we're staying,' I said shaking my head, knowing I am about to be forced through a million embarrassing questions. I lean over to my father's ear.

'Can you please calm Mother down before she meets Lilly?' He nods and goes into the kitchen to do the impossible. I walk Lil quickly into the dining room. My mother had gone to great effort with the table, as she always did on Saturdays, and Lilly was taken aback.

'Does your family do this every weekend?' A tiny look of inadequacy brushed her face.

'Mum likes to make an occasion of it, so we feel guilty enough to turn up,' I explain, trying to lighten her mood. 'Lil, it's just a dinner, nothing really.'

'I didn't realise it was going to be this nice or I would have put a dress on.'

'You look, lovely dear,' my father cut in before I could say anything, he offered her a chair next to him. 'We are glad you're here,' he smiled and nodded for me to sit beside her.

My mother came in, placing food on the table with an unfamiliar look on her face. *What no hysterics? No bombardment of questions?* She simply bowed her head and smiled quaintly. My father must have given her a warning, not something she took easily. I looked at my father for an explanation. He gave me a wink. My mother walked around the table to where we sat and put her hand toward Lilly.

'I'm very pleased to meet you.' She was almost regal, what a performance, Oscar-worthy. Completely unaware of this, Lilly took my mother's hand with enthusiasm.

'I'm really glad to be here. Thank you for having me.'

'You're very welcome,' she said, then, almost sullenly walked back to her side of the table, sitting down without a word. There was something in her movement on the way back to her chair that signalled trouble. I couldn't quite put my finger on it. Something was going on; my mother was clearly upset. It was subtle, Lil is completely ignorant to my mother, but those of us sitting at the table that knew her best knew what whirlwind was coming.

My father shot her a short sharp look, telling her to behave. I took Lilly's hand under the table. I gave her a squeeze to let her know she was doing well. She squeezed back in appreciation. Then slipping her foot out of her shoe, she caressed my ankle with the soft skin of her bare foot, a little thank you. My father passed Lilly a plate. Lil in return gave him one of her devastating smiles. I could see my father was wrapped around her little finger just as I am. My sister then passed her a bowl.

'I'm Rachel by the way, Adam's sister. Why on earth would you want to date my stinky brother?' Rachel tried to bust through the tension, which was slowly building.

'I'm Lilly,' she laughed taking the bowl. 'Sorry, I should have passed… I apologised. And in answer to your question, I feel sorry for him… mostly.' Lilly poked her tongue out at me, so I kissed her on the forehead. My mother, not quite as convinced at Lil's worth, was the first to fire a question.

'Where is your family from? Where did you grow up?'

It was my sister who came to her rescue. 'What does that matter?' quickly passing Lil bread.

'I grew up on Market Street,' Lilly answered unaware she was on trial. I cut in over her.

'Lilly, it's OK you, don't have to talk about anything you don't want to.'

'There's plenty of time for us to get to know each other,' came my father's calming voice, not quite enough this time.

'The food's good, Mum,' Rachel butted in. Mum didn't so much as look her way.

'Can you show me how to make it?' My mother, impatient, answered swiftly.

'You've seen me make it a million times.' At least she tried, I lipped thank you in her direction. I shoot a look towards my mother, she sits unapologetically, cold sweat breaks out along my spine, as I realise, she's just getting started.

'So, do you two have plans for the rest of the weekend?' my father says, trying to turn the tone of the conversation. Lil, seemingly unaffected and oblivious to the recent tension, answered in an upbeat manner.

'No, not really, we are going back to Adam's place to watch some movies tonight…' She winked at me sending an automatic rush of electricity down my spine. My mother and sister looked at each other, taking the word's *movie night* to mean something else entirely. I wish! I thought to myself.

'That sounds lovely.' My father, still on high alert, stops anything unpleasant slipping out, knowing the interaction at the other end of the table is potentially troublesome.

'I noticed Adam has a brother in the hall photographs, do you mind if I ask where he is?' Lilly said, speaking to my father with clear affection.

My smitten father answered, 'Yes, of course not. Adam's brother is married with children. So, he can't always make it to dinner.' My mother snorted, which was met by a stern look from us all at the table. Lilly looked confused at the response.

I move up next to her and said quietly:

'My mother and my brother's wife do not always see eye to eye. So sometimes he is unable to come,' hoping she could read between the lines.

'All families have a little disharmony,' my father said, making light of it.

'I understand.' Lil smiles adding, 'My family has far more than a little.' She laughs. My mother did not find it funny by all accounts.

'What does your father do?' my mother asks as if she already knew the answer. Then it dawns on me my mother does already know the answers. She's heard the rumours, putting two and two together Lilly has already been tried and convicted in my mother's mind.

'I don't know him…' feeling the tension she searches the faces around the table. It takes all I am not to explode, the only thing keeping me calm is the realisation that would make it harder for Lil and upset my father.

'Is that a cross around your neck? You know we're Jewish,' Now my mother is so snide Lil finally catching on.

My father, furious, places both hands on the table, fists tight, and glares down the table. Then changing his expression, he pats Lilly's hand.

'Well, no matter about your situation, you have us. If you're willing to put up with us, that is.' Shooting one more look towards Mum. Knowing when she's beaten, she softens slightly, outwardly only, I'm sure.

'Lilly, you seem to make Adam very happy,' she says. Galled at being cut off, she straightens her silverware. That wasn't so hard was it, I thought to myself? The clattering of forks grating against plates was all you could hear as an awkward hush fell over the room. I looked at Rachel pleading for help. She looked down, then back at me.

'So, Dad.' Rachel stood, drink in hand. 'There is something I need to tell you.' The room fell silent, knowing what was coming.

'Dad, I don't want you to worry, OK? I'm fine... I'm having a baby. Before you say anything I —' like lighting my father sprang to his feet, grabbing her with both hands.

'What? How can this be...?' My father's eyes filled with tears,

'Are you... OK?' Rachel asked carefully.

'I'm happy Rachel, pure happiness. This is good news indeed,' hugging her. 'First, my son brings home this angel and now there is to be new life... what more could I ask for?' Mum held a napkin over her face trying badly to conceal her tears. Even my eyes filled a little, Lilly clapping, congratulations. She hugged me.

'How exciting!' Lilly grinned. I nod back at her.

'A baby, wow!' My father falls back into his chair in disbelief. 'A baby...' he says again.

The rest of the dinner, more or less, moved along uneventfully for which we were all grateful. Mother didn't seem to dwell on being put in her place for once. The news is finally out, overshadowed everything else. I would not like to be in my father's shoes when the subject next comes up, but for now, it's over. Lil offered to help the other women clean up in the kitchen. I watched them walk together, Mum even parting with a half-smile. Rachel looked at Lil, she loved her — I can tell.

Dad signalled quietly for me to follow him into the hallway. Surprising myself, I snuck away without alerting anyone in the crowded room. Mainly because Lilly has the floor, making everyone laugh with a story about a misunderstanding with her brother at the markets. The sunlight shone through the stained-glass windows creating a halo of the blue, red and green light around my father who stood smugly about something. He called me over again, in silence yet with an urgent hand gesture.

'What?' I whispered, as I got closer, instinctively knowing to be quiet.

'I have something for you. It's between me and you.' He fishes in his pocket and I quickly held his hand in place preventing him from giving yet another undeserved gift.

'No Dad, no, nothing else, really, I'm good,' I beg.

'Don't kill the moment for me, I've been looking forward to this.' His eyes sparkle with anticipation. He tugs an envelope full to bulging and I let his hand go for a second, curious to see what it.

'Dad is that money… no, I won't take it!' I put my hands up so he couldn't place the envelope in them. I protest, beyond humbled. 'No, I can't Dad,' I proceeded to push his hands away.

'One way or another you're taking it. You're just dragging it out. We both know I'm not going to stop until you take it!' It slaps against my palm. I look at it there in disbelief. My father's arm wound around my shoulders in its familiar way, speaking low he murmurs:

'Listen it's enough to get you somewhere.' He tried hard to contain laughing with excitement as if it was he, being gifted.

'Dad, I can't….'

He places his hand over my mouth to shut me up. I open the envelope, I stare in disbelief, and I've never had so much money before.

'A new start, take Lil with you.' He grinned, I felt light-headed, and it was now possible. I could form a plan.

'This is a good thing.' My father grabbed me tighter, "You need to start a life —"

'Do you think she'll come?' I questioned rhetorically. Suddenly, things felt perfect and a rush of exhilaration rushed through me.

'Why are you asking me?' My father could hardly contain himself. I hadn't seen him this excited since we moved out of the city and into this house when I was a kid.

'Dad, I'll take the money on one condition, that you let me pay you back,' I insisted, still in shock.

'The only thing I want from you is a phone call. Don't forget the phone call.' He winked.

CHAPTER 27
DARK BEFORE THE DAWN

Dark before dawn,
Sunset before morning,
Fire before ashes,
Empty before full,
Longing before passion,
Want before need,
Heartache before love.

Lilly should be with me, sitting here curled up on the lounge watching TV. Another missed date due to last-minute shift changes. What makes my blood boil is, he does it on purpose. He knows we're together. I've seen his men following me. They stand in dark corners pretending to read their phones but I know who they are! Does John think by making her work it will keep us apart? I've come too far for that — we've come too far for that. Something has to be done; I have to do something… I'm going down there. I'm walking straight into Johnny's place and no one is going to stop me, not this time. I'm doing it!

Here I am, the Black Dragon. The moment has come, a feeling of finality rushed through me. The heat had risen inside me, that familiar hatred. This time it will help me rather than hinder. It's simmering unsympathetically, like a fireball in my stomach. All it needs is an opportunity to spring forward to demonstrate its power. He's just a man. Hands trembling, fear rising. I breathe deeply through my nose in an attempt to control it, to have some restraint over it. Not fear, anticipation, I can do it, I have to do it.

I pushed open the door with all my might as though it's my door to break down, as though I owned the place. I felt the wounded animal inside me, its need to take revenge. In the words of my father: All men are animals. You must learn to control the beast. I did not wish to tame my beast. My animal roared and demanded justice.

On the bottom stair, I realised my entrance was largely unnoticed thanks to the curve in the stairs, loud music and the girls taking everyone's attention. In the corner of my eye, there is a reshuffling of feet and position, a slight panic in the jolted movement. I recognised a bouncer, he's hurrying, flustered, walking more quickly than normal, bending down he whispered into someone's ear. Who else would it be, John!

His table stood elevated from the rest, highlighted by the light of an open door to his office. Like the king, he believes he is. This was his heartland. I took note of just how many men he had in tonight, more than I first thought.

I assume a meeting of some kind must have been taking place. Each one of his men dressed neat and tidy, just the way he liked them. The kind of men you would gladly meet on any street with a handshake and smile. However, under their pressed shirts and neat suits, there was concealed branding from street gangs, homemade tattoos from jail cells and slums alike. He was a genius at finding the vulnerable, the misled and misguided. Giving them a cause, and the family they needed, and in return, they gave him unconditional loyalty. Now I entered his lair. With my blood turning into ice, I sat in the nearest seat. Knowing this was the last stand — it has to be if I am to ever have a life with Lil. It was now or never.

I summoned the anger and hate from each cell running through my blood. I ordered it to stand up and be brave. I commanded my spine to snap into place and my mind to sharpen to the job at hand. There he sat. He bit into a huge piece of steak, of course it was medium rare. The blood on his plate puddles. He slaps his lips and tongue; it turns my stomach to watch him bite into it like a carnivorous dog. It repulsed me that John could have his mouth anywhere near Lilly. He stabbed into it with his knife and fork, he knows I'm here, his napkin slipping from his neck and disappearing under the table. He didn't ask the waitress to retrieve it. On high alert, always, she simply produced another for him without a word or signal. Sensing I am here, he lifted his eyes in my direction. As if I was no more than an annoying fly. He turned back to his plate, not missing a bite. His eyes shift slightly left to a group of men as if to say, get the fly spray. I wait but nothing happens. Do I just go over and grab her hand? I have to think this through. Do I signal for her to come to me, could she? Finishing, he wiped his mouth with his napkin, throwing it into the blood on his plate and shoving it away with some force. It was cleared away before he could stand. The chair grunted with his weight against the floor as he got to his feet. My stomach flipped. Automatically I placed my hand on it. I could feel his eyes moving from her, then back to me, then back to Lilly. I avoided eye contact. The intensity of the bar could not compress nor hide the fervour between us. John's temper was increasing yet steady. From where I sat, I could see him visibly doing his best to taper it. Under that perfectly tailored suit, I knew his heart was ablaze for Lilly like me. He has that same weakness around her.

Lil stared straight ahead stiffly paused behind the bar. She was thirteen again. Her hands kept busy, so there's no opportunity to bother her, even though she realised her effort would be fruitless. John began to approach her, yet Lilly's focus does not move from her task. I put my head down; *leave it alone and it will pass*, my father's voice is speaking clearly in my head. *Wait for the opportune moment and be smart*. I endure a conversation with the regular next to me, yet inside that familiar anger starting to boil again. Lilly looks over my way, just a glance, just for a second but it's enough to know I shouldn't be sitting this one out. It's a call for help, only I understand.

Within seconds of the heat of anger beginning to spit and bubble my fingers start to tingle. A rage from my childhood starts to rise like never before. And I'm back there, I was standing in the snow, John pins Lil to the wall. *The question, the question that had haunted me all these years, do you have the balls to get up and put things right?* This time I rose, not content to sit by knowing the agony that it brings, the anger could not stay lying in its pit a second longer, like a serpent, it rose.

This is for my Lilly, for the first time I can say she is my Lilly. I have to deserve her, I have to earn her. Lilly scuffles backwards. Through the darkness of the corner in which Lil stands, she is trying to wave something away. Johnny stands over her, his massive frame overwhelming her, she's trying to subtly push him back, he is pulling something from his pocket, a box. Is he trying to put something in her hand? She doesn't want it, she's pushing it away, she's wearing her nice face, her agreeable, not to offend smile. Her face slightly flushed… Lips moving very fast, I can't hear the words that are being said. My feet are moving forward, the rest of the bar is a blur. There are people in front of me so I push through them. It's loud, but I can't hear them. I need to get to her, she's protectively laughing off whatever is trying to say. He advances closer, she's in the shadows and I can't see her face any more. I need to get as close as I can get, I lean over the bar, the lights flashing block her face from view. He's just a man, he's just a man, I tell myself.

'Lilly, are you ready to go?' I push my voice up over the music and crowd. She looks at me with pure panic. John looks back at me, I am still of no consequence, an inconvenience. 'Lilly it's time…' I say, louder this time. Johnny looks back over his shoulder, holds his look for a second. This time he is not amused. For a second my stomach drops, and I feel fear, I swallow it down. This is for our future. 'Lil, its time.,' I point to my watch. I freeze; his whole body turns like one huge machine. John's men stand either side of the bar, hidden out of sight, but they are there. They are the silhouettes of cruelty.

'Adam, no…' Her voice is so quiet I could only see her mouth move. That devil that survives in me, the voice that whispered in my ear, louder than my father's, is preventing me from walking away. Call it pride, or just stupidity. My whole life seemed to lead me to this moment; he is just a man.

There was a long silence. John is waiting for me to make the first move; he is trying to make me lose my nerve, applying a strategy. I know this and to a degree it is working; he is just a man, I repeat over and over in my head. He waits but I did nothing. I stood, my mind blank. The range of Johnny's temper seemed boundless; it could fly from zero to a hundred in seconds with the intensity and unpredictability of a toddler. His thick neck veins pulsed with anger as his chest stores oxygen, standing upright to show the true wealth of his muscles. It was a fearsome sight.

I try to snap my spine straight once more. Force myself to stand a little taller, I push my chin up high, trying to meet him eye to eye, I pray he can't see the fear building inside me. Suddenly conscious, I am surrounded by trouble on all sides. I can feel my face started to turn red, but life has come to this, I tell myself over and over, this is the moment. John's men heard me toward the back door, out of sight of the patrons. Boxes stacked high and staff lunch tables now block the doorway to the courtyard where Lilly and me first met. I can still see Lilly standing at her post — it's too late to change anything. I have to let this run its course.

John's patience with me has finally run out. With a long clean stride, he walks up to me, fearlessly, without warning, pulling back his arm like lightning, cracking me straight in the face with a rabbit punch. It took seemingly less effort than it had for him to pick up his scotch. It presses me down. Pushes me downwards. I have no control over my body. I trip backwards over the chairs behind me; the table goes crashing too with everything on it. The momentum holds me down for a second; I struggled to breathe, as though the impact has me in a chokehold. My face is on fire. I feel the warm blood trickling down towards my ear. I will not break under this — this is the moment I tell myself. Although the voice in my head is shaky, with splintered vision I stand. I see Lilly physically reducing, shrinking down into herself. Using the table and chair to prop herself as she fell in slow motion, her mouth paused in disbelief, screwing her fists into her apron. She could no longer hold up her head or make contact with me.

I push up from the ground. I charge. I swing with all the force in me. So frenzied was his reply to my punch, he could have been an Irish prize fighter, stunned for a second. I actually could have believed he'd taken my face clean off. John in stark contrast to myself, stood taller than ever, menacing and heavyset, far quicker than you think for a man his size. No showy moves, no dancing, only expertly executed shots. Lashing out with no remorse or apology, his eyes dark and frigid. Almost leading you to believe that it was your own fault for getting hit.

Standing back, conserving his energy, he didn't need to go crazy. He could destroy me with one punch; I'd never see it coming.

I feel myself howl like a wounded beast. For a second, I'm standing outside my body, I see myself on the floor and John smiling over me. I look small, stark and barren. I am angry at myself: get up you, pathetic little man, get up Adam! Feeling very much in the moment, a surprising calm fell over me, all the noise absent apart from the ringing in my ears, which the punch had left me with. Ironically, this close to death I should be scared but the last deafening blow has smacked the fear right out of me. My insides joined once again with my outsides and I purposely ignore the taste of blood in my mouth. Without warning, as if someone had flicked a switch in my brain, I felt wide awake. I scramble to find the right way up, managing to roll somehow finding my appendages to reach a standing position. I forced my quivering arms to hold the lot into position, affording me a second or two to gather enough strength to call my knees to work. I stand, aided by the table and the upturned chairs I have fallen into.

'Don't! Please don't,' comes Lilly's voice in the distance, leaving me for a moment.

I'm back down, like a turtle on its back. My arms and legs try to find the ground, all seemingly working independently of each other; like a drowning spider being flushed. The world broke into grains of white sand and rolling waves of silver pulsating light. No longer did my arms flail around useless against John's stature but rather lifeless, heavy and limp.

John signals to the barman to ring the bell for free drinks. A flood of legs and shadows storm over the top of me as I flail about on the floor, at the edge of the main room. The smoke and flicker lights confusing up and down.

'Get him out quickly'

Three men pick me up, two at the top and one has my ankles. My brain says fight, however, I no longer have control over my body. I'm outside, the sky is above me, and the sun hits my closed eyes and is still too bright to see. I slump against the wall without strength, barely recognising myself, not sure who I am, where I am. But I know that I am powerless, I know the whip of my own self-loathing has only just begun. The walls of my mind close a little tighter, squeezing, always suffocating, and wrapping its tight grip of madness around me forcing me to gasp.

The air, however, doesn't reach the lungs of my mind it's still breathless. Only the lungs in my chest, which are overworked, ache beyond their capacity, feel part of my body; the rest lays useless and disabled. The world is unclear, standing shakily on my feet. I stumble forward then backwards. The world's a blur and I'm sure I'm not really part of it. My feet trip over one another, yet somehow, I move forward, or am I? The shops meld together as one long strip, they grow tall and lean over me. I feel the twisting of my ankle as my feet face the wrong way, then I bang into a wall and bump into fences, posts, street signs. I stagger, reaching out for the side of a building, it all mixes into a cocktail of I don't know.

**

Time passes, how much—I'm unclear. A knock on the door so soft and light, I can't open it. She can't see me like this. What if she's not alone? John's men will be with her, there's no way he would let her be here alone. No escape, it was always inevitable if I think about it, why shouldn't it end this way? It fits. My ego! Suddenly death seems like an easy answer. What made me think I could stand up to John and all his men? Just me, alone! My head feels like it's splitting, a small tap on the wall as I put my head back is enough to finish me. I let myself slide down the wall until I reach and natural stopping point.

The light tap on the door comes again. I can't move, or I don't want to move, why make it easy for them? I wipe my hand across my forehead. The blood is still warm, wet and sticking. My hand automatically finds my hairline; it hurts as I pull it off feeling a trickle of blood run down the side of my face. I know the door is unlocked, any second they will figure it out. They will burst through the door, and it's all over. I look over to the window. I could make a run for it, but they have done this a million times before, I'm sure they'd be somebody waiting at the bottom, likewise with the roof. I have no energy to run and now there is no Lil, I have no need to run… I hear the door slowly open. The light touches her feet on the floorboards, with my eyes closed and count the steps, I don't need to see her, I know it's her.

'Adam!' she says, gasping at the sight of me. She kneels down beside me, the touch so light and sweet it's almost painful. 'Adam, can you hear me?'

I hear her run to the kitchen and there is a running of the tap and she's back by my side, a warm cloth is placed on my forehead, 'Adam, nod if you can hear me?' I tilt my head slightly. 'Let me help you get cleaned up,' I reach and put my hand around her wrist to stop her.

'There's no point, just leave me.'

'What are you talking about? John's men could be here any second.'

'What…' I have my eyes locked to her face.

'Can you walk? We need to get away?'

'I'm confused, how, this doesn't make any sense?' I look towards the door. Sure enough, there is no one there.

'How did you…?'

'There's no time. We need to get away. That's if you want me. Do you want me?' I can't answer, pure disbelief. 'Adam, I am standing before you with nothing. Only the clothes I wear, do you want me?'

'Yes…' I manage to get out, why not run with this dream a bit longer? She can't be here saying these things.

'If I leave this life I will only have you. Are you sure I will be enough?'

Suddenly the words that she said have clarity, have meaning. With certainty, with everything, I say, 'Yes.' Around to the bookcase, I scramble, 'Lock the door quickly, Lilly, hopefully, that will buy us a little time.' I pushed the books out of the way. I implore Lil to bring my keys and grab the large sports bag from my bedroom; she does so as quickly as possible. Then, using the penknife I keep on my car keys, I rip the low panel from the base of the bookshelf. The money my father had given me was sitting there with a little I managed to put away. I shove it into the bag, along with a couple of books, and the small box containing the buttons, all I needed went into the bag. 'We need to go through the window,' I said zipping the bag and throwing onto my shoulder. Grabbing her hand, I pulled her in the right direction. I open the window looking below me.

'I don't like heights,' she says sounding panicked. I feel her nails dig into my arm.

'Lilly you have to climb down after me — promise. I'm still not good on my feet and don't want to fall on you.'

'OK.' She looks nervously over the railings.

'I got you, it's OK,' I reassure her.

After a shaky landing, I pull her as fast as I can into a side street where I'm parked. I check around me, they must be here somewhere. I open the door almost expecting someone to be inside the car. I'm ready for them if they come, I think, looking at the crowbar in the back seat. Locking the doors, I start the engine and roar down the street, this is not a time for half measures. I tear down Market Street, passing the bars, Lil's old apartment and the bus stop. I passed the school, I passed the nicer apartment buildings that were once part of me, I passed street after street. And I don't look back. We speed past the docks, the line of empty factory buildings, the empty lots and I am racing down an empty highway. It's only then that I can speak.

'Are you OK?' I ask Lilly focusing hard on the road racing before us.

'Yeah…' She nods.

'Are you sure?'

'Yes.'

'How did you get away?'

'I told him I quit and I just walked out the front door, no one tried to stop me. I held my breath the whole way. I think John was so shocked he didn't…' I take her hand into my lap, she's trembling but then so am I. Keeping my foot down, I drive.

CHAPTER 28
A HEART WORTH WINNING

<u>*Note to self:*</u>
All journals but the present one, are hidden under the spare wheel in boot, don't forget!

I pull over into a motel with a cheap sign and a tyre holding the gate shut, noticing its dirty, white paint peeling from along the roofline. Since we hadn't passed another motel and I had become far too tired stay behind the wheel I knew this had to be the place.

Yesterday's adventure had kept me driving for the remains of the day and through the night. Lil barely slept, her hands screwed in knots in the fabric of her dress. I pulled over only long enough for petrol, coffee and snacks. There is no plan, and I'm a guy who needs a plan. My hands were almost numb, my knuckles white with apprehension. I had unknowingly checked the rear-view mirror continually until I realised it was making Lilly's anxiety rise further. In an effort to help her relax, I started telling her every story from what she nicknamed my 'picture-book childhood'. She smiled politely at first but soon she began to visibly ease so we began to laugh and chat a little. It became an unspoken rule not to talk about John and the fact he could have men trying to find us, until now that is. She turned to me as we pulled in:

'It is going to be OK isn't it?' She bit her bottom lip.

'Of course, it is Lilly, we're too far away from everything now.' I felt her hand on my thigh, which helped not only to make me believe my own words but also to start hoping the rooms here only have one bed. Looking at her, so vulnerable, made my temperature rise and my need for her increase tenfold.

Coming to a stop I shut off the engine. Her legs still up on the dashboard, I had been spoilt longing to caress them all afternoon, I didn't want the journey to end. I went into the small room marked *front desk*. A man in need of a shave stood behind the counter. He did a double take, then quickly changed his demeanour to a smile with a friendly, 'How's it going?'

'Just you?' He stretched his neck to check the car.

'And my…' I paused, I wasn't sure what to call her, '*girlfriend*,' I said trying to make the exchange easy. It was only then I realised my head is black and blue, my hands in bad condition and I'm still wearing the bloodstained clothes under my jacket. He's checking out the car for its plates and fellow villains, but only seeing Lilly. He calmed down.

'Oh girlfriend, we get a lot of that here.' He snorted and turning back to the small TV he had resting on a lop-sided table. I don't bother to correct him; I think he believes me to be Lil's pimp or something. I shake my head — whatever. I pick up the key and head back to the car.

To my disappointment she had covered her legs and was sitting upright in the front seat, looking through her handbag. I peer through the open window and jangled the keys. She grinned and reached over to the backseat to grab her bag.

'No, let me do that,' I said, opening the back door, grabbing both bags.

'Oh, a gentleman,' she said smiling at me; our earlier chat seems to have worked.

I gave her the key and we started to search for number nine. It wasn't that hard to find, but I let her walk in front, because I appreciated the view. She opened the door without any trouble and I nodded in thanks, as my hands were full.

'I think we may need to open a window,' I suggested. It was stuffy like the room hadn't been inhabited for a while.

'It's still great though,' she answered, looking back at me.

'It's not too bad,' I said trying to sound upbeat, hiding the disappointment that two double beds neatly made sat in front of me.

'Which bed do you want?' I asked. She pointed to the one near the window. I laid her bag down on the end so she could open it and get her things easily.

'This is going to be perfect.' She sprawled herself over the bed. Her shape curved under her dress and I swallowed hard, looking out the window so as to hide my need.

Later, as the day made an easy transition into the evening, while I was recovering from the shock of her slipping her hand into mine for a few moments and while we walked back from eating at a local diner, I had a pang of sadness at the thought of this ending in a few days. I guess that's how long it's going to take before she comes to her senses and asks me to take her back to her brothers. I decided to put those thoughts to the back of my mind, in order to enjoy the time I have with her.

On entry, the smell in the room seems to have somewhat disappeared. She let me take the first shower, as she wanted to look for a T-shirt in her bag. After I had washed the day away, I sat in my bed with my shorts and T-shirt on, wondering if that's what other men would do. Would they be more aggressive? Would they sit here thinking about it, or would they just do something? Maybe I should make a move? No, that had disaster written all over it.

I crossed my arms, not really knowing how to keep my now useless hands busy and I waited. Unable to relax, I looked about the room and as there was nothing but a menu to read. I began to count the white painted bricks opposite me. I knew she was getting into her own bed when she came out of the shower, so why was I so nervous? As I sat there listening to the water run, I realised a paper-thin wall was the only thing stopping me from seeing her. The vision of her standing under running water was overwhelming. I swallowed hard, excited by the thought. The water turned off and I could hear her rummaging through her make-up bag. I couldn't turn down the volume of my pounding heart. It plugged up my ears like the beats of a drum. She opened the door wearing only a large T-shirt, her hair loosely hanging down with one of her shoulders bare. She was my Venus. I tried not to make my staring too obvious as she passed my bed in order to get to her own.

'Good water pressure,' she said, oblivious to my yearning to touch her. 'I could have stayed in there all night, Ad.'

With no sign of nerves, she jumped into her blankets, pulling them over her and propped herself up on her elbow.

'Not like the city,' I murmur, not quite making full eye contact.

'So, are you ready to sleep?' she said without any sign of discomfort.

She clearly thought of us as affectionate friends, like we were having a sleepover. There had been so many opportunities for us to take things to the next level yet it hadn't happened. My heart sank as my last ray of hope fizzled out. I nod in answer.

'Yeah OK, sleep then?' she said looking at me funny.

'Yeah, sleep… it was a big day, right?' Becoming conscious of my folded arms, I unfolded them trying to look more relaxed.

'Do you have enough blankets?' she asked me in a tone I couldn't quite place. I nodded; small talk really isn't my strong point.

'I could put mine on your bed if not?' she offered.

'No, I'm fine really.' That was sweet of her, I thought to myself, trying to think of something nice to say back.

'Lights off,' she said, reaching over and turning the small lamp on the side table off. I did the same, not really knowing what the protocol was.

'Night,' I said, scrambling under the blankets myself.

'You know what?' she said five minutes later. I started to nod off, comfortable lying on my side.

'What?' I said under my breath, surprised she was still awake.

'I really don't have enough blankets.' I felt her slide into my bed and I didn't dare move. I tried to steady my breathing. Her leg slid over my hip and the warm soft skin of her thighs that I'd been looking at all day was now suddenly upon me. Her arm slipped around my chest. I slowly moved, trying to make it seem natural, cupped her hand to my heart and held it there with a small amount of pressure. I felt her lips on the back of my neck.

Whispering she said, 'Your heart is beating so hard.'

I didn't reply, I couldn't, I was frozen.

'Do you want me to get out?' she said.

'No,' I replied hastily.

'Are you sure,' her breathy words tickled the back of my neck, sending electricity shooting through me.

'Yes,' I said, now wide awake, adding, 'This is the most exciting thing that's ever happened to me,' Regretting my words the second they left my lips.

'What?' she said.

I said nothing, embarrassed. She pushed herself up and around a bit to see my face in the small light coming through the window.

'What do you mean the most exciting?' Her voice was low and sincere.

I tried to clear my throat a little.

'I just mean, I like you in here with me.' I couldn't make eye contact even in the dark. She would have seen my blushing cheeks, giving me away.

'It's no big deal, you've been with other girls,' she shrugged, failing to understand my comment.

'Well, that's where you're wrong,' I said.

'But I'm sure I've seen you around with girls,' she said, thinking she was being lied too.

'No, you've seen me walking my cousins home after hours. You've seen me in the bar watching dancers. You've even seen me playing wingman to my drunken friends, but you've never seen me with a girl.' She looked at me puzzled, trying to recall if that was, in fact, the truth.

'Are you serious? You're not lying to me?'

'Nope,' my tone ringing true.

'So, you really haven't been with any girls?' I shook my head. My awkwardness made it is clear as day I was indeed telling the truth.

'I've had dates but nothing happened on them. I guess I'm not good at that stuff.'

'I'm sorry,' she said. 'I didn't mean anything by it. It's just that I've never met anyone your age that hasn't…' She stopped talking, not really knowing what to say. 'So, do you mind me being here? I won't be offended if you ask me to get out. If this is a Jewish thing, you know, waiting till you are married?' Her sincerity was sweet, but I burst out laughing.

'No, it's more like a — no girl will have me thing.' I could feel her smiling in the dark. She put a head on my chest, her hand back around me.

'I'll have you,' she said in a whisper I could hardly hear. Even though I assume she said it in the confines of friendship. Although I'm still hanging on to a maybe, I put my hand lightly on her head, stroking her hair.

'I can hear your heartbeat thumping… it sounds like a racehorse.' I tried to control my breathing and the urge to roll her on her back.

It took me half the night to get to sleep. I'm almost certain this means she likes me. I'm daring to hope, I've decided. My eyes struggle to focus in the mottled light. I tried to regulate my breathing and stay in the exact same position, not moving an inch so Lilly wouldn't wake up. Her head fits perfectly in the crux of my underarm. I watched her shoulders rise and fall in gentle rhythm. The thrill of having her lay on my chest, feeling her shallow breathing was exhilarating. While having her fingertips almost touching my belt line fuelled an excitement that just wouldn't leave me. My imagination surged. There is a reason to hope for more; we were getting along well before all this shit went down. The pressure from staying in one spot is too much, I move my arm slightly, a shot of sharp pain from a bruise — she doesn't wake.

If I could freeze time, snap my fingers, locking in a moment forever, it would be this one now. Her hand, still on my stomach looked unbelievably sexy, too good to be real. I shivered at the thought and tried to avoid my desires taking control, but it was useless. She sets me on fire. Stretching slightly, her toes curling, eyes opening for a second and smiling with her lips closed tight.

'That was the best night sleep I've ever had,' she purrs, blinking to wake herself up.

'Really?' My voice was still croaky, struggling in the morning light.

'Yeah, I feel so safe with you,' she said, snuggling deeper into me. *Safe with me* I thought. I hooked her leg around to me, trying to make the most of this time before, like everything else in my life; it would be over far too quickly and disappear. I lay, with sleep escaping me. In a few hours, I will sit in a car with Lil. We will drive all day. We'll talk and listen to music. She will be unguarded, and I will try to be the same. It's possible I will be happy. It's hard to believe, but I think I will.

My whole life I have felt to a deep level, misunderstood, alone. Isolated in a cell in my head. No matter how I answer questions, people don't quite get what I mean. It's different with her. No matter how the words

301

free-fall or fumble from my mouth, how discombobulated my thought patterns, she can order and relate to them. I don't have to second-guess myself or explain. It's instinctual with us, almost as if the two of us are an extension of the same thing, rather than a separate being. We're connected, Lilly and me, with a long piece of silk rope. Not a leash; never tugged at or pulled. Instead like an umbilical cord, it's a lifeline, sending me all the nutrients I need to survive. She is more than the moon, sky, sea, and earth. She is season, Mother, Father, and air. She brings a sigh, a sway, an unwavering thought and a deep breath in. I am always found, never forgotten.

Is it possible that this is my new life? A life filled. If I walk into a room and she's not there, my stomach drops with disappointment, the sound of her voice resonates around my brain like an echo. Anytime I hear Lilly's name mentioned my heart actually stops and I have to fight for breath. Surely this is too good, too much for one person to have?

CHAPTER 29
YEARNING FOR ADAM
Thoughts from Lilly's head

Last page of journal

To feel emotion unreservedly,
To offer love entirely,
To receive intimacy utterly,
Yet unable to gather the words.

Adam's body is spread out like a starfish covering our bed. He looked excused most the day and, although I asked him to lie down to rest several times, he had forced himself awake. He's so sweet, saying he didn't want me to me lonely. I think I worry him, I'm not sure why.

Curls of loose hair sit unruly across his forehead. I can't resist touching them. His leather-covered notebook lay under his loose sleeping hand. A tranquil sigh left his lungs and I tugged up the blanket over his shoulders. Reaching out to transfer his most coveted possession to the nightstand for safety, it fell open as I touched it. I paused for a moment; my name was written on the page, a battle with the better part of myself ensued. A battle between good and evil began. Telling myself it was for the greater good, I only wanted to know him better. It was fine to be curious, who wouldn't be curious after seeing their name. Good soon lost. I slide the book, carefully from under his weight, not disturbing Adam's slumber. Ensuring the spine didn't catch on the cotton sheets, I looked down onto the sprawling handwriting, not knowing what I was about to find. Then I read:

The sun fell through the holes in the clouds, silk ribbons binding us with heaven.
A light, a brilliant dazzling light,
A single truth,
It cannot be faked, over marketed or sold,
It's an undeniable, breathtaking sight.
I call it love.
It rests on my pillow in its rarest form.
A glance, a touch, a breath; not dressed up and packaged,
Not analysed to its death,
Pure, simple and redeeming,
It's all these things and none of them.
It's breathing out, then breathing in,
Firing up and calming down.
Its dramatic hand is peaceful; it's being moved without moving at all.
Your undoing and being undone.
Subtle like a whisper with the surprise of a firework.
The start of things, a start that has no boundary.

That's how it feels to have love laid at your feet.

A little way underneath he'd written:

There are no words to justify Lilly. No matter how hard I try, I can't find them. Compared to the above poem, his handwriting was messy, erratic, and darker. As if he'd pushed harder with the pen in temper or frustration?

With some disbelief, I re-read the poem. First in my head then again in a whisper, only my ears can hear. I wish I had the words to say back to him what he wrote about me. Such nice things, such pretty words, more than that, the love… he does love me. Like on TV or in books. I closed the book mindfully, running my hand over the dog-eared cover, inhaling the leather smell deep into my lungs. This is the beginning of something real. I know it. I sit contemplating Adam's work. The way his words trickle from his text to colour my mind.

He lies on his side; one arm drooped, dangling off the bed, eyes closed, flickering in a far-off dream. His face, restful with all the worry absent. This is the first time I've seen him asleep sober. The book attracts my eyes again, temptation, one more page… I let the thick cream pages fall open of their own accord, allowing heaven to choose the page. Movement, he stirs, my eyes immediately switch from book to his body. Re-adjusting, that's all, I go back to the page, and releasing the breath I'd been holding.

There is tenderness to her.

Her heart; wide open with no mask to hide behind.
Mostly due to innocence, the kind that only comes before your first heartbreak sets in.
Before you've wised-up to love, the world and all the people in it.
The time before you can look love right in the eye and yell back.
It smells of sweetness and of vulnerability.
Tattooed with goodness, from head to foot.
It's a beautiful thing,
To have your eyes so wide open yet shut so tight.
Every mark, bruise and scar, vanished under a cloud of exultation.
Doors are unlocked, inviting you in,
No end, to the momentum.
We begin.

I flip through the pages, line upon line of the most beautiful words. The most exquisite emotions captured, I feel each word. He has a way of writing on the page the things that only sit on the tip of my tongue. I skip forward a few more entries. The scrawl almost lying diagonal as if Adam had been hurrying to write down a dream before it escaped into thin air. My name peppered each and every piece of paper, the only word written carefully and with effort. Rapture, that's all one page has in large leaning letters.

His body moves slightly, one arm extending. He's close to waking. I freeze, holding my breath, posed to sneak the journal back. He slips back into a deep slumber. I lay the book next to him, open so I can still read the lines. I curl and stretch my body around his, soaking up his scent — musky and sweet.

Drowsy in the warm light, floating with saccharine.
Dancing with twinkle toes, hovering with delight,
Caressing our skin, free as a tip-toe.
I sink deeper into yearning.

When had Adam written this? Was I sleeping in his arms? Could he see me, or am I the inspiration he runs to, to save him from his day? On the next page not a quite a poem; I'm not sure what you'd call it, ideas, and thoughts?

It's nice to lay here for no other reason than; it's nice to lie next to someone feeling them breathe.
Here in the middle of the day, napping like cats on our backs.
It's indulgent, or at least it feels that way.
I breathe in the smell of sweet sweat and sex.
It's in the air, on our fingertips, on each pause.
Tenderness, from merciful, feather-like caress.
Skimming over what is hard in conversation, filling in the gaps, words don't.
A dexterity of emotion is nearly here.
The agony of waiting for a time of openness and candour.

Page after page, devoted to me. Is this what it is like to be loved…?

The pictures I see in my head when I close my eyes are graphic. Would she hate me for being so soaked in lust? My subconscious filled with moans, groans and craving. I see hands exploring hills and valleys. My need is palpable, all but howling.

He stirs moving his hand, the book now wedged under his arm. The words are no longer visible. I crawl slowly closer to the other side of him. A waft of aftershave fills me with images. I want him. I lay back with his beautiful words zigzagging across my mind. The beautiful words, delirious, haze-ridden poetic words…

Do you understand you have the power to destroy me with one look?

I have seen inside his head. This is the place he goes to when I find him staring. He lays in contentment, every bone at rest. His words have pummelled me like an aphrodisiac. It strikes me that honey wouldn't compare to seeing him undress. On his face, I notice a slight smugness, although it's not happened yet.

CHAPTER 30
BLENDING

First Page of new Journal:

Smoky, drowsy love…
The kind that has you lolloping around with virtually no strength.
Slouching together, skin on skin.
So intoxicated, you say things your ears can't quite believe exist inside you.
A chest so full of enchantment it spills over your tongue.
Heart full, so full it's rounded, beating, unhurried and uninhibited pumping out contentment from deep within.
Slow and steady, thick, heavy love hangs in the air and warms your soul.
Intrigued by every movement, glance, savour and smile.
The act of belonging to each other, to her, to him, to us, to the rightness of this situation, a true homecoming.

Imagine the happiness of a perfect love, comparable to nothing.
Reliable as stone.
Then imagine my shock, the pure disbelief of finding it.
How could I feel so changed in such little time?

I woke to Lilly kissing my neck; I didn't question it. We had fallen back into step; it was as if the whole John mess had never happened. My body sinks out of my control as her warmth covers me and then another feather-light kiss to taunt me. All day she had been affectionate. I'd tried and failed to ask her to sleep in my bed — again! Each time I had felt brave enough to make a move, my mouth and body had frozen solid.

Now, back in our room for maybe the last night, time, like sand slipped through my fingers. She was silent and looked up at me with a pleasant smile. I was hers and she knew it. I step forward, rubbing my now sweating hands on my jeans, trying to regain some kind of consciousness. I should kiss her. I'd waited for this moment for so long, I wondered what other men would do. She'd been with other men. She'd taken them to this moment, had them hanging by a string. What had they done, had they thrown her down on the bed and taken her? Was she waiting for me to make a move? Was she growing inpatient? A mix of nerves and excitement slowly reaches my hand.

Trembling, I scoop my hand around her back pulling her into me almost touching, pausing to breathe her in. My other hand, with only fingertips, touches her cheek tenderly. Laying a kiss on her cheek as if trying to build up resistance to her spell and the nerve to break it. So, I could at last look at her in the face without flinching. With an unsure hand, I stroke her jawline, and then trace the outside of her bottom lip with my thumb. She kissed it, tight-lipped as if I'd hurt myself. Then looking up with a pixie's grin, she parted her lips letting the warmth of her mouth be known to me. I watch eagerly, unable to look away, pushing it in slowly. I am transfixed as she sucks it. I feel the wetness of her mouth and the softness of her tongue roll around my thumb; filling me with a roar of excitement.

I bring my other hand up, cupping her face. She follows the line of my buttons with her eyes, towards my neck, till our faces meet. She looks at me sweetly, that delectable smile I'd always loved. I hover. We paused for a second. My insides are like a washing machine. I couldn't bring myself down upon her — the moment was too perfect. I felt her reaching up to my chest, pushing me onto my back, draping over me, tenderly kissing at first, then becoming hot, demanding. Her tongue draws a line across my lips and sucks at the lower one. I am suddenly overcome by emotion, the need to tell her all I have hidden.

'Lilly, I love you. This is something I know. It's as clear to me as the trees are green, or the sky is blue.' My hands can't be still. Stroking her hair, her back, 'You're not a want, Lil, you're a need. Without you, I am a story without an ending. You're the energy that makes my heart pound, and you are the reason my hands shake. You're a nervous shiver down my spine and the clearing in my throat. If that isn't love, then I don't know what is.'

She looked stunned. However, once I started, I couldn't stop. I emptied my whole being in front of her. I told her exactly how I felt about her. How I had yearned for her. How I couldn't forget her when she left. I knew how it sounded. I was aware, but I didn't care. I had to let it out.

'Adam, I feel the same... but you have the words. I don't know how to say things like you do.' I couldn't speak. I must have misheard. My whole body became too heavy to move. Pausing, my hands shook.

'I'm in love with you.' She spoke with no shame, as you would when pointing out a fact. Pushing a few strands of hair back off my forehead and letting her fingers drift down the side of my cheek. 'I want us to be together.' Her arms snaked around me.

'Yes.' I wasn't even sure what I was saying yes to; just yes, to all things Lilly! My eyes scanned her obviously; her naked shoulders and hair I had ached to touch. I waited for her to object to my attention. She said it again. Seeing my need, she smiled.

'You're my boyfriend, right? So, you can kiss me whenever you like?' In reply, I kissed her neck. She grinned, encouraging me, I think.

'When I look into your eyes, I forget everything, life, time, me, you, there is just a light.'

'Adam, how do you think of things like that?'

'Everyone says things like that… it's you, you bring it out of me.'

'It's a gift, Ad. You need to do something with it.'

***

Sometime later, I waited for Lil in my bed, no shirt for me tonight. That only served to somehow make me more nervous than before. A brave move for me certainly, maybe not for others. She had been affectionate to me all day, and there was a real possibility that something might actually happen. The bathroom door opened, the same T-shirt as before. She walked past my bed and onto her own. She pulled back the sheet and my heart sank. Then turned, smiling.

'Unless you want me to get into your bed…?' I immediately ripped back my blankets. She giggled, sliding in next to me. Her warmth spread through me like a fire. She looked at me for a second. 'Do you want me, Adam?' Something in her was stirring and waking up, I could see it. I sat facing her, the enormity of what she was saying began to sink in. I nodded yes. She leaned over and kissed me, then leaned back to read my face, measuring my reaction. 'Lay back.' Her command was gentle. I did as she asked suddenly aware of the position and angle of every part of my body. Nerves gripped my stomach forcing it to flip, and I hoped it didn't register fear on my face. 'I want you.' The whisper was so sweet it tickled my ear.

She moved slowly over me, never breaking eye contact. I felt my heart begin to thump, our bodies naturally pulling towards each other. I felt the politeness of her touch, only using her fingertips to draw a line across my jaw. I began to drown in her long hair as it started to fall across my face. Tasting her tongue, letting it drift across my bottom lip. The intensity of her kissing increased, her movements more insistent.

My hands suddenly unrestricted moved along her spine. I touched her neck with my lips, tasted her skin. Finally allowed free rein, pushing back clothing I rolled her over allowing my body weight to rest on hers. The soft surface of her skin enflamed me further, securing us like magnets. Her palms skimmed down my chest and I feel each isolated, tiny movement. A primal rhythm starts in my head. As loud as drums it rings out loud. My mind overrun with stirring moans, and heavy breathing, which blocked all else. My eyes turn into cameras, ready to snap from every angle to imprint on my brain what I never intend to forget.

I feel a cutting away of my old life, body and being. I am, at this moment, being reborn. Stripping back the last shred of fabric from her body. It abolishes every doubt, every self-conscious thought. Obliterates each cause to waver. I'm immersed in her perfume, lost in movements. Complete awe grips me.

My impulses take over; electricity bolted and raced with the hunger of fire. I am ignited: every cell and nerve snapped to attention. I feel her legs squeeze around my hips. Her skin seems to cover mine in weightless beauty as she rises above me. Glorious beauty! My arteries pump with a steady and strong confidence that is strange to me. I push her back laying over her and, in that moment, I am a man.

My lungs wait with baited breath. My whole body, hostage, waiting the moment, I am lost in her. I close my eyes. I hear the sound of her breathing. She takes her hand slowly, guiding me into her. I push down under her direction. Slowly I rise and push back down, feeling the heat captures me. The deep-throated sigh left her body, filling mine. I watch our bodies join. Sighs become insistently bolder. They surge forward as I pick up the rhythm. Moving faster, more insistent. I am throbbing from head to foot. My stomach drops, forcing me to take a deep breath. I am swimming in semi-consciousness. Our tempo intensifies. A powerful drive takes over me. Drunk on lust, I forget myself, grabbing her to me. Her desire increases, panting turns to moans driving me on harder. I brace for the ending as her thighs begin to shake. I feel her nails dig into my back. Her head thrown back with an arched spine, her eyes closed tightly with a final squeal. I release, letting go. I am overwhelmed, completely.

I move slowly to the left, resting my face naturally on her breast. I feel her fingers drift to the back of my head and begin to play with the strands of hair. There are no words for what I feel. Her chest rises and falls like a lullaby. I drift into sleep.

CHAPTER 31
HUMBLING SIGHT

New Journal, straight onto the page:

Beautiful ripe words, like rounded peaches, tumbling from my lover's lips; as if they were the first drops of rain, after a sweltering summer. The wettest of kisses on my skin, familiar like home yet as unattainable as myth. Full of hunger but cooling like a sea breeze.

I am overpowered, destroyed and vanquished, a more beautiful place to be — I can't imagine.

The picture on my fridge existed. I had brought it with me, grabbing the poster and folding it into my pocket at the last second before departing my apartment for the last time. There in front of me, it was real, to touch, taste and breathe in deeply. I had gone from black to blue, to hues of pink on a golden sky. Is there anything more beautiful than an uninterrupted horizon? My soul could breathe and stretch out its wings. It was like being born into a new world where my eyes are open and my ears hear the sounds of the sea. I had dared to believe. Now I have been granted her gracious heart...

The edge of day breaks before me. She still lays her head on my shoulder. I feel her deep sleeping breaths tickling my ear. The gentle sway of the car and the sound of her slumber set me into a quite contentment. I have never known before. The words of my father echo in my mind, '*A wise man knows when he has found his happiness and can be satisfied, wanting no more*'. I look down at my hands on the steering wheel, which are like carbon copies of his.

The sun is bigger than I have ever seen it, bursting from the wide expanse, with no buildings in the way to interrupt its morning peacock performance. An array of colours fans across the open sky, stemming from one central light. A small sigh comes from loosely pressed lips. Lilly is dreaming, travelling from the cage of her body to a heavenly place of possibilities. I realise I am smiling. Finally, the future looks good, even with a face like mine, I ponder.

A small bend in the road offers me a place to pull over. I try to bring the car to a slow and gentle stop without waking her. I put on the brake peeling her from me. Softly, I lay her head back on the seat, smoothing the hair from her face. I feel the softness of her cheek with the back of my hand.

This is what love is, a voice speaks so loud and clear in my head it is almost as if some divine being is speaking. Salt spray drifts through the meagre gap in the window with the breeze. It's suddenly all too real, too amazing. My stomach rolls in anticipation. Turning off the engine, I step out of the car, leaving the door to rest on its frame so the noise of a slamming door doesn't wake her. I step forward to the barrier rail. It's a weathered wooden fence with wire joining the posts like lace. It shields me from the steep drop below made of sand dunes. I realise how far the drop is below, suddenly I care if I fall. Keen scrub bushes push their spiky faces through the wire in an act of rebellion against their confinement. There, below me, champagne sands roll out in snaking ribbons making up the last few yards of land before the sea. Even in the dim dawn light, the vastness of the open sea is astounding. I've never seen anything like it before. I am overwhelmed with its beauty, yet humbled that a man like me should witness such pulchritude.

I stand reflective, taking it in. The air is pure and I inhale it, filling my lungs with its healing properties. I hear the waves gently lapping the shore with insects and birds creating morning chatter. The warm heat from the breeze touches my face like a gentle hand, and I breathe in once again. The taste is not smog or dirt or grime; this is the taste of freedom, hope and liberty. I feel a smile spread across my face for the second time that morning. I am unable to articulate this feeling of escape and victory. Deep in thought, I feel her hand slip into mine. Her body nudges its way into my side and the warmth from it travels straight through my chest.

'So, this is the beach?' she sighs, still sleepy, but slowly filling with excitement. I nod; there are no words for what I feel. Why would I waste time trying to think of them when I could be in the moment with her? 'Lock the car, let's go down,' she orders, smiling as she starts to climb down the embankment. I do as she asks, tumbling behind her moments later. I meet her at the edge of the waves, her toes curled, just touching.

'It looks cold,' I state nervously. The sea is far louder and more unpredictable than I had previously realised, unlike the more predictable harbour I'm used to.

'You know we will have to learn to swim now.' She points out, feeling me behind her.

'I think Jews just sink, or so my dad says,' I chuckle.

She looks at me, her face brighter than the sun above us.

'What Lil?' I ask trying to figure out what her sudden happiness is about. Her face makes me smile just to look upon it.

'No, not Lilly, You mustn't, ever, call me Lilly again, I'm leaving Lilly behind in the city.' Her tone is a matter of fact. Bending slightly, gingerly, she starts to dip her toes hesitantly into the water. She pulls the bottom of her dress up to protect the hem from the water. Small waves splashed up to meet her ankles and her face wrinkles. She holds back a squeal.

'Then what should I call you?' I say, putting my hands into my pockets and rocking on my heels.

'From this point forward, I am Sylvia... doesn't that sound delightful? Like a movie star,' she says, spreading her arms out wide and curtsying to the sea like a child would.

I nodded, 'yes,' screwing my face up and laughing. She pays no attention to my attempt at humour. 'If that's what you want — Sylvia?' Grinning, I'm too happy to question it.

'I do,' she declares ignoring my grin, '… and what shall I call you? You can be anything you want,' she encourages.

'I don't know,' I say retracting my shoulders, 'I'm not very good at make-believe games, and you should pick for me.'

'Fine, I will,' thinking for a second as she spins around. Stopping suddenly, a little giddy. 'From this point forward I shall call you, Bram!'

'Bram?' I questioned, shrugging at the strange name.

'That's your name… I got it from Bram Stoker, the man that wrote *Dracula*, it's the only book I've ever read remember!' she persuaded. I couldn't help but laugh and nodded yes to it.

'I like it — it sounds cool,' she said grabbing me around the waist and laying a kiss on my chest.

'OK then, if you say so.' She was the epitome of everything I wanted at that moment; I couldn't not kiss her. She slowly kisses me in return, taking my breath. Then spun away, only to return a few minutes later.

'That's us… Sylvia and Bram…' a slight pause, 'Goldsmith… that's a Jewish name, right?' She turned to check my face for approval.

'Yes,' I nodded laughing,

'Because that way, I can be both silver and gold for you… Like the friend's rhyme on your mother's wall.' She took my arm, using her finger to write on my hand and forearm. Syl-va and gold (Smith rubbed out) it delighted me to watch her.

'Don't you think that sounds lovely? Mr and Mrs Goldsmith?' I pulled her to me for a second, holding her, relishing what she had just said.

'So, we're married now?' I questioned in a whisper, not bothering to hide the overjoyed expression that spread like a rising flood across my face.

'Yes!' she said with full certainty. 'Do you have a problem with that?'

'No,' I said shaking my head. The joy in my heart, large — ready to pop my chest wide open.

'You just need to get me a ring, it doesn't have to be expensive.' I grabbed her even tighter with both hands.

'You're mine then? I'll get you anything you want,' I said trying not to let emotion crash over me.

'Yes,' she agreed, 'I'm yours.'

Joy rippled through each cell in turn, reconstructing the broken parts until there was the fullness, I couldn't help but acknowledge. So strong I couldn't destroy with my normal tactics, the effect was so profound I could hold it in. I felt like a compressed spring. She is sewn into all of my clothes; she walks through each decision. I have set myself, I'm no longer doubtful about who I am, I know who I am, I am the husband and protector of Lilly… I mean Sylvia. It is my pleasure, honour, and duty. We are bound together, this is what I was made for, I am whole and at peace. One last thing to do, I take the phone from my back pocket and dial my father's number. I put the phone up to my ear, using my other hand to block out the sound of the waves.

'Hello. Adam is that you?' The familiar sound fills me with warmth as a smile breaks free from deep inside.

'Yeah, it's me,' I inhale, steading myself. 'Dad, I'm not coming back…'